To

Steve,

Best

Wishes

Mick

13 Days

Michael Robinson

authorHOUSE®

AuthorHouse™ UK
1663 Liberty Drive
Bloomington, IN 47403 USA
www.authorhouse.co.uk
Phone: 0800.197.4150

Published by AuthorHouse   03/26/2015

ISBN: 978-1-5049-3725-2 (sc)
ISBN: 978-1-5049-3724-5 (hc)
ISBN: 978-1-5049-3726-9 (e)

Print information available on the last page.

Acknowledgements

A huge thank you to those that believed 13 days would be printed and to all the people that have encouraged me on the way. You know who you are.

Special thanks to Eilis Searson for a wonderfully inspired book cover and to Laura Ettenfield for her honesty and early editing.

We did it!

Wednesday

It was often dark and damp over by the reservoir. Justin Ivens had never taken much notice, until now, of the broken wall that encircled a small deciduous wood. The emotional pain he lived with continued to cut deep. It was proving too hard to disinter. God it hurt. How Justin felt the hurt. For the past three years, when shaving, Justin had kept his head down so as to avoid seeing himself in the mirror. The daily tears that filled the sink were proof that he still hadn't come to terms with his decision on that day. His life these days was nothing but a carousel of regret.

Although he lived alone, he often received visitors. These were not physical beings, but to him they were just as real. They were neither symptoms of psychosis nor an integral part of his personality but voices of his memories and their anger haunted him. Thankfully, there was one voice that soothed him, that of Fr Hennessey, the priest in charge of the seminary in Dublin where Justin had studied during the early 1980s. An extraordinary individual, Fr Hennessey had been a great role model for young radical seminarians, such as Justin.

"Remember, religious structure and convention is fine, providing it leads you to the heart of God's love. Otherwise it becomes the enemy of spiritual freedom, imprisoning one in a set of static rules," he had said.

After two years of ecclesiastical studies, Justin had begun seeing the world differently from those around him, making it increasingly difficult to continue living in community and achieve holy orders. The prospect of nurturing parishioners' souls had been a constant worry given the fact that he was struggling to cultivate his own. Not even Fr Hennessey had been able to succeed in dissuading Justin from leaving. After departing the seminary, Justin had continued to share in the liturgy of the church. The Mass had become an important element in his life. It helped Justin feel closer to God – that was, until three years ago. Since then his attendance had become almost non-existent.

They were good days, thought Justin.

Justin would never forget the look of disappointment on his parents' faces when he'd revealed his plan to study for the priesthood. Though aware of their son's deepening spirituality, they had never imagined he would want to become a priest. They had been somewhat distraught when he'd forfeited his place at medical college in favour of following a religious vocation. From a young age all Justin had ever wanted to be was a doctor. Hearing their son's wish to give up the chance of becoming a general practitioner, let alone marriage and children, had put them off balance. Once they had come to terms with the seriousness of Justin's vocation, like all good parents they'd given him their support and encouragement. Though, if the truth be told, they had given a collective sigh of relief when Justin had announced that he was leaving the seminary and resuming his original option of studying medicine at Cardiff University.

Yes, thought Justin, breathlessly resting against the weather-worn wall. *Yes, thank God for this place. If only I could feel better.*

If anybody had the right to assume a new life, then Justin Ivens was that person. The only stumbling block to this was Justin himself and his inability to believe he was worth it. This burden was presently proving too heavy. Neither psychotherapeutic nor psychiatric interventions had enabled Justin to free himself from his festering guilt. It seemed he was incapable of letting go and finding a new perspective for his shambolic life.

He walked twenty yards around the periphery of the reservoir and crouched down in the rough grass, scouring the water through his binoculars. The Clough was a reservoir supplying drinking water to parts of Lancashire. Appearing natural, it was surrounded by hills, dry stone walls, farmhouses, broken barns, and little woods. It was hidden within a small valley, providing a sense of its own time and space. It was a place Justin knew well. Every bird living on the moors and all the mammals resting within its spectacular landscape were his to see. Justin believed there was a mystical energy flowing through its landscape, but as yet, he hadn't been able to connect to this as he had during his childhood. Nevertheless, he was glad to have moved back north to the place where he had grown up. London had become too much for him. It now represented the city of many tears and the place of his shame.

The wind as usual was merciless, and the rain soaked his whole body, but he did not care. Having smelt the cold of a mid-November day and watched his breath float out into the world, Justin had in that moment sensed a crumb of peace. For a split second it had felt good. This was a blessing. But it was a blessing he knew could not last, and the feeling of peace extinguished itself with the last drag of his cigarette. Although fleeting, he couldn't deny the moment had existed and that freedom was somehow possible. Change had to come, but once again, he felt unable to instigate such a difficult process.

Sitting down on a large stone, he caught sight of a buzzard majestically circling above its next meal. This great bird waited with patience for the moment to swoop down and take the life of an animal that was unaware of its pending death. The bird was scanning every inch of its very own killing field. When the time was right, without sentiment it made its move. After a few seconds it was back on the wing heading towards the hills with its prey firmly held in its talons. Justin followed the bird closely through his binoculars as the magnificent creature glided by, exuding a sense of pride, secure in the knowledge of its own power.

"I wish I had that much strength," muttered Justin. "I wonder what Nina would have said."

More than thirty years ago Nina had introduced him to his first buzzard flying high over this very reservoir.

I wonder whether it's a descendent, he thought.

Bowing his head as though he was praying, he thought of her. Nina, his older sister, had always protected him. She had provided a great deal of security for Justin when growing up. She had understood his sensitivities and proclivities.

Even on the moors among the green rolling hills, Justin's fears constantly reminded him of his mistakes. They haunted him to the point of collapse. The memory of his actions still burned deep inside him. If only he could have held on to that earlier feeling of peace. It had felt to him like a free moment and not one tarnished with regret.

His best friend, believing life was too short for melancholia, had often told Justin there was not enough time for moping around. They no longer spoke to one another.

They had met at the local college while signing up for their respective courses. They had connected with each other in an instant, instinctively knowing that their friendship was special. They'd finished the day in the local pub where they'd exchanged ideas, jokes, and dreams. It was during this first meeting that Tom had realised Justin had spiritual leanings and was a churchgoer, unlike himself.

The rain was now beginning to wane, although Justin hadn't noticed. The Clough meant more to him than a damp body. Standing up, he turned 180 degrees to face the pinewoods, where he had smoked his first cigarette with Nina. The fun they had encountered over the years seeped into his mind. Justin had always enjoyed humour, but these days laughter was but a ghost from the past. Justin sat on a stone under a pale oak tree but started fidgeting, moving his position. Looking away from the reservoir, his eyes once again rested on the broken wall.

I wonder what happened, he thought. Focusing his attention on the hole, he wondered about all the years of repair and level of skill needed to build and maintain a dry stone wall. Through the hole he could see the swell of the water and birds disappearing every other second underneath the waves. The resident great crested grebes were diving at twenty-second intervals in search of fish. Having been out for over four hours, Justin was acutely aware of the time and how quickly darkness fell on these moors. He thought it was best to head home, and after a swift walk across the fields, he reached his car. The cold was now making him shiver. Before starting for home, he made the customary adjustment to his mirrors and then looked over his right shoulder before proceeding to drive. The journey was soon over. In no time at all, Justin was applying the handbrake on his filthy car. He walked through the front door of his cottage and picked up the morning post before making his way up the stairs to his bedroom. He stripped off his wet clothing and wrapped a soft, large towel around his now-warming body. Spying the letters, he opened a white envelope which had a Dundee postmark. His heart was thumping heavily, making him feel nauseous. There was only one person he knew who lived in Scotland: Tom.

Tears filled Justin's eyes. Crying was not only an emotional pain for him but a fierce physical exercise that impounded every muscle and organ in his worn-out body.

My God, what does he want?

He took a deep breath and exhaled for what seemed an eternity. The only thing that brought him back into consciousness was the noise of a car horn beeping outside. With eyes barely visible under an ocean of tears, he descended the stairs on legs weakened by what he had just read. A search for his cigarettes took him to the kitchen table where he immediately sparked one up. The day had arrived, the one day he had been holding on to in his darkest moments. If only he had not been born Justin Ivens, that decision, that day, would have belonged to another. His hands were shaking so violently he dropped cigarette ash on the floor. The opportunity to speak with Tom had arrived, but rather than joy, a sense of dread filled him. Looking again at the tear-stained letter, a surge of adrenalin hit his aching head.

Well, this is what you've been hoping for.

Justin's nervousness now made him vigorously shake his head, reminiscent of a boxer taking a mandatory eight count. The letter had dazed him, leaving him weak-kneed and uncertain about his future.

Would meeting Tom help my life to change? Can I find the inner strength to meet him? These were only two of the questions Justin now had to face.

The slit in Tom's living room curtains suddenly filled with the enormous, balding head of his tedious next-door neighbour as he passed by the front window.

"I thought I had problems," laughed Tom. "At least I can't use my cap to carry the shopping!"

He smiled wryly. He knew his acerbic humour had over the years upset some individuals. Lessons had been learned. Recently life had been hard for Tom, a continuous struggle to make sense of his and the world's demand for change. In his mind, change had always been a concept left to those moaning malcontents who no longer enjoyed everyday life. Recently, strange thoughts were unhinging him, demanding his attention, calling him to think outside his comfort zone. Life for Tom appeared ridiculously unfair, nothing more than a lottery wheel producing endless miscalculations. Yet for those who truly knew him, Tom was a presence that would always be there when called upon. He just refused to suffer fools gladly. A tosser was a tosser in everybody's language, and he was never afraid to say so. Taking a long gulp of tea, his thoughts returned to the past. As he placed his cup on the table, he felt another of those strange moments enter into his mind. Something had moved him. Whatever it might be, he no longer wanted to ignore it. Compelled to face the future with sincerity, Tom no longer wanted to live the life of the wounded and continue playing the blame game. Finishing his drink, he made his way to the kitchen. As he walked towards the sink, the previous night's excess came crashing through his head. *Shit! I feel terrible. I need to lie down.*

Still knackered after a couple of hours rest, Tom forced himself out of bed. He showered and made his way downstairs to cook something that would help him feel normal again. Stumbling off the last step, he saw that the red light on his answering machine was flashing. *I can't be bothered listening to them just yet. I need to get some food down me*, he thought.

Inside his front door were four letters. A purple envelope with handwritten address was from his only child, Mark. The other three were junk mail advertising credit cards. He quickly discarded these. It pleased Tom that Mark wrote letters rather than sending him e-mails. They seemed more personal than a screen. Opening a letter always filled Tom with anticipation. Tom began reading the letter with amusement.

"Great, Mark's definitely coming back for Christmas." Laughing, Tom continued reading the letter. Mark's literature class was visiting Stratford-upon-Avon the following weekend to see *The Merchant of Venice*. His coffers were dry, and he was wondering whether Tom might send him seventy quid, of which twenty-five would cover the Stratford enterprise and the rest would be spent watching Blackburn Rovers play in Birmingham the following day. Tom loved Mark and missed seeing him on a regular basis. He knew his son; Mark was no spendthrift and had never demanded anything when growing up. Despite being a student living with friends in Manchester, he rarely asked for money. Tom was proud of him. When Chrissie had died, Mark had been a great support, having come to terms with his mother's death more easily than Tom. Even as a small child Mark had been sensitive to other people's needs. Tom had thought he might etch out a career within the caring services and had been surprised when Mark had rejected this idea. More recently Mark had expressed an interest in travelling to Peru once his studies were finished, with clear thoughts of journalism on his return. Believing he didn't have the right to interfere in his son's decisions, Tom took a step back, though as far as he was concerned, he had little time or respect for journalists. At a time when Tom was at his lowest ebb their intrusion had been hurtful, their lack of decency appalling, and their persistent presence bewildering. Given this, Tom was intelligent enough to acknowledge that not all journalists were slugs or all publications, comics. But it had been a long time since he had purchased a newspaper. Putting these thoughts aside, he began cooking a breakfast that was so large a pack of starving dogs would not manage to consume it all.

While still struggling to comprehend his loss, Tom had made himself go back to work after Chrissie's death. Interacting with others had kept him from the perils of splendid isolation. Suicide had been a real option soon after his bereavement, but his desire to see Mark grow up had provided the needed incentive to live. The family house they all had shared in London had become a shrine to her. It had been too painful an experience to live day by day without Chrissie being there. He had loved London, but without her, the city swamped him. Feeling misplaced without his love by his side had been just too much to bear. The light that had been his guide had extinguished. No longer had he been able to live in London. Too many tears had been shed in that city. Having made the decision to move, it hadn't taken him long to relocate to Scotland. This was a place Chrissie had loved, an oasis where he could still feel close to her. They had spent many happy times on the east coast and had talked about retiring there. How he still missed her. At times it was overwhelming. Here in Scotland, people had no knowledge of his history and weren't aware of his loss. This had helped; it meant that they never felt awkward around him or needed to ask uncomfortable questions. Some had become friends from his time in the local pubs; others remained nodding acquaintances whenever he entered the bar.

The jingle of the doorbell brought Tom out of his daydream. Opening the door, he saw the wife of one of his work colleagues.

"Sorry to bother you, Tom – that is your name, isn't it? I'm Viv Charles, Ken's wife."

"I know," said Tom. "I remember you from his birthday bash."

Why has she knocked on my door? Is there some sort of emergency? Does she need help? Something must be amiss, as Viv had no reason to call on him. He said, "Come in. Do you want a drink of tea or something stronger perhaps?"

"Tea would be nice," she replied, taking a seat in the living room.

After fetching two cups of tea, Tom sat down on the chair opposite Viv. Studying her, he couldn't help but admire the beauty of her high cheekbones. He noticed that a hairdresser's bottle had highlighted her naturally blonde hair, making her face even more attractive. Her body was also impressive. She looked strong to Tom.

"What's the matter, Viv?" he asked.

"I'm sorry to bother you, but Ken said he liked you. Apparently, you make him laugh. He loves the stories about your band. What were you called? Wasn't it Think before You Blink? Ken refers to your tales as the gospel according to Sassenach."

Tom didn't know what to think. Although he worked with Ken, he had never thought they were close. Never mind the subject of conversation. This made the situation even more intriguing.

Giving a nervous cough as if to dislodge something from her throat, Viv said, "I think Ken's left me."

"What?" Tom exclaimed.

"I haven't seen him for two days. He's been so moody recently," she said, staring into space.

Poor Viv, Tom thought, wanting to hug and ease away her pain. This was given short shrift as Tom didn't want it to be misconstrued. Instead, he asked whether she had any idea where Ken might be.

"No, that's why I'm here. I think I know what the problem is, though," she replied. "I've never wanted children, but he knew that from the start. He's gone and disappeared. It has to be the baby thing again. None of his friends seem to know where he is. I just hoped you might have some idea."

Tom had absolutely none, not having seen him at work. "When did you say he left?" Tom asked.

"It was a couple of days ago. He was tense. I could tell there was something bothering him. Why has he sneaked off? I'm wondering whether he has found somebody else."

"How important are children to Ken?" he asked.

"Obviously greater than I'd imagined."

"I'm at a loss as to why he just left," Tom said. "I'm sorry, Viv; I really can't help you. I wish I could. What I can do is make enquiries at the pub. I'll see what I can find out. Have you informed the police?"

"Yes, but being fair to them, there isn't much they can do other than to circulate his description around the stations."

Apologising for any inconvenience, Viv made her way outside. For the first time in three years Tom was looking at a woman and sensing something other than indifference. He was smitten, not only with her beauty but also with her personality. She unsteadied him. An excitement he had not felt since falling in love with Chrissie was now flowing freely through him. A feeling of elation gripped his whole body. This subsided as feelings of guilt quickly spread through his mind. He had loved only one woman, but she was no longer with him, although she still lived in his heart and mind. Yet there was something about Viv that couldn't be quelled. She was a presence that had taken a firm grip within Tom's thoughts, which he could not shake off.

Returning to the house, he sat down in the armchair. His marriage had not been perfect, but it had been strong, the sort people believed would last a lifetime. They'd had the usual arguments about where to go on holiday, which friends to invite on a Saturday evening, or how much money they had spent that month. For all this, Chrissie and Tom had been well suited and had recognised that two people could damage one another if they were not allowed to breathe. Experiencing periods of boredom, they would spend time apart. After being given this space, they'd always reunited with vigour and new conversation. That was, until her last few months when she'd changed, not only in a physical sense but also in her personality. Becoming inward-looking, she had no longer been the woman he had known and loved. Brain tumours were a nasty thing. Although not a religious man, he believed in trust. It had always been his intention to be with her for better or for worse. Once he had uttered the words "I do," he had entered into a commitment for life. Nowadays, Tom had ceased asking the question why regarding Chrissie's death. The question had made him ill, and it was futile. His heart was still hurting, and he believed it always would.

———————

Pouring himself a can of beer, Justin thought about Tom and wondered whether he had dated anyone else after Chrissie.

How did he manage to find my address? I'll phone him rather than write, but I won't do it now; I need time to think about it. Maybe I should suggest a get-together. Maybe I should ... Justin had too many questions, and they were raising insecurities, making him anxious. He decided to go to bed and try to get some rest; otherwise he would over think things.

Thursday

The alarm sounded at 8.30 a.m., and Justin slid out of bed. He washed and then went downstairs. The usual tiredness followed him. His body only revived itself after numerous cups of tea and cigarettes. Today he would go walking and bird watching. It was 9.45 and much later than he'd intended by the time he left the house. Making his way past the pub, he took a right turn on to a small road and continued until he reached a gate, which he slowly opened. The large field was full of sheep, all of which seemed content with their lives as they chomped the green pasture.

The day was overcast and typical for the north-west of England. This was beauty, if only people could see it. Pondering upon nature's aesthetic and anaesthetic properties, Justin understood their complexity. Some days he would feel the wind biting his ears, leaving them painful and sore. Yet on others the breeze breathed life into his restless soul. As with the seasons, human emotions also produced extremities from the splendid to the turbulent. Nature and its elements were now Justin's church, the sanctuary of his sorrows, the cloud of his unknowing. Watching a blackbird building its nest on a mild spring day or observing a stoat hunting for prey in the depths of winter helped to soothe him. They all had a story to tell. They all held a truth. This was where God would live, if indeed God did exist. Desperately wanting to reconnect with his faith, Justin somehow had to rediscover his loving heart.

The weather did not stop him from frequenting the Clough. Climbing halfway up the steep field, he could see the start of the Ribble Valley. In the background stood two green domes belonging to Stonyhurst College, a legacy to the Counter-Reformation. To the left in the forefront was Blackburn Rover's Academy, a monstrosity of a building, a symbol of modernity – square, bold, and lifeless. Searching the landscape, Justin could not ease his active mind. It was forever clicking, running, churning out something from his past. He was a prisoner of his memories. Slowly walking towards the reservoir, he entered another field which was home to even more sheep. Alongside them were the territorial lapwings that were once a more prominent feature of Lancashire skylines. Numerous times he and Nina had watched them perform flying feats the greatest pilot could only dream of mirroring.

The huge, cold winter sun hung in the sky, having forced its way through the clouds. Its colour was such a deep orange Justin thought it had fallen out of a Turner painting. The sun seemed to be beckoning him to stare deep into the great ball of fire. The many hours he and Nina had spent debating whether one day humans would visit the sun filled his thoughts. Like Justin, she had developed a deep love of science. From an early age she had decided to become an industrial chemist. Justin smiled as he remembered her fortitude and dedication. Her choice of subjects had been unusual given the expectation of the time that women at university should study compliant subjects like home economics. Her form teacher had suggested she study English literature so that she could at least teach in between pregnancies. Being the force she was, Nina had told her teacher to sod off and then continued to follow her dream. After graduating, she'd started work as an industrial chemist for a small pharmaceutical firm in Blackburn. She had been a natural chemist.

Scotland was cold, very cold. Arriving home early from work, Tom remembered that he had not yet listened to the previous day's messages on his answering machine. *I wonder if one is from Justin.* In a nervous, strangely foreboding way, he hoped one was. For all the pain it had caused, he still missed Justin's friendship. The depth of amity he had once shared with Justin was something he'd not yet encountered in Scotland. He pressed the playback button, and the first message informed him that the five-a-side game that evening had changed from a five o'clock kick-off to six. The second message informed him that the library had the book he was waiting for, *The*

Iron Heel. Great, Tom thought, *I can't wait to read it again.* His father had given him this book as part of a rite of passage into adulthood.

The third message took him by surprise. It was from Ken; he wanted Tom to ring him on his mobile as soon as possible. *Bloody hell,* Tom mused. *What's he gone and done?*

Tom dialled the number. Ken answered immediately and said, "Thanks for getting back to me. Is there any chance of meeting up? I've landed myself right in it. I've completely screwed up."

Tom was initially unsure, as he didn't believe in interfering in other people's business. This time, though, he was going to break his golden rule, especially with seeing how upset Viv had been. He wanted to help her if he could.

"Yes, sure. Do you want to come over to mine now? I've to be at football for six."

"Cheers, Tom, I'll be there within the hour."

Tom hoped that Ken was okay but did not want Viv thinking he was meddling in their business. Sitting with a cup of coffee in the living room, Tom waited for Ken to arrive, wondering why Ken had contacted him. *Yes, he invited me to his birthday party, but we're more acquaintances than friends.* His thoughts were interrupted by the sound of a car engine that had a large hole in its exhaust. The driver looked wired and dishevelled, an unusual state for Ken, or Gucci Boy, as he was known as at work. It was apparent that he'd taken a day off from his immaculate grooming. Rising from his seat, Tom went to open the front door.

"Come in; sit yourself down. You look knackered," said Tom.

"Tell me about it. I haven't slept for two nights. All I've done is sit and think. I'm all out of thoughts. I just feel paranoid."

His weary voice sounded thin, hoarse, and strained, similar to a singer who had not warmed up his or her voice.

"Do you fancy a drink?"

"No thanks Tom," said Ken.

For the life in him, Tom couldn't understand why Ken had chosen him. *Why is this happening to me? Surely he must have friends.*

"How come you've asked me to help? Not that I won't," asked Tom.

"To be honest pal, nobody else seems to want to listen," Ken replied.

"What's going on?" Tom asked. "You look like shit. Are you sure you don't want a drink, or something to eat?" Tom stopped talking, thinking that he might have been a little forward with his remarks.

"No, I'm okay. Later maybe," Ken said. "By the way, I've left Viv."

"I know," replied Tom.

"How come you know?" Ken asked.

"Viv was here asking if I'd seen you; she was very upset."

"What did she say?" Ken asked.

Tom provided a brief overview. Here he was in his own house listening to a colleague from work spill out all his secrets. His attempts to distance himself from Ken and Viv's marital problems were becoming more and more futile by the second.

"Why did she come here?" Ken asked.

"In desperation I think. It seems she'd tried all the obvious people, but nobody had any clue where you were. Are you in some sort of trouble?"

"You know Gemma, the barmaid from the Boar?"

"Yes," replied Tom.

"She's having my baby!"

"Shit," Tom spluttered.

"I know. I need to sort my head out," said Ken fearfully.

You're not joking, thought Tom. "Do you love her?"

"I've always wanted kids, but I didn't want it to be like this," replied Ken, deflecting Tom's question. "I was hoping to talk Viv round, although I haven't succeeded in all the years we've been together. She did tell me her feelings in the beginning, but I really thought she would change and become maternal. All my brothers have children. She adores them but says she doesn't want any of her own. The trouble is I do."

Feeling uncomfortable, Tom fiddled with his hands. *What can I say?* In truth, there was very little he could say. Tom imagined how his wife would have reacted if he had been in Ken's position. Fortunately, they had held the same view; both had wanted one child – boy or girl, it had made no difference. Mark was the product of their life together. And in Tom's eyes he was a very good return indeed.

"I always thought you and Viv were close," said Tom.

"We were," replied Ken.

Tom had to fight back a smirk as he thought about his father's favourite sayings: *No matter how much one person in a relationship wants something, they are powerless without the support of the other,* and *if you're having troubles with your partner, don't get yourself another.* These seemed wise words indeed from where Tom was sitting.

Leaning back, Ken stretched his arms, forcing them outwards as if his life depended upon it – the type of movement used to reinvigorate and ensure there was still some life beneath the worn-out surface. The sun's rays highlighted his greying hair, and its multiple shades represented a November morning sky right there on his head. Ken was handsome in a smooth kind of way, and Tom understood why women were attracted to him. Goth and hippy women wouldn't be able get past his immaculate clothing, which he usually wore so well, but to those women who liked a well-turned-out man, he was the perfect Thunderbird puppet, Scott Tracy to the rescue. Reminding himself to stop taking the piss, Tom refocused his thoughts on Ken. Humour had always been Tom's retreat when under pressure. It was a way in which he covered up his inadequacies. *Still, I am a comic genius.*

"How long has it been going on for?" Tom asked.

"Six months. We started seeing each other on the snooker night at the King's Arms. Do you not remember we lost in the final of the mixed doubles? Mind you, the signs had been there for a while. It just happened."

Though Gemma had a pretty face, Tom thought she resembled a little mouse. Insipid would be too strong of a word, timid would not. It struck Tom that he really didn't know Ken, making this time together even more bizarre. *What am I supposed to do? Maybe there's still time for him to sort it out with Viv.*

"Don't you think Viv has a right to know what's going on directly from you, Ken, and not somebody else?" asked Tom.

"I suppose so," replied Ken. He suddenly let out a noise evocative of a trapped hare that knew its life had just become finite.

"What is it?" Tom asked.

"Shit! Viv's here. What should I do?"

Tom twisted around to look through the window behind him and saw Viv's car pulling up outside his house.

"Talk to her," said Tom.

"I-I can't," stuttered Ken.

"You've no option; she knows you're here. She's seen your car."

"Fuck, shit, bollocks!" shouted Ken.

Tom wanted to laugh out loud at these expletives, but a rapid banging on the door soon killed this desire. "I'm going to have to answer it. Maybe you need to face this head-on," said Tom.

When Tom opened the door, Viv shouted, "How long has Houdini been here? Where is he?" Don't tell me he isn't here. I saw him turn in to the street no more than ten minutes ago. He passed me on the main road. I made a U turn and followed him here."

Pushing past Tom, Viv headed for the living room where Ken was sitting on the settee. Retreating into the kitchen, Tom once again heard his father's voice. *Thy never knows what goes on behind closed doors, Son.*

Maybe she isn't the one for me, Tom thought, referring back to his earlier reverie

"Well then, what've you got to say for yourself?" she screamed.

As they squared up to one another, Tom's admiration for Viv grew again. At least *she doesn't take any crap. What a temper. It's bloody breathtaking.*

"Sit down, Viv," Ken pleaded. "In fact we might be better to go home and continue this discussion there," said Ken.

"Home? It's no longer your home. I don't want you anywhere near the house again."

Stepping into the room, concerned that the argument might turn physical, Tom said, "Listen, I don't mind you using this place, but I think it might be a good idea for you, Ken, to go and get some fresh air and clear your head. You have a lot to deal with. Viv, maybe it would be best if you sit down and take a deep breath."

Remaining in silence, neither left the room. They sat in their own sadness, symbolising the parting of their ways.

————

A little lighter in spirit, Justin headed back home from the fields, having made a conscious effort to concentrate his energies on the wildlife and the physical environment of the moors. In theory, this meant he would spend less time revisiting his memories. Many times over the years Justin had discussed this very issue with his therapist. She had encouraged him to shift his perspective from that of internal struggles to an external reality. Since leaving London and moving north, he had not re-engaged in therapy. Maybe, just maybe, he had made a little progress today; after all, life should not be static. The rain which was inevitable given the heaviness of the clouds started as Justin crossed the face of the dam. Standing still for a moment, he listened to the rip-rap. It seemed to him that the rhythmical lapping waters were chanting encouragement that he should never give up. The rain was sweeping down from the north, hitting his face, paining him, like tiny pins pricking into his raw, flushed skin. It was oddly invigorating. In need of shelter, Justin took cover in the smallest copse and rested on a horizontal tree that had fallen. It was slowly decomposing as the full force of the seasons had first dried and then soaked the dead yet life-giving tree. It was a hotbed for many sorts of insect life, providing a space of rest and sustenance for all manner of creatures, including Justin Ivens.

Nina's smile began to fill his mind. The hours of fun they had enjoyed as children resurfaced in his thoughts. She had protected him throughout his schooldays. Not only popular with boys, she had been equally admired by the girls. Justin was lucky as he had never been bullied with everybody looking out for him on Nina's say-so. She'd had the ability to embrace people who opposed each other, cutting a path through both camps. People had just wanted to please her.

The rustle of leaves and the squelch of boggy ground underfoot interrupted Justin's meandering thoughts. A short but large man with an obvious purpose moved quickly towards him.

"Excuse me, can you help? I've lost my dog and need to find him. Actually, he's not mine; I'm dog-sitting. He's managed to slip my grip and run away. Have you seen a little black-and-white Border collie? He won't worry the sheep, but apparently he'll try to round them up," the man said with concern.

"In that case we're better searching in that field there," said Justin, pointing at a large piece of land ideal for grazing.

"Thanks," said the man.

"What's his name?" Justin asked.

"Barrington."

"Barrington?" Justin repeated. It seemed an odd name for a dog. It made him wonder if the owners had a son named Tristan or something worse like Oscar Tobias.

They both began calling the dog's name.

The man introduced himself as John Taylor, on holiday with his wife and two children. They had borrowed their friend's house in nearby Whalley, a small village nestling on the River Calder. Justin had spent many childhood weekends there fishing and exploring the abbey ruins. Being brought up in the Ribble Valley with its folklore and traditions had helped Justin appreciate nature.

"There he is," shouted John, running towards the dog.

"John, stop! He'll never come back if you chase him. Let him know you're here; then he'll come to you."

"Okay," he replied, oblivious as to how one should handle a dog.

"Barrington, come here, boy," called Justin. "Good boy, come."

Barrington had already gathered the sheep into an attentive and obedient flock. Running towards Justin, Barrington jumped and stretched his slender but flexible legs, barking excitedly, as though he had discovered the biggest bone ever. On reaching Justin, the dog settled at his side, seeking approval for a job well done. With tongue hanging over the left side of his mouth, the dog's eyes mischievously kept darting back towards his conquest.

"The old rascal can shift a bit, can't he?" John remarked.

"He sure can," replied Justin. "He's a real handful. No disrespect, but Barrington, what's that about?

"No idea. By the way, you didn't tell me your name," said John.

"It's Justin. I live down in the village, over there as the crow flies," he replied, pointing towards the field with the rocks.

"I've parked my car outside some cottages next to a very enticing-looking pub. Do you fancy a pint as a little thank you for your help? I reckon I'd be halfway to Blackburn by now, if you hadn't told me to stop running."

"I'm sorry; I can't," replied Justin.

"Come on; I won't take no for an answer," said John firmly.

Justin eventually relented.

Making their way to the pub, Justin explained the history of the Clough. "There's a village under the water," said Justin.

"Get away with you," said John.

"There is, trust me."

"Well, I'll be damned."

Reaching their destination, John opened the door to his car and let Barrington sprawl out on the back seat. With this done, John walked through the door of the pub and immediately went to the bar to talk to the staff about their beers and get their recommendation.

"A pint of …?" John asked, turning to Justin.

"I'll have the same as you please," replied Justin. "I'll go and sit down next to the fire."

After a few more minutes of small talk with the staff, John joined Justin.

"Now then," said John. "Seems like a nice place to frequent, a bit too close to home though, a little too tempting no doubt?"

"Funnily enough I don't usually bother. I'm usually too busy," said Justin.

"I'm never too busy for a pint. It's what keeps me sane," laughed John. "It gets me away from the kids for a while."

"I'm guessing from your accent you're from the West Country."

"It's not difficult," John laughed. "We live in Bristol, Clifton to be precise. Are you familiar with it at all?"

"I can't say I am," replied Justin.

"I couldn't live here," said John. "It's too far out from the hub for me, too many fields. Anne and I actually like city life. There's everything we need in Bristol – great shops, excellent schools, and a bustling nightlife with plenty of music and theatre. We don't have the quintessential dream of living in England's green and pleasant land, but who in their right mind would want to spend time reading bloody Blake on top of some soggy mountain in the pissing rain? Not me. It's all right doing this once a year, but it's not a vision Anne or I have. I don't want a dog and definitely wouldn't want to walk it every day. As far as I'm concerned, trees are trees, birds shit everywhere, and as for cows and sheep, I get what I need from the butchers. What about you then, Justin? The way you handled Barrington suggests you'd be a country boy. Have you always lived with sheep?"

"Oi, be careful. This is Lancashire, not Yorkshire," said Justin.

"That's true," chuckled John. "I suppose the Welsh know what I mean."

They both sniggered, acknowledging that the old jokes were still the best. John's easy nature was helping Justin forget his troubles. And for the first time in three years he was relaxing in company.

"I've spent the biggest part of my life between the Ribble Valley and London. But these moors are where my heart lies," said Justin.

"Well these moors don't quite do it for me, but at least you can get a decent pint round here. It's hoppy but smooth, golden and sweet," John said, beginning to wax lyrical.

"That's enough, John; it's only a bloody pint."

"Hey, watch what you're saying. I'm a bit of a poet, I'll have you know."

"A bit poet more like," replied Justin, thinking how John's sense of humour reminded him of Tom. "Fancy another?"

"I do. However, I won't with drink-driving and all that. Anyway, I need to get back; I promised Anne and the kids we'd go to the Indian restaurant tonight. We always save enough money to eat out when we're on holiday. It saves the washing-up."

"No problem. It's been nice meeting you. Oh, and enjoy walking Barrington – not," laughed Justin.

"Take care," replied John as he walked out the door.

It wasn't just the weather on the east coast of Scotland that was thunderous. For the past hour there had been a torrent of insults lashing down in Tom's house. The atmosphere now seemed less fraught, with exhaustion having taken over. The two warring sides were unsure whether they still had to face further battles. For the moment, both seemed content for their bodies to rest and take relief in their own silence. They could no longer summon enough energy to confront their immediate futures. Tom looked over toward Viv who appeared traumatised, like a post-operative patient. He imagined Viv was unable to make sense of what had just taken place and thought she must be struggling to know where she was and to coordinate her thoughts. *What will you do next? Tom thought.* Admiring her beauty, Tom breathed in her distress and wanted to blanket her emotional exposure. Her flittering eyes, which had been hostile, were now still and as red as her lipstick. Wanting to rescue her, to reassure her, to hold her, Tom had to feel her hurt from afar. There was little movement from Ken, who lay in the foetal position in the middle of the settee. The only thing amiss was the sucking of his thumb. His eyes were tightly shut, as though he was attempting to block out the reality of what he had done. He was far too exhausted to speak. Viv leaned back into the chair and let her gaze settle on the ceiling, as though contemplating emerging doubts. Her eyelids looked heavy, as if her many tears had irritated and made them sore. Hoping that they could work through their differences and begin again, Tom made his way into the kitchen, leaving them to rest. Over the years, he had seen friends argue so intensely that they had become emotionally bankrupt, keeping them destitute for many years. Ten minutes had passed by the time he entered the living room with a tray of tea and biscuits. He alerted them to his presence with a small cough. No matter what the problem, this ritual was sacrosanct – homemade biscuits and cake with hot mugs of tea. Speaking softly, Tom handed each a cup and chocolate flapjacks baked and delivered two days previously by Gladys, one of his neighbours. Fearing he was not looking after himself, she had expressed her concerns to him that day. She was a lovely elderly woman with a heart the size of Scotland, and Tom felt ashamed when he'd realised it was his drinking habits that so worried her. What Gladys had seen that day was nothing more than a throbbing hangover, a state he was becoming too accustomed to of late. His binges were burdensome. Bored with throwing alcohol into his tired body, he wanted to stay sober, although deep down he knew he could never take the pledge. All he wanted to do was to find some other pastime and save his liver on the way. When his wife had been alive, he had gone fishing, but since she had passed away, he seemed unable to find comfort or enjoyment in hobbies. It was time to start afresh and find new interests; his mind now craved stimulation from something other than alcohol.

Sitting apart in silence, Viv and Ken avoided eye contact. They drank and ate within their newly defined, very separate spaces. Perturbed, Tom had not expected this. Somewhat naively he'd thought they would find a way to bury their differences and realise seven years was a strong enough basis to fight for and rebuild their disintegrating relationship. That had been his hope. The reality was that Ken had cheated on his wife.

Why should Viv forgive him? Would Ken do the same if it had been on the other foot? Tom doubted that he would. What he did know was that today was not a good day for them. Aware of the time, Tom also knew he was unlikely to make it to the five-a-side game. It didn't feel right asking them to leave at such a delicate time.

"Look me in the eyes, and tell me you no longer love me," Viv demanded.

Looking at them, Tom wanted to tell them they needed to give the situation time, take a day or two to come to terms with what had happened.

"Well?" asked Viv.

"You know I've always wanted children," Ken said.

"Answer my question!"

"I would if you'd let me," Ken shouted.

"I've had enough of this; I don't want to go over it again. I don't need to hear any more."

Viv quickly gathered her coat and made her way towards the front door. Before Tom could speak with her, she was already in her car and setting off down the road. Caught in his emotions, he was glad the memories of his own marriage were happier than that of Viv and Ken. Lingering by the front door, remembering his wedding day, he pictured his bride. Their big day had been eventful. The ceremony itself had been fantastic, but after the service it had turned farcical. By the time the wedding party had arrived at the restaurant, the chef had been so inebriated he had fallen asleep on the kitchen floor. When the best man had enquired about the delay, he'd found two men and three women trying to lift the twenty-stone beast of a man out of the way. They had laughed about it afterwards. The assistant chef had provided a top-class meal.

Strange noises distracted Tom from these recollections of happier days. He returned to the living room where Ken was pacing up and down. The sounds coming from him were incomprehensible – primeval and guttural. Bent over, he was biting the back of one hand while grabbing hard at his hair with the other.

Bloody hell, Tom thought, fighting back his laughter. "Ken! Ken, what the …! Ken, listen to me. Come and sit down. You're going to hurt yourself."

Tom led him by the arm to a chair and went to pour him a brandy.

"My God, I needed that," said Ken in between large gulps that made him frown. "I'm so tired."

"Right, go into the spare room and have a sleep; it'll do you good. What time do you want waking?" Tom asked.

"About seven," replied an exhausted Ken.

"It'll be better for me if it's about half past eight. I'm going to play five-a-side from six until seven, then nip for a pint with the lads afterwards. If I set off now, I'll only be five minutes late. I need to stretch my legs, get some air," said Tom.

"Aye, that sounds a good idea. Thanks, Tom. I don't know how I'm going to repay you for this," replied Ken.

"That's okay. I'm sure you'd do the same for me. Listen, I'm off; see you later," said Tom, grabbing his sports bag from the cupboard at the side of the front door.

Just after eight thirty Tom walked into an empty house with no note or any hint of where Ken might be. Hoping he was okay, Tom couldn't help but wonder whether he was with Viv or Gemma. Tom poured himself a beer and began dissecting the game. Although he enjoyed playing football, he had very little skill. What he lacked in that department he made up with enthusiasm. Rigorously rubbing his sore ankles, Tom rightly knew that age was the enemy of the game. As he drank a glass of water in an attempt to rehydrate himself, his thoughts rested on Viv, hoping that she wasn't hurting too much.

Friday

When he woke the next morning, Tom was still unclear as to Ken's whereabouts. As usual, Tom arrived ten minutes early for work. He felt a strong inclination that Ken was likely to turn up there today. Removing his overcoat, he reflected on his life. Over the past few days he had felt more alive, as though he was being prepared for another age, another time. Philosophy had never been Tom's forte; although academically bright, he had always referred to self-searching as some type of hippy bollocks. Yet here he was sitting at his workbench deep in thought about what change might mean for him. No longer could he deny the inner rumblings of his psyche. It was as though he sensed an inner light but presently was not able to understand its meaning. Tom could no longer deny this; he had to accept it was there. It was like a metaphor, a representation which hopefully, in time, would lead him to a peaceful consciousness. Never having been one to suffer delusions, he knew life was tough, sometimes unbearable, but he was sure it was more than the material, the shallowness of consumerism, or the countless nights when he drank too much. Since he'd lost Chrissie his world had become opaque, where every day was the same irrespective of the season. Colours were now faded, shapes had wilted, and people silhouetted. Direction no longer existed. But today Tom felt differently. It was a new day.

Analysing the day's jobs, he would first strip down one of the machines used for canning fruits, in this case, raspberries. The motor needed replacing, but as yet there had been no talk of further investment. For now he had to make sure it continued functioning. It was work Tom enjoyed. The other workers on the whole were good people, and they shared a laugh together. The responsibilities Tom undertook kept him busy throughout his shift. Picking up his spanner, he thought about Ken and, of course, Viv, making him feel disloyal towards Chrissie. But the more thinking he did, the more it seemed he should be with someone else.

"Thanks, Chrissie," he said, knowing that she had given him encouragement to fall in love again, something he had not contemplated until meeting Viv. He was very lonely and needed comforting but had still not given himself permission to move on.

"Well then, my old mocker," someone said.

Tom raised his head to see Gucci Boy standing in front of him. He seemed well considering his recent antics. He was different from yesterday, when he'd appeared to be a shadow, a nervous wreck, like the proverbial rat cornered with nowhere to hide. This was no condemned man wrestling with his conscience. No, it was the opposite from the previous day. Ken was boasting, almost smug. His attitude surprised Tom.

"Viv's left me, but to be honest, Tom, we've both been unhappy for a while. I just feel totally relieved. At least me and Gemma can get on with our lives," said Ken.

Genuinely shocked, Tom could not understand how easy it seemed for Ken to cut out seven years of his life. His dismissal of Viv seemed almost brutal, and Tom found it difficult to understand his uncaring attitude. *He's like a different person from yesterday,* thought Tom. Today he was arrogant. The thought that one day Ken might inflict the same treatment on Gemma rushed through Tom's mind.

"Well, I'm glad everything's worked out for you," Tom lied. "By the way, how is Viv?"

"She's gone to stay with her mother, who no doubt will be happy; she never liked me," replied Ken.

Callous bastard, Tom thought. A swell of resentment rose within him like a river in flood, peaking, bursting its banks, and ready to discharge its venomous fury all over Ken.

"Well, good luck to you. I hope you'll be happy," Tom lied again, wishing a plague of locust would visit, suck him dry, and leave his carcass for the jackals to strip bare.

"Aye, thanks. I've got to go; I've a lot to arrange. Maybe see you later," Ken said.

"Maybe," responded Tom.

Shaking his head in disbelief, Tom picked up his screwdriver, but it immediately slipped out of his fingers. Irritation was pumping sweat into every pore of his body. His hands were quivering. He felt overpowered by his feelings, dizzy and light-headed. *The situation between Ken and Viv is none of my business, so why am I acting like a schoolboy?* Tom thought.

His feelings for Viv were real. They were unstoppable. By contrast, his brooding anger towards Ken flowed through his body like mercury – slowly, heavily, and poisonously. For a crazy second, he wondered whether Viv might be his soul mate sent by some benevolent force in the universe. This soon passed. What he was feeling was pure, unadulterated lust.

———————

Justin prepared himself to walk the Clough. He needed the morning air to revive his senses. Today, he walked half a mile up the road and entered it from a different angle. As he reached its peak, a green woodpecker flew across the road towards a collection of elm trees. It flashed by in all its glory – yellow, red, and green; bright and beautiful; an incandescent sight against the backdrop of a colourless sky. Resting on the stile, Justin was able to observe the entire reservoir. This was his favourite view of the valley; the water looked as though it had been there from the very beginning of time. Maybe the human race had some redeeming features after all. The life of the Clough was testimony to that.

As the morning unfolded, there was a stirring wind and a complete lack of sunshine, but it was fine. No matter what the conditions on the moor, it was perfect for Justin. Coursing his way down the field in the direction of the reservoir, he thought about the telephone call he was to make that evening to Tom. He was more than a little anxious. A loud honking sound made Justin look skywards where he spied a skein of barnacle geese flying by. Justin wished that he could be a migratory bird heading for sunnier climates, where a new life would be waiting for him. The need for security was chipping away at Justin, leaving him to face the dilemma of fight or flight. In this instance Justin had to fight, not literally with fists but allegorically. He had to face his responsibilities that were weighing heavily on his weary shoulders. These days his best friend was little more than a name. His regrets regarding Tom were many. He believed they both had buried their relationship under misconceptions and misgivings, symbolising the director's cut lying at the bottom of the waste bin, destined to be lost forever. What had happened was an undeniable fact; he lived with his memories, and they were hideous. Many people had defended Justin's actions on that day, claiming it to be an act of love, yet they could not have known it would leave him drained of moral strength, that it would cause his belief system to break down and die. Justin was Justin no more. No matter how much spiritual water he drank, he could not forgive himself. Recently, he'd attended Holy Communion, but by the end of the Mass he'd felt neither sustained nor, more importantly, forgiven. He thought the act more emblematic, as a kind of last refuge for the scoundrel.

He looked at the reservoir through his binoculars. The water was shining, moving to the rhythm of his heartbeat, fast, furious, and unsettled. In his loneliness, he wanted to shout at the top of his voice that he was sorry for the hurt he had caused. Since that day, Justin had become obsessed with the shortness of human life, acknowledging that even if he were to live for a century, his life would be less than a microsecond in infinity. Gathering his thoughts, he peered down towards the ground where he spotted the skeleton of a sheep, its bones a testimony to an existence extinguished. In life, they had been white, but now, having been exposed and ravished by the elements, they had turned grey. Predators had stripped them bare, only too eager to sustain their own lives, devouring every inch of flesh in fear of their own deaths. The screech of a curlew made Justin look skywards. The bird had started its descent, its wings flapping furiously in an attempt to attain the perfect landing. A flock of reed buntings scattered in utter terror. The moment lifted Justin's spirit. The curlew let out a call warning other birds to stay away, making Justin wish that his life could be that predictable. Deciding to take to the air again, the curlew was finding it difficult to level itself. Ever the master of aviation, the bird twisted its body to the left and without sound headed towards the opposite bank of the reservoir. After witnessing yet another uncomfortable landing, Justin turned and walked down, aware that he could easily fall. It was such a treacherous place in winter; many times he had finished on his backside viewing the sky. Finding the gate that led directly to the reservoir, Justin stopped for a few seconds and leaned against it, taking time to view the smallest piece of water, the one he thought looked the more natural. On reaching the reservoir, he walked down towards the water's edge, where he stood at the side of a wooden jetty. In a state of disrepair, it was a crumbled testimony to the art of fly fishing.

Scanning the water, Justin thought about the many trout caught over the years and how many had been monsters. The trout angler's dream was always to catch the Ferrell, the fighter that is wild and uncompromising. There had always been big fish in this water. Thirty years earlier he had witnessed a young osprey lift a huge brown trout out as if it were nothing more than the tiniest of minnows. The raptor had lost its bearings during migration, and instead of hunting on the loch as expected, it had contented itself with a fortnight's break at the Clough. This brought back fond memories of Nina and the time they had sneaked up to within ten feet of the great bird. Crouched behind some gorse bushes, they had marvelled at its power as it had slashed at the flesh of its conquest. It had been magical. Today, there was no osprey. Instead, a magpie flapped its wings incessantly in a creepy way. The chak-chak-chak-chak of its voice freaked Justin out, especially with the bird being no more than five yards behind, as though it was stalking him.

Where's the second bird? You've got to be here somewhere. What am I doing? I'm not even superstitious. For Goodness sake, man, get a grip.

Fear was now engulfing him. It had nothing to do with how many damn magpies there were. His mind had returned to those memories he so desperately wanted to leave behind. Justin quickened his pace, hoping to relieve his spinning head, to no avail. Meanwhile, deciding it had terrorised him for long enough, the bird took to the air and flew into the ruins of a barn. With his head down Justin continued to walk briskly.

"I bet that bloody bird's spying on me," he said under his breath.

The field where the hawthorn tree lay came into his eyeline. *That'll help me ground myself,* he thought. *I'll rest underneath it.*

Whenever in the hawthorn tree's field, he would stop and say a prayer, hoping that this might reconnect him to his faith. This had not yet been the case. For much of his life, he had acknowledged Calvary as a selfless act, an act of love, a lesson for the world that showed love mattered. To love one another was a simple commandment, but Justin knew that people formed prejudices and experienced hurt over the course of their lives. Love in such a scenario could so easily be misconstrued.

Out of breath, Justin stopped walking, thankful that he had reached the tree. Sitting underneath its leafless branches, he took extra care not to catch himself on its sharp thorns. There had been many times over his lifetime when he had torn his skin on a protruding branch. The silence around him helped to slow his heartbeat. He tried to rid his mind of damaging thoughts that shot through his head with precision and cunning, a mishmash of sadness, desperation, and non-forgiveness. Antagonistic, they disturbed his logic, telling him he had failed, that he had deviated from the truth, that he had lost his faith.

My God, where are you?

Even with all such supplication and self-examination, Justin's condition remained the same. Once a vibrant person, he had now become lost in the choices of his life. The faith that had guided him through rocky seas and impregnable mountains had given up its tenancy of his soul. He needed an offensive against this moral erosion. From being a believer to now feeling the outsider, Justin's lack of ability in dealing with his conscience had left him spiritually homeless. No longer could he find an absolute for his sickened soul. No longer could he tell the world in certainty that love was a verb, a doing word, an action that was supposed to present a positive affirmation to a broken world. Even by the reservoir, where he was trying to forget himself, Justin couldn't stop dissecting the nature of love. Having to live with his recent past meant he was disconnected from his spiritual self. A deep inhale on his cigarette mirrored the heaviness of his spirit. Seeing the abandoned crow's nest above his head reminded him of the time he and Nina had raised a young jackdaw that had become separated from its mother. Both children had shown adept parenting skills. Feeding it dead chicks purchased from the local abattoir, they had guarded the bird against predators, eventually releasing it back into the wild after nursing it for six months. Many local ornithologists had expressed their displeasure at such an action, believing the bird would lack the necessary skills to survive, but survive it did.

What fun they had shared over the years. Whenever Justin and Nina had been together, their discussions had always been energetic and meaningful. Although very close, they had held different values and certainly had diverse belief systems. Many times sitting by the hawthorn tree they had disagreed with one another as to the meaning and value of life. They had, however, found common ground in believing that religion was a man-made institution. Where they'd fundamentally disagreed was in their understanding of the purpose of existence. Nina had firmly rejected Justin's premise that spiritual purpose could be a force for good in the world. She'd also rejected his belief that seeking God was integral to human existence. When he would explain his relationship with God, she would accuse him of subjectivity. For her, faith had been nothing more than intellectual blindness. It seemed only yesterday that he'd suggested that the great Einstein had acknowledged the existence of a creative force within the universe. Nina, bright and ready as always, had countered that Einstein had never accepted the concept of a personal God.

"I'll tell you something for nothing, Justin. God is not dead, because God has never existed," she had told him.

For Nina, talk of a deity that could transform lives was nothing more than an illogical proposition put forward by those too frightened to take on the world. The existence of a benevolent spirit was not only irrelevant but also bloody stupid given the state of the planet. Any talk of a God-love had made her even more scathing. All her antipathy towards faith had never deviated Justin from embarking on a spiritual journey he'd thought would provide some relevance for his life. Unlike Nina, he had seen no conflict between the pursuit of scientific reason and a path that led to self-discovery and spiritual grace. Up until the day his faith had catapulted out from his being, the concept of love for Justin had meant God. To love was to have experienced the presence of God. How he wished for such a renewal of faith.

Tom was taking a late afternoon break, having been busy discussing the need for new machinery with the managing director. Normally, he enjoyed spending his break exchanging banter with his work colleagues, but today he was experiencing a side of himself he did not like. A slow dawning resentment against Ken's recklessness was overwhelming him. Waves of jealousy surged through his body like electrical currents, making him feel sick. It seemed to him that Ken's decision was neither logical nor sensible. Tom was projecting the feelings of loss he had for his wife as disdain for Ken's behaviour. *How could Ken disregard Viv so easily? How could he take life so much for granted? It was something to be cherished and nurtured.* The loneliness of Tom's existence revealed itself even more greatly when in Ken's company. *What a cock you are, Ken.*

"Do you fancy a pint after work, big man?" asked Ken, appearing from nowhere.

"Not straight after work, thanks, Ken. I need to get home, so that I can change, and then I'll head over to the Boar," replied Tom. "I'll see you then."

"No problem. Gemma's working this evening. I'll buy you a pint. See you."

"Okay," replied Tom without looking up. It wouldn't bother him if he never saw Ken again. Ken could go to hell and stay there as far as Tom was concerned.

With his thoughts now on Chrissie and wanting to hold her again, he returned to his work. He wanted to get home. He wanted Chrissie but knew this to be impossible. *Why did I let you down?*

In moments such as these, he wanted to punish himself. Chrissie had always understood Tom much more than he could ever understand himself, and with this in mind she had left him a letter which he had read every day since her passing.

"What are you still doing here?" asked Tom's foreman. "Go home."

"Bloody hell, is that the time? I didn't realise it had got to that."

"I don't suppose you fancy any overtime tomorrow, do you?" asked the foreman.

"No thanks. I'll be having a few beers tonight," replied Tom.

"I thought as much. See you on Monday."

"You will," said Tom, who by now was putting his tools away.

It was blowing a gale outside. Walking out of the factory towards the car park, he hastened his steps against the fierce wind. Unusually tired, Tom arrived home at 5.45 p.m. and literally threw himself on to the settee. Closing his eyes, he started thinking about Chrissie.

With all his heart he wanted her to be with him getting ready to go out together for the night. These thoughts brought him closer to her. Or that was what he believed. Her love had been a blessing. On these occasions, Tom imagined telling her they were going somewhere special, to a place where the ravages of pain could never reach or hurt her. In these private moments Tom reinvented a perfect world for himself. Unfortunately, these fantasies effectively reinforced his fears of endings and loss, holding him in time and making him struggle to confront the change that was needed to move forward.

The ringing of the telephone brought him out from these thoughts. On picking up the receiver, he heard a familiar voice.

"Tom, it's Justin. How are you?"

"Well then," replied Tom, surprised.

To have one's fantasies disturbed by the ringing of a telephone was shock enough, but having to face the past, present, and possibly the future all in the space of ten seconds was almost overwhelming. Tom readjusted to the moment.

"I read your letter and thought I'd ring. I hope you're well. What are you up to then?" Justin asked.

"I'm working at a canning factory in Dundee, looking after the machines. I'm really enjoying the change from a suit and tie," replied Tom. "What about you?"

"I haven't worked since … you know, since—"

"What, not at all?" Tom interrupted.

Justin took his time to reply, not thinking this was the place to get into a deep conversation. He still believed that Tom had played a large part in his loss of freedom. The rejection he had felt from his friend had been mirrored by an unsympathetic judge.

"It's been difficult … So where to now, Tom? I'm sorry to be blunt," Justin stuttered, feeling vulnerable. "How about we meet in a week on Saturday?"

"Okay, that sounds fine," replied Tom. "I'll ask for some time off work. Do you want to come here? You have my address. Do you know how to get to Forfar?"

"Yeah, I'll come to Scotland. I've got a road map," replied Justin. "I'll be fine. See you then."

"See you," Tom replied, placing down the receiver.

Tom was so relaxed it made Justin suspicious. He wondered whether Tom might be playing some sort of mind game with him, which didn't help the feeling of paranoia racing through his veins. It was unsettling.

At least I've made contact with Tom. That's one barrier down. This had been a task he had been dreading. It was now out of the way. Dispensing himself a scotch, the drink's calming effect soothed his nerves. Sitting with his eyes closed in a state of solitude, he began playing out various scenarios. Some of these set in motion a deepening fear of the future, and all attempts at countering these were initially met by further bouts of fear.

I'm not listening; I won't listen, Justin silently repeated. *I must be strong. I will be strong. I have to be strong.*

Tom was pleased with himself. A month ago he would have shown much greater hostility towards Justin. His perception had clearly shifted. Standing statuesque like a heron, Tom scanned his brain for reasons as to why thoughts of reconciliation were regularly invading his mind. Something was happening that he didn't understand, but the feeling was a good one. Little by little he was allowing his fury towards Justin to dissolve. He desperately wanted to speak to him. His head was still hurting, but his body no longer felt like exploding into a rage when he thought of him. He looked at his watch; it was much later than he had anticipated.

Friday night, pub night, he thought.

This had been Tom's routine for the past twelve months. It helped to keep the shiver of loneliness on the other side of an increasingly creaking door. Tom knew it was important to socialise, and he enjoyed company. Since his encounter with Viv, he had begun to sense a change in himself. It was like the rain on a sweltering day, surprising, welcomed, and utterly longed for.

The Boar was already busy when Tom arrived; the weekend had commenced. He began drinking his first pint at 8.45 p.m., much later than usual due to his conversation with Justin.

Alistair, the pub landlord, appeared relieved. "I was beginning to get worried. It's unheard of, you being forty-five minutes late! Good job I hadn't pulled your pint. What happened?"

"I was busy, that's all," said Tom defensively, not taking kindly to what he perceived as an interrogation.

His earlier optimism had disintegrated and given way to his nervousness at having arranged to see Justin. The earlier softening of his attitude towards his old friend did not negate the sheer terror Tom was feeling. There was now no escape; he would have no choice but to come face-to-face with his own ghosts and betrayals. These fears were always present in his life, and soon he would have to acknowledge them instead of his usual denials. They were there, brooding, prodding, and incessantly fighting his efforts to accept the possibility of change. Their malice made his resolve weak, possessing his brain, and they were utterly ruthless in their exploitation of his anxiety. At times they were unstoppable. Standing at the bar, Tom was in a lone battle for his future. The ship of negativity was now circumnavigating his newfound optimism and trying to sink it with violent cannonballs of panic.

Alistair sensed Tom's hostility and wisely backed away, recognising that this was unusual behaviour for Tom. Tom was drinking heavily; his plans to curb his intake were now no more than a distant memory. A melting pot of emotion, he wanted to scream out and tell everybody in the pub about his life. They did not know him. People had no idea about his existence prior to him moving to Forfar. How could they? The four pints of ale and the subsequent double whisky chasers were quickly taking effect. Alistair kept a close eye on him, knowing this was not Tom's usual drinking style. Sure, he would sink more than a few pints, but not at this speed or intensity. Concerned, Alistair asked Gemma to also keep an eye on him. Lifting his head from his glass, Tom ordered another pint with a double chaser, raising his voice to make sure that whoever was serving could hear him. Gemma placed his drinks on the bar in front of him and pleasantly enquired as to whether he was okay.

"What's it got to do with you?" retorted Tom. "You might be better worrying about yourself, glasshouses and all that."

"I was only asking," replied Gemma with tears welling in her eyes. "There's no need to be so rude."

"Well, don't ask," Tom yelled. "It's none of your damn business; keep your nose out. You've done enough damage as it is. I can handle my own affairs, thank you!"

At this verbal assault Gemma ran from the bar sobbing.

"Cow!" shouted Tom, struggling to hold his balance. Within a few seconds he was lying on the floor nursing a throbbing head. Standing over him holding a bottle in his right hand was Ken.

"Speak to her like that again and you'll be nursing more than a sore head. Now apologise," demanded Ken.

"Fuck you," Tom shouted as he tried to get to his feet.

"Apologise now!" Ken screamed. "No one speaks to her like that. No one, do you hear me?"

Dazed and struggling to stand up, Tom knew he'd stepped over the line, but there was no way in hell he would allow Ken to humiliate him in this way. He had a feeling he had done that of his own accord.

"Tom, mate, come with me," Alistair said, taking Tom by the arm.

"Not until he's apologised," demanded Ken.

"Leave it out," said Alistair. "Go and have a beer and calm down. In fact, take Gemma home. Julie will take over. Come with me into the back, Tom; let's sort you out."

Turning away from Tom, Ken shouted for Gemma to join him as Tom staggered to the back of the pub.

"Hellfire, Tom, what's going on? Do you want to tell me what the hell that was all about? This isn't like you," Alistair said.

"How long have you got?" said Tom sarcastically. "You don't know the half of it."

"Anyway, let's look at your head. You took a heavy blow. I've always thought Ken was a head case. He reminds me of a wannabe gangster, all suits and brogues."

"I feel like finding him and giving him a good hiding, sly bastard. Bottling is way out of order. At least I'm not cut, but I've a hell of a lump forming on the top of my head. And just to think I helped the prick last night."

"It's a big lump all right," said Alistair. "Do you need to go to the hospital for a check-up?"

"No, I'll be ok. It ain't half sobered me up though. I'm sorry about the trouble I've caused. I know I was out of order. I'll apologise to Gemma as soon as possible. I'm just really tetchy at the moment."

"I know, mate. You weren't in the best of moods when you arrived. What's going on? Wait there; I'll get us a brandy."

Saturday

Tom was in his living room rubbing his sore head. It felt as if he had a ball on the top of his crown. He walked into the kitchen and settled at the table. He giggled to himself, reminded of a joke he had heard many years ago in which a man went to the doctor with a huge boil on the top of his head. When the doctor enquired as to how long it had been there, the boil replied, "It grew out of my arse yesterday."

Although in pain, he was somewhat upbeat and couldn't help but smile at the ridiculous situation he had found himself in over the past few days. Knowing he was out of order the previous evening, he would apologise to Gemma, but as for Ken, the least said, the better. They would never be friends.

Tom made himself a cup of tea. Finding no milk in the fridge, he made his way to the front door where a fresh bottle stood. As he straightened, the beeping of a car horn made him jump. He didn't recognise the driver at first. It was only on the second beep that he saw it was Viv Charles who was waving at him. She parked in front of his house and stepped out of the car, quickly making her way towards him.

"Hello, Viv," he said nervously. "What can I do for you?"

"I've just heard about last night and was wondering whether you're all right. From what I heard, you took a fair old whack." Laughing, she pointed at the lump on his head. "Damn! I wish I'd brought my clubs."

"Very funny," replied Tom. "Do you want to come in and have a cuppa? The kettle's boiled."

"Aye, okay. I'm sorry about last night. Is it true you called Gemma a cow?"

"I think I did. Who told you?"

"I bumped into Alistair in the supermarket. He said you didn't stand a chance. Ken hit you from behind with a bottle."

"I always thought Ken was the quiet sort; I'd never have thought he was a thug."

"You don't know him. When I first met him, he had a reputation as a hard man, the sort you see at nightclubs, always looking for trouble. His behaviour became so problematic that we had to move from Glasgow to Forfar. Last night was the first time since moving that Ken has been violent, well, as far as I know," said Viv.

Continuing to chat, Tom moved into the kitchen where he made them both a cup of tea. He bid Viv to sit down and then handed her the drink. Any concerns he might have held about Viv not coping with the breakup were disappearing fast. Spending this short time with her reassured him that she would be fine. Tom was sure there would be a string of admirers eager to have her on their arm, Tom included, if he was to believe his churning stomach. Looking at Viv, he was baffled that somebody of her character would ever be with a knob like Ken who was neither bright nor caring. *What had she seen in him?*

It struck him that men were stupid bastards. Having now lost his relationship with Viv, Ken was entering into another with Gemma, bringing with him all his insecurities and the same old baggage to make the same mistakes again. As far as Tom was concerned, issues needed resolving before taking a new partner, or the bag could be a very heavy one to carry. Chrissie had been special. Since her death, he'd never thought loving someone that closely again was possible. But now looking at Viv, he wasn't so sure.

"Tom?" Viv asked. "I hope you don't mind, but are you all right? You seem sad. Tell me to mind my own business if I'm prying."

Sitting opposite her in silence, he didn't feel affronted; it was quite the opposite. He was pleased that Viv was taking the time to ask him personal questions. Unlike last night's drunken incident Tom felt comfortable in Viv's company. Both took a sip of their tea and smiled at each other. Tom knew that Viv would be trying to make sense of her new life. That was the key for Tom, a new life. Tears were starting to form at the back of his eyes. He fought hard to contain them, hoping they did not show. After all, he barely knew her. But it was a useless task – they flooded out, not in a dribble or a drip, but like a waterfall in the depths of a torrential rainstorm. They would not and could not stop until his eyes had spilled their last droplet. Viv's long and comforting hug brought him back to earth.

"I'm sorry. I don't know what came over me," Tom lied. "The trouble is, I've been holding on to all these feelings of loss, anger, and guilt. That's why last night's debacle happened."

"Do you fancy going for a walk? Let's get a bit of air into our lungs, clear our heads. Come on," insisted Viv, reaching for his hand.

Following her outside into the biting winds of a Scottish winter, new emotions were now exploding inside his heart. Powerless to her charms, he was beginning to feel alive again.

As they arrived at the field leading to the riverbank, Viv was talking about her new life and fresh aspirations. Both stopped simultaneously to breathe and take in the view. They were standing close to each other, so close that Tom could smell her. The fragrance was sweet; it was subtle and very pleasing. Taking a deep breath, he wanted it to linger and rest in his subconscious where he could relive that moment at any time. The woman standing beside him not only was physically beautiful but also, much more importantly, radiated an inner glory that shone like the Milky Way on a cloudless evening.

"It's lovely here," said Viv. "Do you fish? I used to as a girl; my dad took me down to the canal. I really enjoyed it."

There was so much Tom didn't know about Viv, but he could imagine himself sitting with her for years to come still spellbound and fascinated. *If only I could spend more time with you,* he thought.

"I used to fish when my wife was alive. She used to insist I go. It gave her time to herself; we never lived in each other's pockets. When she died I had to get away from London. It was never the same without her. These days I don't seem to have the motivation to go fishing. Maybe we could go one day."

"Aye, maybe we could." Viv smiled. "I'm sorry about your wife. I had no idea."

"You weren't to know. Why would you. I do miss her though."

"I'm sure you do. What was she called?" Viv asked hoping not to appear too forward.

"Chrissie and she was one hell of a character," smiled Tom.

A silence descended between the two that seemed more reverent than awkward. This provided a moment for both Tom and Viv to scan the river and take stock of their individual lives.

"Do you fancy a drink at the pub? It's not far, just across the path." Tom pointed breaking the silence.

"Sure," replied Viv, "I'd love to."

"Come on then."

Having enjoyed an hour chatting in the pub, they arrived back at Tom's house. He built a coal fire and then made his way to the kitchen to brew a pot of tea for them. Gazing through the hatch, he caught Viv's eye. She was kneeling by the fire rubbing her hands.

"You all right there?" she asked.

"I certainly am," he replied. He finally felt comfortable enough around her to broach the question he had been avoiding throughout the day. "Would you take Ken back if he asked?"

"No. He's hurt me too much. It's horrible being rejected and also bloody embarrassing. His arrogance has really angered me. Anyway, thank you. I've enjoyed myself today."

"You're not going yet are you?" Tom asked with more than a hint of desperation.

"No, not unless you want me to," she replied.

"Are you hungry? I'll rustle something up," said Tom, hoping not to appear too eager.

"It'd be the first time any man has cooked for me," laughed Viv.

When Chrissie had been alive, Tom had undertaken all the cooking; it had been a sign of his affection for her, and she had loved it.

"Well, in that case, tonight you shall dine in style. What about seafood risotto and then Gladys's homemade apple pie – she's my neighbour. How does that grab you?" Tom asked.

"That sounds great."

"What can I get you to drink?"

"Vodka and orange please, that's if you've got it."

"I tell you what Tom. I'm looking forward to trying out different things – you know, simple things, which I never did with Ken. That's the weird thing about the split. It's come when we were due to spend more time together. I'm a kick-boxer but have now retired from competition. It means I won't be travelling here there and everywhere. I've had a good time, but I was ready to retire," said Viv, gazing at her hands as though searching for something.

That's why you look strong, he thought. *No wonder you're so toned.*

"I best not give you any cheek then. I don't fancy getting a good hiding," laughed Tom. "How did you get into kick-boxing?"

"Initially to get fit and it just went on from there. My instructor encouraged me, told me I could make the grade."

"How long have you been fighting?"

"About ten years."

"I bet you've won a few competitions. Haven't you?"

"One or two," she replied modestly. "Anyway, I don't want to spend all night talking boxing. I only go to the gym to work out these days."

"Well, you must have been good at it; you don't have a flat nose," roared Tom.

"You might in a minute if you carry on," Viv said with a huge beam on her face. She held her fists together as if ready to punch him.

"Point taken," laughed Tom.

"Just one more question, and then I'll leave it alone. Is Ken a kick-boxer?"

"He was, but he suffered a foot injury, which put an end to competitions for him."

"Instead, he's taken up bottling for a hobby," said Ken sarcastically.

"How is the head?" asked Viv.

"It's still sore, but I'll live."

Tom could not help but notice that she was still wearing her wedding ring and wondered whether Viv had not yet given up hope of reconciliation irrespective of what she had just said. One thing was for sure; she could never be boring. In fact, the opposite was true. There was vibrancy in her exchanges, which stemmed from deep within her warm heart. These special properties were given life through Viv's smile.

Admiring her, Tom could see Viv was genuinely unaware of the light she emitted out into the world. It was extraordinary. *How could she be so unaware of her inner beauty? Ken's held her light under his own bushel all these years. I'll bet he's the jealous type. What a bloody bastard.*

These musings only compelled Tom to want to delve further into her mind, to be seduced by her thoughts and devour her recollections.

He fantasised about them going fishing together. Tom, unlike the fish that would struggle and fight, would surrender as quickly as possible to her. Continuing his daydream, he suddenly sensed her presence behind him. In the moment he also connected to her grief. Turning in her direction, he witnessed her tears.

"Are you all right?" Tom asked, wanting to embrace her.

"I'm okay, thanks. It just feels odd being looked after for a change. And being in the company of a man other than Ken is kind of weird. If I'm honest, I actually don't miss him. It sounds callous in some respects, but I think I'd become too used to routine and being Ken's wife. He had such a low boredom threshold. He would demand I entertain him. If it wasn't sex, we would sit watching awful videos. The rubbish I've had to endure is mind-numbing," said Viv.

"No videos tonight then?" Tom smiled. "I must admit I don't watch a lot of television. I love music though."

"Me too," said Viv.

Viv was now enthralled with Tom and could feel a sense of excitement welling up in her stomach. She did not know this man in front of her; she might even be ten years younger than him, but it did not matter to her. There was something dynamic about him. His developing beer belly would have been a turn-off to her in the past. One thing she could say about Ken was that he had a great body. The only image she could conjure up of Tom and a six-pack was of him carrying it from the off-licence. Different from the men she had known, he was unconventional, the opposite of what her life with Ken had become. Taking notice of his face, she thought Tom was handsome, although he would not be seen as pretty or owning classic good looks. His dark complexion could easily be mistaken for Romany. Surprisingly, he had few grey hairs. It struck Viv that Tom's deep-blue eyes were unusual in that she would have expected them to be brown.

"There must be something I can do to help," she said bringing herself back into reality.

"There is; go and put some music on, then sit down here and talk to me while I'm cooking. How does that sound?"

"Good to me," she replied. Moving into the living room, she speculated as to what music he and his wife had listened to and whether they had had a favourite tune. The way Tom talked about her made Viv wish that her partner had loved her that deeply. If she had died, Ken wouldn't have held such feelings for her. Even in life he had never expressed such love, such understanding; otherwise, he would still be with her. One thing Viv could never envisage was Ken expanding himself intellectually or in a personal capacity in the same way that Tom had. They were very different animals. Tom was intelligent and thoughtful, a new phenomenon for her. He spoke kindly of people and was not the type to be taken for granted; he was strong where strength mattered, in the heart.

Flicking through a huge catalogue of music stacked on three shelves, she became aware of the room's shape and content. Photographs covered the old oak sideboard in front of her. *I wonder which photo is Tom's wife,* she thought. Within a few seconds she answered her question as she caught sight of Tom's wedding-day photograph. She picked it up. Standing next to him was an eye-catching woman with long, dark hair and a smile that would have seduced many. Out of respect she quickly returned the photo to its rightful place. She selected a CD, placed it in the rack, and pressed play. Distracted by the photograph, Viv hadn't taken much notice of the music she had chosen. The sound of a keyboard spilled like a wave eager to take the listener on a journey. A rolling guitar from The Edge joined it, setting the scene for a talented power that sang stories about a more hopeful existence which was still out of reach.

"I wanna run; I wanna hide. I want to tear down the walls that hold me inside," sang Tom in a voice not quite as tuneful as Bono.

"A top tune," he shouted.

———————

For once, Viv was feeling wanted, and she had her suspicions that Tom liked her. For a moment or two her brain overloaded with voices warning against rebounds and rash decision-making. The split with Ken had made her realise that there was a world calling for her to come and enjoy; whether as a single woman or not made no difference. Though being a romantic person at heart, she would want to love again but the next time on a deeper level where the body hurts when there was separation – not the self-indulgent love spawned out of narcissism or the obsessive destruction of personality found in tragedy but rather a love grounded in belief and surety based on a life shared together. Having spent some time with him, she believed Tom and his wife would have taken into account each other's needs. She liked the way Tom spoke about his marriage; it made her realise what a special person he was. Viv wished she had seen Tom and his wife's interactions. Her marriage had only just broken down, yet here she was with Tom, as though they were long-time lovers.

"I love this album; it never dates," said Tom, catching Viv's figure in the corner of his eye.

Though he'd never dated a blonde-haired woman before, he knew he could make an exception for Viv. His liking had always been towards the dark Celtic look. Chrissie's hair had been almost black, her eyes brown, and her skin Mediterranean. When holidaying abroad, the sun's rays had always seemed to make their way directly to her, and usually after four days other tourists had begun mistaking her for one of the locals. Chrissie would always smile when people approached her. Tom put her complexion down to her Irish heritage from Spanish Point, County Clare. Both sets of Chrissie's grandparents had left the Emerald Isle and settled on England in their search for a better life. For that, he would be forever grateful. She had been his best friend.

"What are you thinking about?" enquired Viv.

"Nothing, I'm concentrating on not burning anything," he replied, aware that she could soon become bored with his sorrow. "Okay, it's time to sample the first course; come on and take a seat."

Warm and satisfied sitting opposite Viv, Tom was feeling better by the second. Until meeting her, his heart had belonged to another who had been spontaneous and passionate. Chrissie had been a wild one; it was she that had introduced him to a nocturnal lifestyle. She had always been last to leave the party. Her stamina was legendary, as were Tom's memories of her. He had so many stories to tell. Now here in Forfar he was gazing at a woman who was quickly taking his heart.

"Well? What do you think?" Tom asked.

"Excellent," she replied. "You can cook for me anytime."

Tom liked her response. To be the centre of someone's attention was like being in another world for him. He wanted to hold and caress her, but his ability to read signs of reciprocation had always been atrocious. The culmination of apprehension and innocence had kept his romantic desires locked away until Chrissie, kind and loving, had expertly provided the key. Here with Viv, he might be older, but he was still just as nervous. What Tom wanted to do was explain his longing for her, but he didn't want to make a fool of himself. Voices of vulnerability resurfaced within his racing thoughts, triggering ever more caution and nervousness. Even at forty-four he could not stop himself from re-experiencing those calamitous days from his teenage years where he had been far too shy to ask a girl out and had become the blabbering idiot whenever he'd tried. Chrissie had helped him feel safe; she had been his security, his comfort, the one who had encouraged and cradled him during his down times. Even towards the end of her life, when her spirit had been crumbling under the constant barrage of pain, she had held him. Tom hadn't coped well during Chrissie's illness, especially when the pressure on her brain had started to change her personality.

"Hey, tell me some tales from your music days. I've heard some of your stories from Ken, but I'm still not convinced they're true." Viv smiled, bringing him back to reality.

"Whatever you've heard is true. But you know bands; whatever happens on tour stays on tour," replied Tom, tapping his nose with his index finger. "Anyway I want to know more about you and your roots."

"I'd be here forever answering all that," replied Viv. "But okay, I'll give it a go. I was born in Glasgow, but when I was five, we moved to Jedburgh. Being Glaswegian, my father missed the city. When I was eleven, we went back to Glasgow, but within a year my mother had left with my two younger sisters and gone back to Jedburgh to be with her lover. They are still together to this day. I stayed with my father, not just for him, but also because I didn't want to move schools. When I left at sixteen, I managed to land a job as a cashier with Clydesdale Bank, and I've worked in finance ever since. Ken and I met when I was twenty-five at the boxing gym. He was a poser but in those days made me laugh. The rest is history. As you can see,

I was stupid enough to marry him," laughed Viv. "What about you? Come on; don't be shy."

"Where do I start? I wasn't born, but discovered alongside other fossils."

Viv smiled.

"I was raised in and around Blackburn, Lancashire. My employers at the time sponsored my university course, where I passed a degree in mechanical engineering. I was already going out with Chrissie, who was two years older than me and in her final year when I became an undergraduate. I really missed her because she was at Sussex University while I studied at Salford. After graduating I stayed in the north-west of England to continue my job and because Chrissie was working for a local chemical firm. Within twelve months I'd been made redundant. I was already in the band by that time, so we decided to take off. It was great to start with. For about three years we constantly gigged throughout Britain, Ireland, and the Continent. We'd been chased out of so many places that the band decided to call it a day. On top of that we were sick of seeing each other. There were four in the band plus partners, about three of them. Me and Chrissie wanted to stay put for a while. I tried with other musicians, but it never felt the same. Then our son, Mark, who is now eighteen, came along. He's doing a degree and lives in a flat with mates in Manchester. There you have it, the concise life of Tom Riley."

Standing in his kitchen, Justin could see the moon through the window. It was a spectacular sight, a beacon shining for the inhabitants of the fields below and a source to soothe his worn-out soul. The light of the moon meant the closing of the day, which could never come quickly enough for Justin. Winter was a godsend; it gave him a legitimate excuse to shut the world out as early as 4.30 in the evening. Staring into the dark sky, his thoughts started multiplying. They teased him and made him sweat, working against him and igniting his misgivings. Fighting them, he thought about Tom, his life and regrets. *Surely he must have some. Otherwise, why invite me to see him?*

Being able to make this connection was a definite step forward. Their histories were indelibly interlinked, and they had once been closer than kin. Even this truth did not stop the outpouring of resentment that choked and later rendered their emotions into a singular expression of anger. Justin knew this force for destruction only too well, and it was hardly the best way to solve problems. The conviction that anger was a potential vehicle for social change, through channelling societal resentment into political issues, had once appealed to him. People could make a difference. Anger was an effective method to get something done, but within the realms of individual relationships it was nothing more than a barrier to kindness and acceptance. Continuing to gaze out the window, Justin squeezed his hands together in an attempt to ground himself. An overburdening sense of loneliness was attacking him, leaving him feeling self-conscious and hypersensitive. The crux of his problem still rested with not being able to deal with that one specific day and the subsequent spillage from it. At times he lost his rationale, believing that everyone was presiding over him as judge and jury. Even the most innocuous question felt like an attack on his integrity. This had been a major reason for leaving London. Whether empathic or disgusted, every gaze, stare, or glance from people reinforced his insecurities, allowing his overworked brain to cloud his judgement. This resulted in him assuming a trench-like mentality. Although he had loved London, the city had hurt him. It had failed to heal him, to liberate his soul. The moors opposite his house were now his hope. The wildlife and livestock asked no questions, nor did they demand a reaction from him. He could walk for as long as he wished without meeting many people. Clear reasons for him to have moved back north.

―――――――――

Being able to laugh helped Viv feel comfortable in Tom's company. What a great night she was having.

"I'll call a taxi. It's getting late," said Viv, not wanting to outstay her welcome.

"Why don't you stay the night? Mark's room is free. In any case, you can have another drink, that is, if you want to," said Tom, hoping he wasn't speaking out of turn.

"Are you sure? I'm really enjoying the night so far and wouldn't say no to another glass or two," she replied.

"Great, hold out your glass; I'll fill it up. And while we're at it, let's make a toast."

"Okay, what to?"

"Let's say to new beginnings."

"To new beginnings," repeated Viv. "That's a nice thought, Tom."

As he listened to her talk, he wondered what it was that made her different. Clearly she was a woman who was able to skilfully verbalise her opinions and was obviously someone who was focused, having been a kick-boxer. This was another deviation from his usual choice of women, having always been attracted to the anarchic hippy type. In retrospect, he was that wanky teenager who had spent a lot of his time hanging out with so-called radicals. Remembering them made Tom smile.

Where are they now? I know exactly where they are, thought Tom. The boys were driving BMWs and wearing suits to the jobs Daddy had found them at the end of their studies. The hippy trippy girls either married the BMW revolutionaries or switched the uniform of freedom for the power suit representing commerce and consumerism. All the same, he could never deny that Woodstock women with long, flowing hair and free expression were the type he'd fancied during his developing sexuality. As for revolutionaries, Tom thought they were precious with a short lifespan, usually the length of time it took them to graduate from university. Still, he had little room to talk. Politics had come later for him, when his friendship with Justin had been developing, although he had been less interested in changing the world than his friend had been.

"Do you like living in Scotland?" Viv asked.

"To be honest I came here so I could be near to Chrissie without having to breathe the tragedy every day. The home we shared in London was a tribute to her style, and her presence was everywhere. It just became too much. I couldn't move without sensing her. Everything I touched brought tears to my eyes. I won't ever forget her. Even after three years I'm still struggling to come to terms with the situation ..." Tom trailed off. "But to answer your question, Scotland is good."

"You really loved her, didn't you?" Viv said, instantly regretting her candour.

"Yes," Tom replied.

"Healing is a process you have to initiate yourself, Tom. You've started by talking to me."

"What about you? Surely, you must feel anger, even hatred, towards Ken. What he did is unforgivable," said Tom.

"To be honest I actually feel a sense of freedom. He was boring to live with. What we had was a mutual need. He had to move away from his life in Glasgow; otherwise he'd now be in jail. At the same time, I needed somebody that would accept my life, the kick-boxing competitions, training, and travelling, which often took place in the evening. That's a big commitment to endure week in, week out, and to be fair, Ken was supportive. On the one hand, I feel relief, on the other, a failure. I know what people will think. *She denied her husband children, selfish cow, why did she get married if she didn't want kids?*"

"Viv, Ken was unfaithful, not you. You told him you didn't want children from the start. He still chose to marry you. It's not your fault."

"Yes, but I can't ignore my part in the break-up. I don't hate Ken, but at the same time, I certainly don't love him. I wish it was a few months down the line, that's all."

Sensing her anxiety, Tom decided to be a little more tactful. He was about to give the speech about how time was a great healer when he realised it had done nothing for him. His ghosts were still haunting him; they had not been laid to rest. In fact, time had done nothing for Tom other than elongate those feelings which were stifling his recovery.

"Maybe we can help each other. What do you think?" Tom said.

"I'd like that, a sort of support group without the group," Viv smiled.

"Precisely. By the way Viv, I've enjoyed spending this time with you. You've made me feel alive again." Tom blushed, turning his face away.

***

Tom's embarrassment made Viv think of a little boy at school that became red-faced when a classmate decided to tell everybody about his secret fancy. His childlike qualities intrigued her. One thing Ken had not been shy about was his need for sex. Taking a gamble, Viv embraced Tom. His body instantly relaxed, giving way to her arms. In her embrace his breathing became more and more rapid. This was not sexual; in an instant the passing of distress and anguish rebounded throughout her body, setting Tom off crying, as though for the very first time. Understanding he was hurting, confused, and as frightened as a newborn, she continued to hold him. No longer the foetus, secure within the womb of a loving mother, he had been thrust into the world like a baby, relying on others to provide care and nurture. Some people would think it strange that she was not walking the streets in black playing the aggrieved and spurned wife. It was hard to explain, but she had no need to pretend. Ken had done the dirty, and Ken had gone. She didn't want to fight for his return as she no longer wanted predictability. Her life had provided plenty of that over the years. No, she wanted somebody that would use his imagination with little things. In fact, when she thought about it, she didn't need a man at all. Whatever life she wanted, she was free to choose, although she could not deny the chemistry so evident between Tom and her. Earlier in the day she had spent some time considering a career change, maybe teaching, counselling, or community work. She wondered whether to enrol with the Open University and gain a degree. One of her teachers had tried to encourage her to stay on at school, but at the time it had been too soon for her to contemplate. She had wanted to earn money in order to support her sporting endeavours and have decent holidays with her friends.

Suddenly aware of the strength of his arms around Viv, Tom relaxed his grip. "Sorry, Viv, can you breathe?" he asked.

"I can now." She smiled.

"I'm pathetic," said Tom, embarrassed about his crying.

"You are if you think crying is a weakness, but you'd be downright stupid to think that. What is it about men and tears? We're nearly in the twenty-first century for God's sake. Go on, fill up my glass. You're a decent man, Tom. Don't be afraid of tomorrow; otherwise you'll struggle to enjoy today. I think that's why I'll be okay. My future lies in my own hands."

"You're an inspiration. Cheers," said Tom, passing her a drink. "I tell you something, you're not only intelligent, brave, kind, and a deep thinker but also very beautiful."

Realising he was at it again, he turned red once more, but rather than retreating into his shell, he let out a laugh while pointing to his face.

Viv felt flattered that Tom had listed other qualities first before her physical looks. People would find her egocentric, possibly even narcissistic, for admitting to knowing the power of her physical beauty. Aware of her good looks from an early age, she had had to fight off lecherous attentions from men of all ages. Her experiences with them had told her men thought that the harder their stump, the greater love they felt. This image made her snigger.

"What're you smirking at?" Tom asked, feeling uneasy.

"Nothing," she lied.

If the truth be known, she wanted to tell him that the majority of men were dirty bastards, but she thought it best to keep quiet for now. Instead, she told him that she was pleased he had mentioned qualities other than her looks.

"That's the whole point. I may fancy you, but to be honest, if you had nothing else, I wouldn't want to spend time with you," replied Tom.

"Flattery will get you almost everything," said Viv.

Stretching her legs out, she wondered whether he had ever done anything extraordinary in his life. What she now wanted was to spend time with people who thought about the world, those individuals who weren't afraid to ask questions about life. She believed Tom had such qualities.

"You're looking thoughtful," he said.

"I was fantasising, wondering whether you'd ever done anything spectacularly crazy."

"I've travelled through Europe and been arrested for stealing food, things like that. I doubt that counts, does it? Anyway, I wouldn't mind experiencing a little more of the world, like that Michael Palin, lucky bastard; he seems to get everywhere. Where would you travel to if you could?"

"I'd definitely go to the States. I'd hire a Harley Davidson and ride as many routes as possible," said Viv with a warm smile. "Imagine New Orleans, with all those street musicians. I can imagine being there all right."

"Too true," said Tom. "Can I come?"

"Only if you ride pillion," she replied.

"What do you mean? You're a woman. You'd have to be on the back. Biker's chicks always sit there," said Tom deadpan.

Falling for the bait, Viv shook her head. Looking over at Tom, she realised she'd been had. "For a second I was taken in. I thought you were a real arsehole."

"Ha ha, the look on your face, yes, that felt sweet," said Tom, rubbing his hands together like a little boy.

"Be careful; you don't know who you're dealing with. Just watch your back; that's all I've got to say," said Viv.

"Promises, promises," he replied.

"Listen, Tom, I've had a brilliant evening, but I really need to sleep. You don't mind if I go to bed, do you?" Viv asked.

"Of course not, I'll show you to your room."

Sunday

It was seven o'clock in the morning when Justin made his way downstairs. With it being Sunday, Justin normally would have been preparing himself for Mass, but this was no longer the case. He put on his walking boots along with his waterproofs and set off. Being late November, the rain was in full flow. Even with this, he felt nature calling him to wander among her beauty. This would take him through muddy fields, slowing down his movement and hopefully his thoughts. Never still for long, Justin's mind was locked in a constant struggle to keep his thoughts from turning toxic. What he wanted was to assume a new identity – not merely a name or an occupation but a new inner self. This needed courage, and to have such courage meant stepping out into the world no matter what the consequences. Turning this knowledge into a vehicle for his restoration was something still unattainable. The exact time and place where he had tainted his existence was etched deep into his consciousness. Up until that day, he had lived a blessed life.

The humming of a small aeroplane overhead interrupted his thoughts. Scanning the sky, he spied it dashing between the clouds directly above his house. Standing still, Justin stared intently at the huge clouds as they changed into patterns, allowing his imagination to wander. Leaning his head backwards, he could see the shape of a dragon. For a second he was transported to an arid land and could see himself walking as though a pilgrim searching for enlightenment. The truth was there for Justin to see. There could be no transformation without him slaying his inner dragons. His was a soul aching for rebirth, a soul tattered and fed by three years of guilt manifesting itself as a life wasted. Time provided nothing for Justin except a reminder of his past actions.

That's it, thought Justin. *That's it! Let it go. Today is the day. There is no other day. There is only today.*

Not wanting to waste another minute, let alone three more years, he set off walking. The hurt he carried every hour and every second of each day was a reminder of what he had done and not a measure of himself as a person. Wanting more than anything to escape his life, he had been sucked into a void. For him, future goals had become nothing but empty rhetoric, a by-product of self-imposed stagnation. At least for the next few hours, Justin would be outside walking through the fields – the same fields he and Nina had trodden many years earlier. The love they both had shared for the natural world had come directly from their father. Every Sunday morning for a couple of hours after Mass, he would take them either birdwatching over the moors or fishing in the brook that meandered near to their house.

Returning his mind back to his surroundings, Justin decided to rest a little and try to calm his thoughts. The gate was a perfect height for him to lean against. Grouped together at the left side of the field were five horses, warm and content under their winter rugs. As with Justin, they didn't seem to notice the rain. Being herding animals, they were happy in the company of their own kind, relying on each other for security and nourishment. Staring out into the beauty of the moors, Justin wondered about his own interactions, or the lack of them. His inclination to lock himself away was not healthy. There was no denying that everyday conversation had become more difficult for him. He avoided mixing with others in the event that this led to questions around his conduct. The time had come to stop the cascade of guilt by boxing and outmanoeuvring his past and beating it into a final submission. Yet the past was still wreaking havoc and keeping him in a straitjacket of guilt.

He opened and then subsequently closed the gate as he headed down to the top end of the pinewoods that overlooked the reservoir. This was the place to view the hundreds of starlings as they provided an aerial ballet of amazing grace and timing.

———

The morning sun poured into Mark's bedroom, waking Viv from a good night's sleep. Rubbing her eyes, she quickly became aware of two things: she was in the home of a man she barely knew, and the knot in her stomach told her that she could no longer deny how much she liked him. Yesterday had been lovely, but the reality of her life came flooding back in a moment of panic. Her marriage was over, and now she needed time to digest this, to step back and contemplate her next move. The feelings she had towards Tom worried her; they were growing too quickly, and she had no wish to lose control.

I know Tom has feelings for me – God knows I've had to battle with enough advances throughout my life to know the signs.

Logically she had to agree that a day together hardly constituted love. Tentatively she made her way downstairs. The gruffness of Tom coughing greeted her as she entered the kitchen.

"Good morning, Viv. Slept well I hope?" Tom asked, gazing at her.

"Aye, really well, thanks," she replied.

"What do you fancy for breakfast?" asked Tom.

"Tea and toast please."

"Coming up," Tom smiled.

Stepping out into the garden, Viv drew in a large gulp of fresh and wet morning air. Extending her arms, she leaned backward and her lungs began to respond to the new day. She performed these daily exercises as part of her kick-boxing routine. They also helped to ground her thoughts. The coldness of the day was sharp, forcing her to beat her arms across her body in an attempt to keep warm.

———————————

Taking a few seconds to study her from the kitchen window, Tom was not at all surprised to see her alert and active. There was no doubt that she was an athlete, something he could never have been. *My God, she's beautiful, Tom thought.*

Knocking on the window, he beckoned her to come inside and eat.

"It's cold out there," she said, laying her hands against his cheeks.

"It is that," he replied.

Slowly moving her hands towards his mouth, Tom blew warm breath onto her strong fingers. Upon kissing them, he suddenly sensed hesitation from her. Letting go, he took a step backwards; the teenage Tom consumed him, making his body rigid. Viv asked him to sit next to her.

"Tom, I do like you, and I do want to see you again. I'm just afraid about throwing myself into a new relationship so soon after Ken," she explained.

Initially mortified at yet another miscalculation, he was disappointed, but he was also heartened that she wanted to see him again. That was enough for him; he could deal with friendship. After all, he hadn't slept with a woman since Chrissie had died. He missed her closeness, her breath, her love. Chrissie had been his life, his closest companion. She had known him more than any woman had. Viv's company was as important to him as her body, and her presence was enough to satisfy him, even if this meant they might never be lovers. Some of his best friends from schooldays had been girls he had fancied. Tom had learned to live with their rejections, believing that they were people worth his time. It was likewise with Viv.

"So can we be friends for now?" Viv asked. "I just need time to sort out my life. I need to speak to Ken and find out what his plans are. I'm going to move on from him as quickly as possible."

Hoping that these words were only metaphorical, he wanted to ask if she had any intentions of moving from the area but thought this might sound self-seeking. As far as he could see, she had no need or reason to leave Tayside. Fixing his eyes on her, he knew she was a rare person. He had already experienced her kindness. Both of them were ready to walk out into the world and embrace change. For him to step out would be an act of bravery, and today for the first time in three years, he was ready to be brave.

"Are you going?" Tom asked, accepting the inevitable.

"Aye, I must be off. I'm going to speak to Ken and start the ball rolling. I'll ring you in a day or two."

"If you need anything, somebody to talk to, drink with, whatever, call me, d'you hear?"

He held out his arms, and Viv accepted them. They hugged for what seemed an age, both content to rest in each other's arms.

"I've got to go, Tom. Thanks for being you."

Waving as she was leaving the house, Tom willed with all his heart that this was not the end and he would see her again. He continued to watch her as she set off down the road in her car.

———

On entering the pinewoods, Justin was startled by the cry of a crow. He tripped over a felled tree and landed on his knees in the stream that fed the reservoir. "Bollocks!" he shouted.

A responding cackle from the big bird seemed almost personal. If Justin hadn't known any better, he would have sworn the crow had planned his accident. Taking refuge on a huge log, he removed his boots and then proceeded to wring out the water from his socks. Dispensing with his initial anger, he giggled, seeing the funny side. He pictured the bird telling its pals that another human had fallen. From the corner of his eye, he noticed that a giant pine tree had dropped cones around its base. He picked one up and studied its shape. One Christmas he and Nina had searched for pine cones to make decorations for the dinner table. It had been a good Christmas. The zeiss binoculars each received had been their perfect Christmas present. Justin smiled remembering that Nina had also received a microscope which she used to examine pond life. In the morning after Mass, he and Nina had walked nearby their house doing a spot of birding. Although they had encouraged one another, their closeness had also held an edge of competitiveness, and that particular Christmas morning's task had been to spot a redwing. The first to do so was the winner and the loser had to hand over their chocolate smoking set, which each had received that morning. For the life of him, Justin couldn't remember who had won. After eating Christmas dinner they had ambled over the Clough.

Carrying on his walk, Justin suddenly stopped dead in his tracks. Three yards in front of him was a great tit. It was flapping wildly, changing direction at speed and obviously in danger. To Justin's amazement, a sparrow hawk swooped down, lifted the terrified bird into accepting claws, and quickly disappeared to the other side of the wood. Within seconds the hawk had landed on a gatepost, where it proceeded to eat greedily. It took a few moments for Justin to get his breath back. With his sight still on the hawk, taking care not to startle it, he walked further into the trees. Unfortunately his left foot inadvertently crushed a fallen branch. The crack shattered the silence. Within a split second the hawk was in the air and soon disappeared over the gate into the open spaces of the moor. Checking his watch, Justin saw it was 3.50 p.m., and daylight was slowly giving way to darkness. Stepping out from the wood, he marvelled at the sight of the distant winter sun fading into the horizon in a pink glow.

A brew sounds good, sweet tea in front of the fire, with a book. Once again, he was reading John Wyatt's *The Shining Levels*, a book that never became tedious. It had the ability to transport him miles away from his troubles.

As Justin passed the pub, he noticed a roaring fire. It was alluring, and rather than going home, he walked through the door and ordered a pint of bitter.

"How do?" said a friendly voice from a man sitting at the end of the bar. "We don't often see you in here."

"I'm usually too busy to spend time in the pub," Justin quickly replied, recognising the man's face. Justin thought he might live by the roundabout at the bottom of the village.

I wish you'd leave me alone, thought Justin, beginning to feel tense, his instincts warning him about this drinker. *He's far too forward for my liking.* This made Justin guarded, worrying that this unknown might pry and raise awkward questions. *Come on, Justin; stop being so paranoid.* Relaxing a little, Justin offered the drinker a cigarette.

"No thanks, I've given them up. It's a filthy habit," said the man.

"Health fascist," replied Justin louder than he had intended.

"Sorry, what was that?" the man growled.

"Nothing," Justin replied in defiance.

"Something about fascist?" the drinker shouted, tensing his body.

Conceding his rudeness, Justin thought it wise to present an olive branch. *When will I learn that not everyone is out to shame me or question my integrity? Get a grip, Justin.*

"Can I buy you a drink?" asked Justin.

"Go on then. Why not," the drinker replied. "I'll have a pint of lager."

Taking a table nearest to the fire, they began chatting.

"You're a bit fiery," remarked the man. "I wasn't sure what all that was about, but we'll leave it there, shall we?"

Feeling relieved, Justin slowly relaxed. It was unusual for him to go to the pub. One thing he didn't want was to start upsetting the regulars, especially if going to the pub proved to help his recovery and go some way to repairing his dysfunctional interactions. This small step was in essence a gigantic one for Justin.

"By the way, I'm Graham, Graham Jones," said the man, extending his hand.

On accepting it, Justin immediately felt its power. Graham was around six feet in height, stocky, with a squat neck. His hand was rough, likely a side effect of intense physical labour. Justin couldn't help but notice a huge scar that had disfigured the whole right side of the man's face, giving him a menacing look. If Justin had seen the scar in the first instance, he would have been a bit more careful with his words. Even though the man's face was blemished, Justin had a feeling he had met him before, but he couldn't be sure, although the man certainly looked familiar.

"So, Justin Ivens, long time no see. You don't remember me, do you?" Graham teased.

"That's it. Of course, now I remember! You're Graham from the farm. Bloody hell, it must be well over thirty years."

"Yep, the family's no longer farming. I'm a builder now, and a busy one at that," boasted Graham.

Justin remembered that Graham had been a tough child, always ready to trade punches whenever called upon. Never a bully, he was more a friend of the bullied, loved by the underdog and feared by tormenters. Possessing such a sharp sense of justice so early in life was very unusual for a child. Talking and listening to him, Justin now knew the child had become the man.

"Well, my old mate, I hear you've had your fair share of problems," said Graham.

Feeling as if he had been smashed in the stomach with a large mallet, Justin fiddled with his fingers. Sensing his body weaken, he made no attempt to stand up, knowing his legs would not support his frame. Instantly his mouth became dry, forcing him to take a large swig of beer.

How much does Graham know about my past? Is he playing mind games? Maybe I should just get up and leave. That'll stop any further prying.

But for once, Justin remained seated, reaffirming to himself that he wouldn't leave. He gripped the side of the chair to hold himself down.

"What about you?" Justin asked, desperate to change the subject.

Thankfully it worked – Graham went into great detail about his divorce and talked affectionately about his new love, a French woman called Paulette. Within minutes they were harking back to their childhood, remembering their encounters and the many laughs they'd shared. They had played numerous games and tricks on unsuspecting neighbours. They were interacting as though it was only yesterday they had seen each other. Graham seemed to be in his stride.

"Do you remember the pizza man? Ha ha. They'd only started delivering a few weeks earlier. It was like a new thing. It was so funny. Was it you or me that rang the order through?"

"I think it was me," replied Justin.

"Yes, you're right," said Graham.

They had ordered a pizza unbeknown to the man living opposite Justin's house. They then had knelt behind the curtains in stitches watching it being delivered. The neighbour clearly had been puzzled and had refused to accept the pizza. Irate, the delivery man had started shouting and insisting the neighbour had to pay. After a few more minutes of arguing the neighbour had chased the man and his pizza up his driveway, all the time shaking his fists.

Enjoying this venture into the past, Justin and Graham next laughed at the time they both had received a clip round the ear from the local bobby for throwing fireworks at each other. Reckless and stupid, they had been completely unaware of the dangers. Needless to say it was an act they had never repeated.

Before Justin could make his excuse to leave, Graham signalled to the barman for two more pints.

"Good health," said Graham.

"Cheers," replied Justin.

Their venture into the past continued with them remembering the summer holidays they'd spent together on the farm haymaking. As with most people's recollections, their childhood summers had been sunny and had seemed to last forever. Building dams in the nearby brook and fishing for small brown trout had kept them busy. The occupants of the house on the edge of the brook must have been child lovers. Despite the crowds that had descended there, they had never once complained. Graham asked Justin if he could remember Nina slipping off one of the bales when they had been climbing the hayloft. Justin smiled. Nina had banged her head and broken her arm from the fall. The road to the farm had consisted of nothing more than a few tons of rubble on top of soft mud, and the ambulance had struggled to get to her. Yet Graham and his father had been able to manipulate their farmyard vehicles around the dodgy bits with incredible deftness.

"So when did the family stop farming?" asked Justin.

"About fifteen years ago. They were fortunate; they sold at the right time. A couple of years later they might not have fared so well. They now live in Clitheroe. They're happy enough."

Graham's parents had been kind people who had always made Justin feel welcome. If one had been lucky enough to arrive at breakfast time, Mrs Jones would have provided home-cured bacon sandwiches. She had always insisted Justin eat them up. They had been stereotypical farmers. A large woman, Mrs Jones had been very friendly. No matter what time of day Justin had seen her, she'd always had an apron on. Alongside her domestic work, she had tended a large flock of ducks and a brood of hens. A small but wiry man, Graham's father had been lean, with a red, weather-beaten face. Stooping slightly, his gait had suggested that he had carried many heavy things over the years, but this hadn't stopped him from being strong and capable.

"I suppose you're wondering about this thing here," said Graham, pointing to the huge scar on his face.

"I suppose so, but I wouldn't presume to ask," Justin said.

"I don't mind telling you. I find it stops people from staring – not that you were gawping," said Graham.

"Well, if you want to tell me, then go ahead. I've no objections."

"I was minding my own business walking through Blackburn when I saw a man lying unconscious on the floor. Three lads were kicking the hell out of him. I ran over yelling at them to stop when one of them turned and slashed out with a Stanley knife. He kept on doing it until I managed to knock the lot of them out. It hurt like hell. There was blood everywhere. All three were laid out unconscious by the time the police and ambulance arrived. The guy who was beaten suffered brain damage. He now has to live in a residential home with twenty-four-hour care, fucking bastards. I can talk about it now, but it took me a long time to come to terms with a face that was no longer my most appealing feature. You have to admit, Justin; I was a good-looking lad. All the girls at school used to fancy me. At first it was hard having people gawking at me – so much so that I stopped going out. When I did start again, it was to a period of heavy drinking. At first, people felt sorry for me, but as time passed, they started showing their disgust at watching me stagger home drunk every night. Anyway, I'm used to the scar now. Paulette says it gives me character."

Sitting still, sipping his beer and not making any comment, Justin was transfixed with Graham's story. Graham's insight into pain and its effect upon his life was eye-opening for Justin. Graham's ability to demonstrate compassion also impressed Justin. The revelation that hiding from the world meant Graham was hiding from his fears resonated deeply with Justin.

"I have to admit," Graham said, "that the drink eased my hurt in the beginning, but after months of getting pissed, I realised that every morning the pain started all over again. I'm sorry if I'm going on a bit, but I need you to understand that life can change. Justin, I know what you've been through. You must be hurting like hell. I, for one, respect your decision. You have to learn to cope. Don't lock yourself away. What you did, you did out of a sense of right. You cannot be persecuted for that, but if you are, those who condemn do it out of ignorance."

Nervousness overtook Justin when he realised that Graham was alluding to that day. In some ways he was glad, as he no longer needed to worry about what Graham might be thinking.

"Listen," Graham continued, "I'm not religious, but in my mind there's only one sin in the world, and that's wasting your life over something that's gone. You were a good friend to me when we were kids. Unless you've changed out of all proportion, then the boy is essentially the man."

"I was only thinking the same about you. Yes, I believe the boy became the man. The same old Graham still standing up to be counted, no matter what the consequences," said Justin.

"I have changed; I've had to. In the beginning, it was terrible. Before the scar, I'd been a womaniser, which obviously created a problem for Dawn, my ex-wife. She used to get jealous, and sometimes I used it to wind her up. Childish I know, but at the time,

I didn't understand what being in a relationship really meant. Since then, I've become more aware of my actions towards those I love." Graham stared directly into Justin's eyes.

The time pressed on; conversation slowed. Graham did not elaborate any further and refrained from asking any awkward questions about Justin's situation. Justin was thankful for this.

"Well, my friend, I must be going. I've got the boys for tea. There's my phone number," said Graham, passing Justin a business card from his wallet. "You can ring me anytime. Maybe we could go birdwatching or something. The last time I went must have been with you all those years ago."

"Sure," said Justin.

"Anyway, must go. See you later! Ring me," Graham said, walking towards the door.

"I will. Oh, and thanks, Graham," replied Justin.

Justin ordered a scotch at the bar and returned to his seat. He mulled over what Graham had said to him. After several more drinks, it was 8.30 pm when he finally staggered out of the pub bouncing off every inanimate object in his way. Approximately ten yards from his front door he fell over and banged his knees on the tarmac. Rather than screaming in pain, he screeched with laughter. He lay on his stomach shouting incoherently at the top of his voice. His head spun uncontrollably as he attempted to get to his feet. His laughter became louder and louder and its intensity so invariable that revellers from the pub came outside to see what the fuss was all about. Thankfully, Justin didn't have far to go as he lived next door but two to the pub. He had no idea about the commotion he was making. At the third attempt of lifting himself off the floor, he felt an arm steady him, then pull him up on to his feet.

"Come on, mate; let's point you in the right direction," said an unfamiliar voice. "There we go."

Justin managed to open the front door and once again lost his balance. Staggering into his living room, he landed on the bureau that stood in the left-hand corner of the far wall, cracking his head against it as he fell to the floor. Lying on his back motionless, he started laughing again but within seconds was breathing heavily and snoring loudly.

Monday

It was 8.15 a.m. The factory was already busy, and the wagons were full of cargo. Ken, the warehouse supervisor, was giving the drivers their instructions. Snappy and offhand with them, he insisted there be no cock-ups. The deliveries were for new clients based in the south-east of England. In between his shouting, Ken thought about Viv and their previous day's meeting. It had been uncomfortable, especially her insistence on a clean break. Later in the day she would be starting divorce proceedings. Although it had been Ken who had made the decision to leave, he was angry at how quickly she wanted their marriage to dissolve. Ken now recognised that Viv was discarding him, and he didn't like the thought of it. In fact, when he stopped to think about it, he was incensed. No one ignored him, never mind cast him aside. *How dare she, the cheeky bitch! Seven years is a long time.*

"Get a move on," Ken shouted to the drivers. They gave him a collective stare that would have frightened other men, but he was used to their reactions. They did not scare him.

"Bingo," said Tom to himself, having found the fault on the machine.

A sudden bang on the door startled him. Ken stared down at him with menacing eyes. They were cold, projecting a deep level of loathing Tom had not experienced before. The look sent a shiver through him. His heartbeat rapidly increased, and his hands suddenly became damp, leaving his nerves jangling. Swiftly turning without speaking, Ken made his way out of the workshop.

Ignore him, Tom thought, trying to calm his nerves. Continuing to work, he didn't look up again.

Viv had gone for a three-mile run, taken a shower, and finished her breakfast and was now going through her usual morning routine. Applying her makeup, she rubbed in the foundation with caution, followed by eye shadow and lastly blood-red lipstick. Natural beauty needed very little help. Having made an appointment to discuss divorce proceedings with a local solicitor, she had taken the morning off work. An odd feeling enveloped her when she walked into Foster, Briggs, and Rigby specialists in family law. This was a new experience for her, though it was an exercise her parents and some friends had already undertaken. In a bizarre way, she felt excited. Today her priority was to discuss what might be considered a fair settlement. The future was about her. No longer did she need to be an attentive wife or consult her husband about everyday trivialities. She was entering new territory, and nothing would hold her back.

"Well then, from what I see, there's no problem. Your husband has clearly breached his marriage contract. What are you looking for – an amicable agreement, or do you want blood?" Mr Rigby asked abruptly.

"I want what's mine and nothing more. At the moment, I'm thinking of keeping the house, but this could change depending on my circumstances. Also I'm not sure whether I can afford the repayments. What I want is to start the ball rolling. Once this begins, I can then speak to Ken and come to some sort of agreement," said Viv.

"I'll serve him a petition which will let him know your intentions. The divorce I mean," replied Rigby, opening the door for her.

A sharp pain shot through Justin's head. It woke him with a start and then reached a crescendo in the middle of his eyes. Shutting his eyes, he scrambled on to the settee, using all his will power to stop from throwing up. He slid back on to the floor and crawled on all fours through the living room towards the stairs. Kneeling on the bottom step, he told himself there were only thirteen to tackle and that with effort and concentration he could make it. On reaching the top, he managed to edge into his bedroom with his head a mass of pain and a gut that was on fire. "Oh God, my head," he groaned, falling on to the bed.

His nausea became tangible as he spewed remnants of the previous night's profligacy all over the duvet. "Shit," he screamed as he jumped off the bed, immediately falling over.

His knees were sore, but he couldn't fathom out why. Perching himself on the edge of the bed and taking a deep breath, he only just managed to strip the bed before being sick again on a chair that held some of his clothes. Rolling down on to the floor, he let out a huge groan. He crawled into the back bedroom and managed to scramble on to the lowest bunk, where he fell into a long sleep. It was 4.00 p.m. before he stirred with a mouth as dry as the Sahara. Feeling as if he had been poisoned, Justin lay still not wanting to move. It felt horrible.

The day had once again gone quickly for Tom. He took time to clear his bench, wanting his tools to be ready for tomorrow's shift. Thinking of Viv, he slowly wiped them clean. He hoped that her visit to the solicitors had not been too upsetting. His impulse was to give her a call, but he didn't want to make a nuisance of himself. Feeling as though somebody was near him, Tom looked round to find Ken standing in a threatening position about to say something.

"What do you want?" Tom asked.

"I just want to apologise for the other night. I don't know what came over me, though you shouldn't have said those things to Gemma. She was only being friendly," said Ken.

Is this his apology, or has Gemma told him to make one? Tom wondered. There was something not quite right about it. Maybe it was Ken's tone, which gave Tom the impression that he didn't give a toss. *I feel like smacking him with my hammer, but I know it's senseless. It would make me just like him.* At the same time, Tom wanted to see Ken sweat.

"Ken, why are you here?" Tom asked. "It's obviously not easy for you to apologise and mean it. I would prefer you not to bother."

At this, Ken smirked. Tom was fuming.

"You're an insincere bastard!" Tom said. Remembering what Viv had told him regarding Ken's inability to back down from confrontations with men, Tom put some distance between them. "Anyway, I've spoken to the police, and they'll be speaking to you shortly. I'm pressing charges."

"What!" Ken screamed.

"You heard," replied Tom, picking up the hammer. He didn't have any intention of using it. It was just a negotiating tool for safe passage out of the factory, if needed.

After a few seconds of silence, Tom agreed to drop the charges, advising Ken to get some help for his temper before he did any real harm. Marching away military style, Ken didn't say a word or look back at Tom.

Tom left work and went home. On entering the kitchen he switched on the kettle to make a cup of coffee. Glancing out the window, he noticed that the moon was huge and dominated the sky. It was a magnificent presence that filled him with awe. By now his thoughts were wandering. Life had taught him that certainty by its nature created uncertainty. Peering at the moon made him think of its power. It was a huge magnet in the sky that pushed and pulled the ebb and flow of the sea. Having been an angler, Tom knew that the tides were extremely unpredictable. As with human existence, there would always be contradictions, times when a situation was misread, creating danger. The memory of one fishing trip on the North Sea off the coast of Whitby sent shivers down Tom's spine. As Tom had happily fished away, a gigantic wave seemingly from nowhere had hit the boat, washing his friend Samuel into the sea. Thankfully, with the help of the skipper, Samuel had managed to scramble back on board before the next huge, life-taking wave had descended. Samuel had said that during the ordeal, albeit short in real time, his overwhelming emotion had been one of powerlessness. Simultaneously, Tom was able to tell many positive stories about the sea, especially relating to his wife, Chrissie. When on holiday in Spain, they had always gone swimming and snorkelling together. Many times they had lain on their backs, hand in hand, allowing wave after gentle wave to lift and slowly drop them back into the healing waters. The sea had restored their love and lifted their spirits.

Life is water, Tom thought, wondering where the hell such words were coming from and what they might mean. Once again, he was saying things outside his usual remit. He was conscious that his life was taking a turn into territories previously untapped. Up until 1999 everything he had ever wanted and needed had been his.

Wishing to be close to his wife, Tom removed a photograph of her from the sideboard. Moving his index finger around her figure, he gently kissed it. The moment overwhelmed him, and he bit hard into his bottom lip, knowing that given the chance again he would have made a different choice on that day.

Tuesday

Tuesdays were always Viv's busiest day at work and were usually spent interviewing clients and then giving them a decision on whether they qualified for a personal loan. Today she was uninterested in work and wanted her shift to end. This was a very different state of affairs from her usual approach. The client sitting on the other side of her desk was a large man who kept sniffing loudly. Wanting to tell him to find a tissue and blow his nose, Viv was exasperated, particularly as it seemed his wife was impervious to his poor social skills. *I couldn't put up with that. I bet the poor woman's been worn down over the years. He needs a good slapping,* thought Viv. She wondered what Tom's bad habits might be. *I hope he doesn't constantly pick his nose, especially when driving. Mind you, the only way I'll know is if I spend more time with him.*

Although Viv had told him that she needed space to think, she was already missing him. He was in her mind all the time. *I'll phone him tonight.*

"Well then?" the large man said, bringing Viv out of her daydream. "Do we qualify?"

"Yes, Mr Clay, you qualify. I'm sure you'll have your new caravan by the end of the week," she replied.

Viv was concerned for her customers. Her job over the past couple of years had changed somewhat. She had seen an upsurge of lending and more credit availability. It was as though the banks were encouraging customers to buy things they didn't really need. Viv could see that encouraging people to borrow more and more was doing nothing other than extending their already-spiralling debts.

Maybe now is the time to find a new career. Well, at least explore different possibilities, she thought.

It was a new day, and Justin no longer felt ill. Collecting his boots and waterproofs, he was ready for a walk over the Clough.

"Today is the day. Today is the only day," he repeated to himself as though it was a prayerful meditation. This was Justin's attempt to create positive affirmations. It was a continuation from his thoughts on Sunday and would hopefully become his starting point for every day. No doubt this would appear peculiar to some people, but he had to begin somewhere.

The sky was colourless and dull, the kind of weather that saw sane people pursue an indoor hobby or, for those with square eyes, the television. Not one for TV, Justin believed it to be 'the opium of the masses', in essence an ingenious capitalist invention to keep people passive. After locking the front door, he took the narrow road to the right of the pub. This was Justin's favourite lane in the area leading to Black Wood, where there was a lot of wildlife to be seen, especially within its blackberry bushes. A favourite sight for Justin was watching a wren shyly rear its head in anticipation of marauders. How he was able to empathise with this creature, bobbing in and out of cover, its tiny frame too afraid to stay exposed for long periods. Like Justin, it was forever on guard, conscious of the natural dangers around.

"Good morning, young man," a voice came from over the wall.

It was the retired sergeant major, a talkative man with many stories to tell. Some were funny; others, horrific and poignant. Stan had seen action during the Falklands Conflict and had come close to losing his life. He had lost friends in battle. Although Justin believed most wars to be morally indefensible, he could not help but feel for those families that had lost loved ones and for those in the armed forces who had been killed or maimed.

"Morning," Justin replied. "Been out long?"

"I've been out a couple of hours. I thought the fresh air would do me good before I start the late shift. How are you then? Keeping well I trust?"

"I'm okay, thanks, just stretching my legs, filling my lungs," replied Justin, feeling less guarded than usual. These were genuine questions with no hidden agenda.

"Anyway, must be off. Enjoy your walk," said Stan.

The morning was changing as the fighting sun peered out from behind a gigantic grey cloud that was slowly breaking apart. There was now a hint of blue in the sky and with it a slight rise in temperature. On reaching Black Wood, Justin sat down on the wall and scanned the Ribble Valley through his binoculars. Spying the River Calder edging its way towards the ruins of a monastery, he thought about its journey to the sea. Long before the industrial revolution and its pollution, this had been a fine salmon river. Knowing that monks had always purposely built their monasteries where food was plentiful, he was pleased that after many years of pollution, salmon were once again starting to use the river, albeit in small numbers. Before joining the seminary, Justin had contemplated becoming a monk. The thought of dedicating himself to the world through prayer had appealed to him. Such a thought these days filled him with regret, knowing that if he had followed this inkling, he wouldn't be responsible for what had happened on that day. He would have been locked away in a monastery. Lighting a cigarette, he drew in the smoke deep into his lungs. He gasped for breath. *Maybe I should stop.* But at this moment in time, it was an impossible task. He needed to smoke; it provided a comfort only smokers could understand.

Standing in the middle of nature started Justin reminiscing about Nina and their anticipation of a positive future. A full hour passed. Jumping off the wall, Justin made his way into the wood where the light quickly vanished under the protection of giant pine trees. It gave the place a damp feel. Even at the height of summer the ground was soft and the air oppressive. Many of the locals believed Black Wood's name had a double meaning, allegedly relating to the practice of witchcraft. Local rumours stated that the devil had become trapped in the wood after being tricked by a local clergyman. During the 1980s a goat's head and several black candlesticks had been found, starting a rumour that a coven existed for local dignitaries interested in power. In some ways Justin could believe this. There was a sense of eeriness about the place. In truth, the people responsible for the objects were probably less like occultists and more like the local swingers wanting to screw each other in a different place. Whatever the reality, be there a coven or not, Justin was aware of the foreboding presence of Pendle Hill, which dominates the landscape of East Lancashire and a place well known for its infamous witches of centuries past.

Breathing in the muggy air was now causing Justin to cough repeatedly. Deciding to rest under a pine tree, he momentarily closed his eyes. A sudden scream from the treetops directly above his head unnerved him for a second. Opening his eyes, he could see two rooks attacking each other with venomous intent. Their continued attempts at disempowering each other came to nothing, forcing both birds to take a step backwards and reconsider their positions. After Justin's heartbeat returned to normal and the birds retreated, he stood up to stretch his aching back. The dampness from the tree had wet his backside, but Justin had greater things to concern himself with. The birds' fight made him wonder why people spent their time seeking power. His thoughts took him back three years to the day that gave him the opportunity to relish the rawness of this. The truth of the matter was that being able to wield power had left him feeling sick with remorse. Walking further into the wood, his eyes filled with tears of regret.

"Today is the day," Justin repeated. "Today is the only day."

Standing in the depth of Black Wood, Nina's face flooded Justin's mind, reminding him of the countless hours spent challenging each other deep into the night. Many times he had accused Nina of closing her mind to the realms of the supernatural and the possibility of a spiritual realm. She had countered that she was a scientist to the core and did not like religion. For her, it had made people believe beauty and goodness were consigned to some far-off being outside of the physical world. Nina had believed there was no distinction between religion and spirituality, as Justin had argued.

Oh, Nina, how I miss you. I don't care what you say. You're here in spirit. I can feel you. He'd told Nina that her argument had little bearing on the development of faith and that by its very nature religion had to be corrupt, as it had been created by human beings. But this argument had had no effect on her. According to Nina religion was a curse. People, she had rationalised, needed to express their ideas and thoughts from their own experiences, not within the constraints of an institution that served those in power. Justin had agreed with her, although he had reminded Nina that not all spiritual people were creationists or believed the world was a mere four thousand years old.

Nina, sweet Nina, Justin thought, staring into the darkness of the wood.

The wind was now blowing deep into this darkness, unsettling the trees and lifting small fir cones off the ground. Justin shivered. Further memories of Nina gate-crashed his thoughts. They had spent so many happy times together. Yet on some occasions, when she had been drinking, her tongue had been very cutting. This usually had taken the form of her belittling his faith in Jesus Christ. At these times he had felt she gave him little respect.

Justin stopped dead in his tracks. He thought he saw a shadow move in the corner of his left eye. "Nina," shouted Justin, disorientated.

Stop it, he thought, leaning heavily against a tree. He lit a cigarette. The coldness of the wind made him clasp his arms around his body, shielding himself from its icy sting. Memories of Nina were battling for supremacy in a mind that refused to relax. Sliding down the tree on to his backside, he bowed his head under the weight of his thoughts. Here he took a moment to pray but was soon distracted, calling to mind one particular evening spent with Nina at his house in Whitechapel. Once again, she had been claiming God couldn't exist, that faith belittled rationality, and that religion was morally bankrupt, having shown itself to be a hindrance to scientific progress. Closing his eyes, he recalled the look on her face when he'd argued that the Nazis had used science as a rationale for their murderous regime, showing science didn't have the upper hand when it came to probity. Standing in the darkness of the wood, Justin still believed that many of Nina's arguments were irrelevant. What did it matter if the world was not created in six days or whether we descended from primates? As far as Justin had been concerned, God had transcended all such nonsense. In Justin's eyes science had been no different from religion in that central to its advancement were human beings. In that case, science had been neither progressive nor a tool that would answer the existential questions of life. On the other hand, spirituality had transcended the banal, the human element of religious dogma. If only Justin had such surety now. If only he could rise above his past.

Moving his head to the left, he spotted a treecreeper walking from side to side up the tree. It was comical how it moved so adeptly, and it made Justin smile. So sure of itself, it didn't cling to the trunk in fear. It was confident as it almost danced its way up the tree. This helped Justin to refocus his thoughts on the scenery around him. It was time to start making his way home. Now on the small road at the opening of the wood, Justin walked slowly along in the hope of catching sight of the kestrel that hunted in the field opposite his house.

Another couple of hours and I'll be home, thought Tom.

Another busy day had seen him attend to three broken machines, each taking the best part of two hours to fix. They were at least thirty years old and quite frankly knackered. Their breakdown had meant a loss of production. Laying his toolbox on the workbench, he sat down and then poured himself a coffee from his old but trusted flask. It had seen many days and been to numerous places. Thankfully, it was not able to tell tales. Closing his eyes, he pictured one of the times he and Chrissie had gone on a picnic. They had finished off with a period of vigorous exercise in the middle of a field with only the elements and wildlife as observers, or so they had thought. At the height of climax they had heard sniggers from a group of static ramblers, not one of them younger than sixty-five.

Tom recalled another time during a walking holiday in Pembrokeshire when they had been meandering along the coastline. Suddenly Chrissie had begun to feel horny. Both had struggled down a steep cliff face into a cave, believing it to be miles from civilisation. Once again, to their embarrassment, they had misjudged the situation. With Tom's pants around his ankles there had come a cough from the darkness. When he had turned around, three cavers with grins the size of the Cheshire cat had welcomed them. "Don't mind us," one of the three gawping men had sniggered, giving a dirty laugh. The only thing that Tom and Chrissie had been able to do was to readjust their clothing and get the hell out of there. The echo of laughter had seemed to follow them along the pathway for miles. After about an hour of intensive walking they had sat down, looked at each other, and fallen about the ground laughing. Their stomachs had creased to the point of physical pain.

"Hey, Tom, do you want to share your thoughts?" asked his foreman. "Something's tickled you."

"Sorry, Jimmy, I was daydreaming," replied Tom.

"I know that, but what about?"

"Oh, it's nothing. By the way can I take some holidays starting next Monday?

"I'll look into it for you," replied the foreman.

Having returned from his thoughts, he realised that it was time go home. As was his usual practice, he packed his tools away, making sure that his workbench was tidy for the following day. Ending the twenty-minute drive, Tom parked his car and took the few steps into his house, ready to relax.

I'm seeing Justin on Saturday. I hope things go well. My God, I do. For the past three years, Tom had used Justin as a scapegoat and a way of dealing with the whirlwind pain that tore at his heart. The time was approaching when he could no longer keep blaming his old friend. The overwhelming need for truthfulness continued to creep into his consciousness. *Is it you, Chrissie? Are you telling me to sort myself out? My God, how I miss you.* "What a prat I've been," Tom said aloud as though to a father confessor.

Random thoughts multiplied in Tom's head by the hour. In the present moment, he was thinking about the afterlife and the fact that Chrissie wouldn't be bothered that her ashes still lay in a jar at the back of his kitchen cupboard. Tom had asked her on numerous occasions where she wanted her ashes scattered. Chrissie hadn't cared. As far as she had been concerned, she would say her goodbyes to him and brace herself for eternal extinction.

"Dispose of them as you feel fit, love," she had said.

The truth of the matter was he couldn't face letting her go. Her ashes reminded him of her and were the last symbol of their life together. Some might say this was morbid, but for Tom it meant Chrissie was still close to him.

Oh, Chrissie, why did you have to die? Why did you have to leave me?

The knowledge that Chrissie had loved him, as much as he had loved her, helped Tom face the next day. He knew that to have been loved so deeply had been special and was something many people had never experienced in their lives. Tom knew he had been blessed. The thought of life after death had been nothing but pub talk to him over the years. Yet today, he was curious. *If there is a heaven, would or even could you still love me? If you exist somewhere else on a different plane, can you still see me? I know you don't believe in the afterlife. But what if you're wrong? What if you're there now? Is human love different in the afterlife? Does love exist?*

More of an agnostic than an atheist, Tom's understanding of theology was no more than the knowledge acquired at school and then later snippets of information from his friendship with Justin. The notion of being together after death had never been a concern for Tom. Even after Chrissie's departure it had not occupied a moment's consideration until now. For the past three years, Tom's fear of the future had slashed him like a knife, cutting, hacking, and ripping at his thoughts, slowly bleeding him, leaving his heart in an emotional coma. All this self examination had made him face his failings and accept that he had stifled the chance for grieving. It had been on his terms, retrospective and wholly self-indulgent. His defensiveness had been a barrier against him taking responsibility, which, in turn, justified his actions in blaming others.

I wanted Chrissie alive no matter what her condition. She was my life! I couldn't imagine life without her. Maybe I should cancel seeing Justin. I don't know if I can face him or myself for that matter. I mustn't though; I can no longer ignore him. Chrissie wanted me to stay close to him. Christ, what am I to do? If I love again, who do I spend eternity with, my first or my new love? What the fuck is happening to me?

Not being a believer in a divine power meant he had no theological answers. What he did know was that the huge gaping hole that Chrissie had filled was slowly becoming packed with Viv's presence.

You'd like Viv, love. I know you would. She's fun just like you were. So many thoughts swilling around in my head; I feel like my brain is overloading. I need to stop them, but I don't know how.

These thoughts were like parables in miniature, asking questions of him, probing and painful.

I'm so sorry, Chrissie. I don't know if I can carry on like this anymore. I know it's me. You've always wanted me to move on. But I feel like I'm a traitor to you, to your memory. I know I'm alive; I'm breathing, but I don't feel like I'm living.

For the first time, Tom accepted that his life since Chrissie's death had been lived through his grief. This had protected him from other people's arrows, shielding his own shortcomings and weaknesses. His ineptitude on the 19th day of March 1999 had been nothing short of spineless. He was now ready to admit that his past excuses were unworthy of someone who wanted to live and love again. They were nothing less than pitiful. Yet even with this newfound optimism, Tom was still feeling weak – not just physically but as a human being, as a man, husband, and friend.

Without thinking, he had poured and guzzled two large helpings of scotch, making his head light and his balance unsteady. It was proving difficult for Tom to admit that Chrissie was no longer a life-giving force, no more the provider of emotional comfort, although she still filled his mind. These reminiscences were reruns of their time together, burnt deep into his subconscious, where he could re-enact them whenever he wanted to or when needed to ease his pain. They had made his life worth living, but they no longer did. It was time to acknowledge that these revolving memories were not enough to develop him as a human being. For all his faults, he believed he was worth saving. Too many years had passed producing the same feelings without ever taking him beyond the barriers he had built and unwisely defended. The stirring of love for Viv had now awakened him. The battle for his heart and mind was beginning to shift from that of memory to a dynamic and existent person in the form of Viv. Instinctively, he wanted to embrace her as his saviour, his freedom, his escape, but he was conscious that Chrissie had once worn that very same mantel. His reliance upon a woman for salvation had already blown his life apart. This time he wished for love to transcend his own needs. The whisky was now playing tricks on his mind as he sat down and tried to steady himself. Shutting his eyes, an image of the world spinning around the sun entered his head, reinforcing his own dilemma, that Tom Riley needed his very own Copernicus revolution. "What's happening to me?" Tom shouted out loud as he reached for the whisky bottle.

He poured another large measure, and taking a swig, he scowled as it scorched his throat. Strange revelations were challenging the foundations of his life. Pushing back his chair, Tom stood up and let out a shout. This was more of a chant, a celebration, an understanding that something good had occurred. In this moment, he comprehended that truth was easy to acknowledge yet so very difficult to achieve.

The cold was penetrating his skin, making him shiver and rub his hands together. It had reached into Tom's bones, so he decided to build a fire. The ritual of fire making was something he had always enjoyed. That within a few minutes he would be snug and warm fuelled his anticipation. Sitting in front of a roaring fire gave him permission to daydream as he spotted all manner of weird and wonderful shapes within the dancing flames. Many nights he had stared deeply into the blaze and been captivated by its colours. Tom attributed his perfect blood pressure to this pastime, as it was relaxing and clearly good for his heart. Feeling more at ease, he went into the kitchen and poured himself a beer. He lay in front of the fire and closed his eyes.

Viv sat in her car outside Tom's house with a Chinese takeaway. She was trying to pluck up the courage to ring him. Taking a deep breath, she picked up her mobile phone and dialled his number.

"Hello, Tom, it's Viv," she said nervously. "Are you busy?"

"No, why?" he enquired.

"Hungry?"

"I haven't eaten yet. In fact, I'm not busy, but I'm hungry. I'm also a bit pissed, though. Why?"

"I'm outside. Do you fancy some company?"

"Come on in. The doors unlocked," replied Tom trying not to appear too excited.

"You don't mind do you?" Viv asked as she walked into the house.

"Of course I don't," replied Tom greeting her.

"I thought you might like to share some food. It's not homemade, but it's pretty good," she said.

"Here, let me take that from you. Come into the kitchen." Tom put plates on the table and asked, "How did you get on at the solicitor's?"

"Okay. He's going to write to Ken. Rigby was arrogant really. I felt quite intimidated by him. I've also spoken to Ken."

"Good. I'm glad things went well," said Tom.

There was an awkward pause for a moment or two.

"The duck in plum sauce is gorgeous," said Tom. "By the way, I've got an old friend coming to stay at the weekend. Have I mentioned Justin to you before?"

"I'm not sure," said Viv.

"He was my closest friend, but I haven't seen him for three years. I've decided to make contact again as there's something we need to sort out," explained Tom.

There was another brief moment of silence, allowing them to gaze at each other. In that moment both knew that tonight felt right.

After taking a shower, Justin sat down in the armchair next to the front window where he observed people walking to the pub. A tall man passed by whom Justin thought he might know. After further memory searches he identified him. *Roger Stapleton. Blimey, he was really short at school. He must be six foot five. I wonder what he's up to now.*

Not quite having the courage to step outside and talk to him, Justin envisaged that one day he would. This in itself was a victory. Maybe this marked a turn, a deviation and a small conquest that provided the tiniest sliver of hope. His time with Graham in the pub had helped him to refocus his life a little. Justin would be seeing Tom soon and therefore needed to gain courage to face him. Maybe he should follow Roger into the pub. This he soon dismissed. Even though his mantra that today was the only day had helped him, he didn't quite feel ready to venture into the pub following an old school friend. It was now dark, and the world needed shutting out for the night. Looking out at the cars parked opposite his house, Justin believed he was slowly beginning to deal with his guilt, but he could not quite yet turn defeat into victory.

"Never!" shouted Ken. "Viv and Tom? You've told some tales in your time, but this one I can't believe."

"I'm telling you," insisted Old Donald, "I saw her go into his house no more than an hour ago looking all cosy. They were smiling and laughing."

Ken was struggling to come to terms with this news and called Donald a meddlesome old fool.

We'll soon see, thought Ken. *It'd fucking better not be true. Viv and Tom, no way! The bastard! That's my wife he's with. It didn't take her long. Bloody bitch, I wonder when that started. Right!*

Ken quickly downed his pint, wiped his mouth with the back of his hand, and left the pub.

"We'll see about this. I'll kill him, the sneaky bastard," shouted Ken as he walked towards his car, forgetting that he no longer held any claim on his wife and showing himself to be Neanderthal-like. The desire to give Tom a good hiding fuelled Ken's thoughts. Images of somebody else touching his wife stoked his anger making him feel sick. With every breath a surge of hatred flowed through his body, muddling his sense of perspective. Never experiencing humiliation like this before, he was ready to put a stop to it.

"She'll come home with me if I have to drag her," he said in his rage. "Divorce me, will she."

Pressing his foot down on the accelerator, his mind was now speeding faster than his car. Swinging it around a tight bend, he gripped the steering wheel so hard that his hands were turning red.

———————————

Glancing at Tom, Viv knew what made her want to be with him – respect; he gave her respect. In his eyes, she was a person, not just a wife, and he made her feel special. This was new for her. She was enjoying it and wanted more.

"Fancy a drink?" Tom asked.

"Why not. Have you any white wine?" replied Viv.

Stretching downwards, Tom reached into the booze cabinet and pulled out a bottle. "Give it ten minutes. I'll chill it first," he said, placing it in the freezer.

"Okay," she replied. "I bet you're looking forward to seeing Mark. Catch up on things and see how he's getting on. You must miss him."

"I do, very much. No doubt he'll have a few tales to tell. He usually does. Mind you, I can't talk; we got up to all sorts at university. Real silly things," chuckled Tom.

"Out with it," demanded Viv laughing.

"It's where to start," said Tom.

"How about you start at the beginning," Viv smiled.

"Okay." Before he could start bullshitting, there was a thud on the front door. Startled, they both jumped up. "Who the hell can that be?" Tom asked, turning to Viv.

"I haven't got the foggiest," she replied.

Making his way to the front door, Tom was scratching his head as to who might be calling at this time of night. On opening it, two hands grabbed him around the throat, holding him so that he couldn't move. Within a flash, Ken swung his right knee into Tom's groin, immediately dropping him to his knees, allowing Ken to then kick him in the head. With his right hand he closed the door cutting off any escape route.

On hearing the commotion, Viv rushed to the hallway where she could see Ken standing over Tom. "What have you done?" she screamed, running towards him. "Get off him!"

"So it's true then, eh?" Ken said, pointing at Tom. "Get your stuff, Viv; you're coming with me."

"I'm not. What I do in my life has nothing to do with you anymore," said Viv.

"Come here," he screamed, making a lunge for her.

Too fast for him, she moved closer to Tom, who was groaning and still on his knees.

"Going to see how lover boy is?" Ken scoffed.

"Go on; clear off home to Gemma. No wonder I don't love you; you're a bully. I don't know why I stopped with you for so long."

Ken made towards the front door but then quickly turned. Grabbing hold of Viv, he tried forcing her towards his gaping lips. "You'll miss this," he sniggered.

"Viv!" Tom shouted, trying to get to his feet.

Distracted by Tom's voice, Ken slackened his grip, giving Viv the chance to break free and send him spinning backwards. Now firmly on his feet, Tom shouted at Ken to leave.

"Ha ha," Ken scoffed, composing himself. "Call yourself a man."

"I've told you once; now get out," shouted Tom, pointing to the door.

"Ooh, I'm shittin' my pants," mocked Ken, pretending to shake.

"You will be," countered Tom.

"Come on, Viv; you're coming with me."

The mistake had been made: Ken had taken his eyes off Tom. Like lightning, Tom rushed towards Ken and threw him over his right shoulder.

"Quick, Viv, the door," he shouted. "Open the bloody door."

Within seconds of her having done so, Ken was sprawled on the pavement outside.

"Now piss off," Tom screamed before slamming the door shut, shaking the house to its foundation.

"That's the second time he's had me. He's a real nasty piece of work," Tom said as he entered the kitchen, rubbing his head and balls, which were now very hot and no doubt red. "I've a feeling we haven't seen the last of him."

"Come here," said Viv with her arms out. "Let's have a look at your head."

"Never mind my head. How about taking a look at my bollocks?" Tom said.

"Maybe later," Viv said with a smile, helping to lighten the atmosphere. Both Tom and Viv laughed out loud.

Her stout defence of him impressed Tom. Never in a million years would he have envisaged being in the middle of a love triangle. Not him, no, he had been content to live his life with one woman without complications. He wanted that again. He wanted Viv but was now questioning whether it was all worth it given Ken's violence.

They finished off the bottle of white wine and laughed about their earlier fracas with Ken. Tom's head pain had settled a little, and so had his knackers. The lump from his earlier encounter with Ken had up to that point been getting smaller. If truth be told, the lessening of pain was more to do with the large amount of alcohol numbing his senses rather than any ability to take a punch. Feeling content with Viv by his side, he leaned back on the settee and closed his eyes.

"What are you thinking about?" Viv asked.

"You," replied Tom. "Since meeting you, my world has changed. You've brought me back to life again and shown me that life shouldn't be squandered."

Conscious of what he had just said, Tom turned his head leftwards and gazed at Viv. She had her eyes closed with a large smile on her face. On opening them, she moved towards Tom and kissed him on his forehead, sliding her right hand over towards him. Moving closer, she then rested her head against his shoulder.

"Are you okay, Tom?" Viv asked.

"I am now," he replied, fighting back his sexual impulses, willing his rapidly growing bulge not to expand any further. Knowing this to be a special, if not precious, moment, he didn't want to ruin it. Holding Viv in this way was everything he had wished for. Ken could give him a good hiding every day if this was the prize at the end of it. Cupping her hands around his chin, Viv kissed his forehead and worked around his face until their lips met. Fighting hard not to come, Tom let out a sound of orgasmic proportions as blood pumped through the whole of his body, shaking it with sexual excitement. They stopped kissing and looked at each other.

"Thank God that's over with," said Viv.

"Cheers," replied Tom sarcastically.

"I don't mean the kissing, I mean the situation. There's no need for us to feel awkward anymore."

"What about this morning and you not wanting to rush things? Are you sure about this, Viv? My God, I hope you are. If so, then you've made an old man very happy." Tom's endorphins were now partying to their maximum. Only a week ago he wasn't fit for human integration. Now, he was sitting on the threshold of the greatest prize of all: love. "Do you not want to know my age before you commit to anything?" asked Tom.

"Are you fishing? Do you want to know my age?" Viv replied.

"No," Tom said.

"I'm thirty-four, and you're in your forties. I don't give a damn how old you are."

"Well, I'm forty-four."

No longer could they hold back their suppressed passions. Within seconds they were fumbling each other, their bodies aching and pounding with impatience. Tom moved slightly away from Viv, wishing to look at her before they made love. The moment was monumental, and he could not help but smile. The evidence of his desire was substantial – one epic hard-on that was ready to split his underpants, rip his trousers, and smash through the roof in search of relief. Things would never be the same again.

Miracles do happen. I can't believe it. Concentrate, you idiot. Concentrate. Keep breathing. Breathe, breathe.

Smiling at him, Viv pressed her hand against the swell in his pants, making him work overtime as he breathed in rapidly.

"Be careful, Viv; it's been a while. I don't want to finish before I've started," Tom said, slowly unzipping her skirt.

Moving to the edge of the settee, he pulled her towards him. In response, Viv started undoing the buttons of his shirt, making Tom delirious as she slowly moved her hands across his chest, running her fingers up and down his stomach. Viv laughed

"What're you laughing at?" Tom spluttered in between gasps of air and her loud laughter.

"You," she said. "I know you'll think I'm stupid, but your belly made me laugh. It's a" – she let out another laugh – "beautiful belly. I'm sorry, Tom; I just didn't know what to expect." She laughed some more.

"You're a mad cow," said Tom, sliding his hand underneath her bra on to her right breast.

"Come on, Tom; let's go upstairs," she said.

Wednesday

"Oh no, its eight o'clock and I'm late for work," shouted Viv in a panic. "I've never been late for work in years. Bloody hell, it's Wednesday. I've got a meeting with the manager just after nine. You're a bad influence you are, Tom."

"You're late? What about me? I should have been at work at seven. I'd best ring and let them know I'll be going in. We could be even later. Come on; give us a kiss."

"I'll have a quick shower; then I must be off. I'll see you tonight, okay, love?" Viv said, thinking that she should be more like Tom and not worry so much. The hot shower helped to waken her. Downstairs, Tom was waiting with a cup of tea and a slice of toast for her.

"There we go, love," Tom said. "We can't let the workers go without their breakfast. I wish we could stop here all day and cut the world out for a while."

"Aye, but we can't. I don't like being late for anything, never mind work," Viv replied. "Hey, Tom, be careful today. Ken will be at work; just watch your back."

"He can go fuck himself. I'll smack him this time. Little shit," Tom mocked.

"I mean it, Tom; be careful. You've seen what he's like. I don't want to get a phone call telling me you're in hospital," Viv shouted, heading for the door.

"Wait a minute," Tom said. "You've forgotten something."

"Oh yes, my purse," Viv replied.

"No," Tom said with his eyes shut and lips ready for a kiss.

"I haven't time to piss around," she said, gently kissing them.

"Ring in sick," demanded Tom.

"No. I do that when I'm ill. You'll have to wait until tonight. See you later," Viv said, leaving the house.

Tom rang the factory and informed them he would be late. His foreman told him not to worry; he liked Tom and knew he was one of the better workers. Jumping into his car, Tom began the twenty-minute journey. The factory soon came in to view. He parked his car and then walked to his department. On reaching it, he unpacked his bag on the workbench.

"Well then, ye lazy bugger," laughed the foreman. "You have too much ale or what?"

"Something like that," laughed Tom.

"By the way, it's okay for you to take some time off. We can cover your shifts."

When Chrissie had been alive, Tom had lived for his holidays. How different he had become. *We had some great holidays. Didn't we, Chrissie?* What a different person he had been with Chrissie by his side.

The thought of seeing Justin was now beginning to unsettle him. Trying to calm himself, he thought about Chrissie, but also the previous night's exploits. *My life is changing, love. But you'll always be with me.* Chrissie now represented Tom's past; she was a memory. Although he could sense her spirit, she was no longer flesh and blood, whereas spending time with Viv was real. He could hold and caress her and listen to her breathing. Tom couldn't wait to see her again and hoped that she was feeling the same.

"Oh, Tom, there's a problem with the machine in the building next to the depot. Can you go and take a look?" the foreman asked.

"Sure," Tom replied, collecting his toolbox and briefly scanning the area in case Ken was lurking. Passing the depot, Tom could hear Ken shouting at the drivers. How they put up with him was a mystery to Tom. These men continued to be humiliated on a daily basis by a bully who never had respect or a kind word for anyone.

"Tosser," Tom whispered as he entered the building.

After tidying the kitchen, Justin sat at the dining table with the morning paper. He had not bought one for the past two and a half years. This in itself showed the extent to which he had withdrawn into a world of one. Taking a drag on his cigarette, he blew the smoke out from his lungs with a sense of purpose, almost hopeful. Yet this did not last, as the daily visitation took hold of him. His internal scars slowly smouldered until they burst open, becoming more brutal as the day progressed. In the beginning, Justin's response had been to use every antidepressant medicine available to help dowse his growing anxiety. They had helped in the short term but were unable to eliminate any long-term angst. Being a medic, he knew that medicine could never cure guilt. Justin Ivens was dying, not physically, but slowly decaying from the inside, infected by the disease of non-forgiveness. Many people over the years had suggested he pull himself together. Those with such opinions had never made moral decisions that could break a man's heart, where each fragment was a reminder of what he had done.

Thirty minutes late with her head full of figures and other people's debts, Viv read her diary. The office was so hot that the staff could feel the bacteria fermenting in it. It was a boring place with no spirit, and her job had become dull without any prospects.

Never mind, I'll get the meeting over with, and then it'll soon be lunchtime.

Having fixed the machine, Tom began walking back to his department, keeping his guard up with Viv's words of warning in the forefront of his mind.

"Hey, wanker," came a familiar voice.

Ignoring it, Tom continued walking.

"Watch out, lads; it's Casanova's granddad. Lock up your wives," Ken shouted.

"Shut the fuck up, and leave him alone," Dave, one of the drivers, said. "You can be a real prick at times."

"Says you," replied Ken. "Anyway, it's fuck all to do with you. Keep out of my business."

Maybe this is the time to confront Ken, thought Tom.

"Here he is, Peter Fucking Pan. This man's been at it with my wife. How long for? Fuck only knows," said Ken, pointing his finger in Tom's direction.

"I've told you once: give it a rest," Dave intervened.

"And I've told you to keep your fucking nose out," Ken said.

"It's okay, Dave; I'll sort it. What do you want, Ken?" Tom said.

"No wonder you took me in, trying to sweeten me up, you bastard," Ken said, squaring up to Tom.

"I've done nothing wrong. You're the one who cheated on Viv."

"That doesn't give you the right to steal my wife, you thieving fucker!" Ken screamed.

"I don't think this is the time or the place. Do you?" Tom said, aware of the crowd gathering around them.

It was as though Ken didn't care, as if the jealousy running through his body was too great for him to suppress. Taking a step forward, he threw a punch at Tom. If Tom hadn't ducked, Ken's fist would have landed flush on his chin. Tom gave no retaliatory swing; he wanted to keep his job.

"One more of those and you're fired," shouted the managing director. "I want both of you, in my office, now!"

––––––––––

There on Justin's fence sat the fattest song thrush he had ever seen. Keeping it overfed for years was a continuous supply of snails from Justin's garden. The bird was that fat it had to run before it was able to take flight. Peering out into the garden allowed Justin's mind to wander. He remembered a visit to Morecambe with Tom and their old friend Tim. Two oystercatchers flying low over the bay had proved to be nothing for Alec.

"They're birds, just birds," Tim had said.

Being a townie, he had believed the countryside was a place best left for those with a perverse sense of smell. Making a cup of tea, Justin continued thinking about incidents from his past. He recalled the time his classmate Ben had yet again copied his maths homework. Rather than making the customary adjustments so as not to arouse the teacher's suspicions, Ben had presented a perfect piece of work, which was unknown for Ben. Justin's suggestion that he get five of the questions wrong had fallen on deaf ears. The teacher wasn't stupid and had called Ben to the front of the class, accusing him of copying. Of course Ben had denied this, but like a fool, he had asked the teacher to prove it. His humiliation had continued as the teacher next had written the questions on the board for Ben to do. Of course, he had been unable to answer them. But instead of accepting defeat gracefully, he stupidly had given the teacher further cheek, saying, "So what're you going to do about it?" There had been no verbal reply, only a fist that had landed on Ben's face, leaving a red mark for the remainder of the day.

Why do I keep remembering things from way back in my past? I must be going mad. Ben was a character, though. I wonder what he's up to now, he thought as he climbed the stairs, ready to change into his walking gear. He would once again visit the Clough, try to gather his thoughts, and attempt to banish his fears regarding the weekend ahead.

———————

The managing director was not impressed. "How old are you two?" he asked.

Both Tom and Ken stood in silence.

"Here, a written warning," said the managing director, handing Ken a piece of paper. "Any more of that behaviour and you're down the road. Do you hear me? I won't tolerate it. Right, back to work. You wait here, Tom. Go on, Ken; back to work."

Once Ken had left the room, the managing director asked Tom to sit down. "Take some advice, Tom; steer clear of him. Between you and me, he's good at his job but not indispensible. Next time, I won't be as generous. Okay? That will be all. Now back to work."

Tom headed back down the stairs, through the courtyard, and into his department. There sitting on Tom's workbench without any shame was Ken.

"I'm telling you, you're history. Finished," Ken sniggered. "That's it, Pops; go and sit down before you fall down. Oh, you can't; my feet are on your seat, oh dear."

Fortunately, the foreman popped his head around the door, enquiring whether everything was all right. Tom nodded. Not saying anything, Ken made his way out into the corridor, all the while looking back in an attempt to intimidate Tom.

"What can I do for you?" Tom asked the foreman. "Has another machine broken down?"

"No, lad, I was just a wee bit concerned about you after that fracas. I also wanted you to know we're all behind you. The drivers were hoping he'd get sacked. There's a lot of people who like you here, Tom. As for Ken, he's burnt his bridges," the foreman said.

"Thanks, that's good to know. I like working here. Ken's beginning to plague me, and one day I won't be answerable for what I do to him. He's a real arsehole," Tom said.

"You're not wrong there. I know I'm being nosy, but are you really seeing his missus?"

"That'd be telling," Tom replied.

Stepping out from the bank, Viv breathed in the polluted air that reeked of car fumes. It was still fresher than the air in the office. Heading towards the sandwich bar, she thought about her future. With Ken gone she was now able to make her own decisions. The previous night with Tom had her looking forward to many more. Her enjoyment had not only been sexual. The laughter and closeness she had felt when lying next to him had been special. On entering the sandwich shop, she ordered a chicken salad. Her normal routine – weather permitting – would be to sit in the park and eat her lunch, but today she decided to eat at her desk. Back at the office she sat down and closed her eyes in an attempt to clear her mind so that she could focus on the paperwork that was piling up in front of her. Eating her salad while continuing to work, the previous night with Tom kept invading her thoughts. And it felt good.

Justin placed his rucksack on the ground and removed his flask from it. As he drank the coffee, he leaned against a wooden fence, on the other side of which was a small stream feeding the reservoir. The tree facing him held good memories. It was here with Nina that he had spotted his first cuckoo, initially misidentifying it as a young sparrow hawk. When the bird had taken flight, Nina had told Justin to study its wing movement. Following her instructions, he had seen that they were faster than that of the hawk and never lifted higher than its back. She had been a good birder and had always been generous in sharing her knowledge with Justin. Finishing his cup of coffee, he packed the flask away and headed along the bank of the stream. There were no visible signs of life in the water other than the odd mallard.

I think I'll move on. There doesn't seem much around today, Justin thought beginning to walk northwards along the bank.

The canning factory had just received good news. The managing director, standing in the canteen, informed the workers that he had signed a supply contract with a major American company.

"That's the only good news you'll have today," Ken said from behind Tom's back.

Turning round, Tom saw Ken heading out of the building. Looking at the clock, he thanked God that there were only two hours left to work. The sooner he went home, the happier and safer he would feel. The day had been one of those that should, in essence, be infinitely forgettable, and it would have been except for a persistent irritation under his skin. Not only was he a pain in the arse with his constant barracking, Ken was proving to be the chief of all tossers.

Spying a mound at the top of the hill, Justin slowly made his way in that direction. Looking across the reservoir, he spotted a farmer pouring sheep feed into three metal containers. This was a regular occurrence throughout the winter. The biting cold made Justin blow hard into his hands. There was little of the sun left in the sky as the fiery ball descended over the valley. This was Justin's cue to head home before darkness set in. As he slowly walked sideways down the mud-laden hill, the cry of a woodcock startled him. Losing his footing, he slid on his backside to the bottom of the hill. Getting to his feet, he caught sight of the bird's underbelly flashing against the dim sky as it flew towards the reservoir's open mudflats. Unlike Justin, this bird had the sense and instinct to know when to move on and find nourishment.

"Hey, Tom," shouted his supervisor. "The machine in the building next to the depot is on the blink again."

"I'm not surprised. I told them I'd fixed it temporarily. It needs new cogs, which I've ordered. It's about time new machines were bought," said Tom.

"I know, but you'd be out of a job. Oh, and keep away from the depot."

Smiling, Tom said nothing. As Tom entered the courtyard, Ken's assistant asked, "Can I have a word Tom?"

"Yeah, sure, what's it about?"

"Ken's been shouting the odds about you and Viv. I'm telling you, I've worked with him for five years and never seen him so mad. He's almost crazy. Just watch your back!" the assistant said.

"Thanks for your concern, but I'm not going to hide myself away. The bastard's had me twice now. It won't happen again. I'll have him next time," said a defiant Tom.

"Tom, listen to me. Ken's the type to hound you. Even if you did manage to have him, which I doubt, he'd just keep coming back for more. He's a bloody animal."

"Thanks for your concern," said Tom.

"I don't want you to get hurt. Believe me, Ken's a mad bastard. I know because I've seen his reaction to things over the years. He used to be well known for fighting," warned the assistant.

"Where is he now?" Tom asked.

"He's finished early. Why do you think I'm talking to you? He'd make my life hell if he saw me."

"Thanks for your concern," said Tom again, walking away.

———————

"Hello, gorgeous," said Ken.

"Oh, it's you," replied Viv, continuing to walk towards her car.

"Hold on, Viv; we need to talk. Come on, love; at least give me a minute," pleaded Ken.

"I haven't anything to say, especially after last night," she replied.

"Please, come for a drink, and I promise I'll leave you alone once you've listened."

"We'll have one drink and no more. I suppose we need to come to some arrangement regarding the house. Let's go in here."

The best part of forty minutes went by, and Viv felt nothing for Ken. She was frustrated at his lack of subtlety and sickened by his threats of violence towards Tom.

"Listen to me, Viv. I want you back. What do you say?" he said.

"I've told you; it's over," said Viv, by now bored with Ken's pathetic attempts at reconciliation. "If you don't mind, I'm going home."

"What about the house? What do you want to do about it?" Ken asked.

"I'd like to buy it. What about you?" Viv said.

"So would I. We'll need a place when the baby arrives," Ken said.

"Right, that's fine," she replied, not wanting to play his games.

———————

Taken aback, Ken back-pedalled, having no intentions of buying the house. Why would he when he believed that he would win her back? Her resistance would melt once she spent more time with him.

"Is it okay to come round on Saturday and collect some more of my things? I've no key, so you'll have to let me in," Ken said, plotting her seduction.

"I'll ring you on Saturday. Now I must be going," said Viv, putting on her coat and making her way out the door.

"See you on Saturday," shouted Ken. He then headed for the Boar, deciding not to tell Gemma about this meeting with Viv.

Once again Ken's thoughts returned to Tom. His determination to seek revenge grew ever darker as he thought of the Sassenach with Viv.

The Boar had not yet become busy when Ken walked through its doors.

"Hiya, love," said Gemma, leaning over the bar to kiss him. "Pint?"

"Aye," he replied.

"Are you all right?" she asked.

"Yeah, why wouldn't I be?" Ken snapped.

"No reason. Anyway, what do you fancy doing later?"

"Whatever," he said with no thought for her. His mind was now focused on Tom Riley.

The pub quickly filled up with revellers, which meant Gemma was no longer able to continue speaking to Ken. This suited him just fine. Sitting alone in the corner with his pint, brooding over a multitude of poisonous thoughts, he worked on a plan as to the best way of getting rid of Riley. He would wage a campaign of intimidation against Tom and whenever possible frighten the hell out of him. If that didn't work, then he would use his fists. This had been Ken's problem when he'd lived in Glasgow. He would strike out first, and then make excuses for his actions afterwards. Memories of such conquests now stimulated Ken's darkness. It felt like old times, glorious times again. Tensing his biceps, as though showing them off to a non-existent audience, he lifted his glass to his lips and downed the rest of his pint.

———————

Viv parked her car outside Tom's house and knocked on his front door.

"Come in, Viv. It's good to see you," he said, holding her tight and kissing her forehead.

"And you," she replied.

"Fancy a cup of tea?"

"Please," she replied.

The kitchen table was becoming a place of sanctuary for Viv and Tom, a space where they were able to share their burdens and talk about brighter times ahead. Tonight this included the impromptu visit from Ken and his attempts to get her back.

"Here we go, Viv, one cup of tea," said Tom, holding out a cup.

"Thanks, love," she said, reaching across the table and touching his lips with her finger. "Let's enjoy ourselves tonight."

"We will. But I have to tell you what happened today."

He quickly relayed this to Viv, including the support from his foreman and his encounter with Ken's assistant.

"I told you about him. He's not going to give up easily," said Viv.

"You know they call Ken 'Gucci Boy' at work, all suit and brogues. You have to admit he is a bloody poser," Tom laughed.

"You're not wrong there. It takes him hours to get ready. I was always sitting around waiting for him. Listen, Tom, I want you to know that if Ken was the last man on earth, I would never go back to him," Viv insisted.

Tom relaxed his shoulders, not even realising he had been so tense.

"I want to spend time with you, Tom, not him. Do you hear? You," she repeated.

I'm living the dream, thought Tom. Thanks, Viv. You've saved my life.

They held each other in a long embrace. There seemed to be no need for words; they knew exactly what each was thinking.

"Listen," said Viv, breaking away from Tom's arms. "I know I keep saying this, but be careful around Ken."

"Okay," he replied.

"Tom, promise me. I mean it. Promise me. Say, 'I promise.'"

"I promise. Come here; let's forget about him, shall we?" he said, holding out his arms.

"We will," she replied.

"Right, let's have something to eat. Go on, love; put some music on," Tom said. "By the way, Viv, you must treat this as your home. I'll get you a key cut if you like.

"Maybe one day, but it's probably a bit soon, don't you think?"

That was one thing Tom didn't think. If he had his way, he would move her in at this moment in time and keep her there by his side.

The weekend ahead now seemed less fraught for Tom. Even if nothing was to come of his time with Justin, there would still be Viv. The thought of her was keeping him focused. Only a week ago his empty moments had been filled by reliving happy times in his head. Those precious memories with his wife had sustained him, but only by holding him in time. Given this extraordinary chance with Viv, he now intended to fight with all his might to hold on to it. Watching her flick through his vinyl collection, Tom couldn't help but feel grateful that providence had finally decided to shine down on him.

───────

Sitting alone in the front room of Gemma's flat, Ken was brooding. She had gone to bed after sensing his aggravation. Furiously tapping his right foot, he focused his malice on Tom. Ken was not a thinker that sought deep answers to life. Those which he did seek usually gave him an advantage. He was the bloke that could fix things or, when this was not possible, would always know somebody else that could. He was the type of character every town, village, and city had. This made him popular with those who traded on the black market. He believed this gave him a certain amount of status. The proof was there to see. Whenever out in the town, people were always stopping him, wondering whether he could get what they needed.

What can I do about, Tom? he thought, grabbing a bottle of lager from the fridge.

Walking back into the tiny living room, he dropped down on the settee, propping his head against the cushion. The image of Viv and Riley was still there in his head, and it wouldn't leave him. He wanted Viv back despite her earlier lack of enthusiasm. Any power he had once had over Viv was disappearing fast, and he was now planning ways to restore this. This was a feeling he didn't like. Riley would pay for what he had done.

Thursday

"All right, love?" asked Viv.

"Yes, but I'm starting to get a little nervous about Saturday. You know, with Justin coming," replied Tom.

"I noticed you were tossing and turning for much of the night. I thought it might have been Ken's behaviour that was keeping you awake."

"Well, I suppose it doesn't help. Anyway, let's not talk about him. Give me a good-morning kiss," said Tom, reaching over towards her.

"You've only two days to go. It'll soon be weekend. Do you fancy going to the cinema tonight? It'll help take your mind off things, and we won't have to keep talking about Ken," said Viv.

"Yeah, why not, it sounds a good idea. We could have something to eat in Dundee beforehand. What film do you fancy seeing?" Tom asked.

"I'm not sure what's on. I'll pick up a local paper and have a look."

"Okay, love," said Tom. He climbed out of bed and made his way to the bathroom.

———————

I hope Ken's going to work, thought Gemma.

What a life she was now leading. She was too afraid to leave her bedroom, a prisoner in her own apartment. *I'll stay here until he's gone,* she thought. *I can't look at him.*

"You stupid bitch," shouted Ken in the direction of Gemma's bedroom. "There's no bread."

Gemma sat up, holding the duvet up to her eyes. "Please don't come in. Please don't come in," she repeated in a very low voice. It was her prayer, her cry for help. She bit hard into the duvet as Ken kicked her bedroom door.

"I know you can hear me," he screamed. "Make sure you get some bread for later. I need to eat. I'm off to work."

"Thank you, God. Thank you," she repeated mantra style with tears running down her face.

Ken closed the front door of the flat so violently the whole building shook. Tears continued to cascade down Gemma's cheeks, dropping off the end of her petite nose. They wouldn't stop. Her heart was broken, and her nerves, shattered.

"I'll sort Tom out today," Ken said to himself as he started the engine on his battered car. He was talking to himself but didn't acknowledge this. As far as Ken was concerned, he was being wronged by everybody. The world had turned on him. It was time to fight back.

Why did Gemma not make sure there was bread for my breakfast? Viv would have done. Useless woman! Anyway, Viv will soon be cooking for me again. That's for sure.

"Fuck off," Ken shouted to the driver of an oncoming car that had to swerve out of the way. Ken had been going too fast and had crossed the white line in the middle of the road.

This didn't make him slow down. On the contrary, he kept his foot on the accelerator. At one point on the A90 he reached over 100 miles an hour. Like the swimmer that pays no attention to those less gifted, Ken expected all other drivers to move out of his way.

"You're all a set of bastards," he screamed to nobody and to everybody.

"Right, Tom, I'm must be off. I'll see you tonight. I'll have a look to see what's on at the cinema. It'll be nice to go out. It'll be like our first date," laughed Viv.

"Yeah, that's true. Should I wear a carnation so you know who I am? " said Tom following her out of the house.

Once outside, Viv felt the coldness of the morning. Winter was here. Shivering, she gave Tom a kiss and climbed in to her car. She was right to have put on her woollen cardigan. Before driving off she looked at her diary. It reminded her that she needed to try and rearrange the afternoon's meeting with a colleague from mortgages as her line manager wanted to bring forward her supervision session.

———————

"Good morning," said Ken's assistant.

"What's so good about it?" Ken replied sarcastically. "Get back to work."

Without any reply the assistant sat behind his desk and began making phone calls to customers. Standing in the middle of the office, Ken stared hard at a group of drivers chatting to one another. Their loads complete, they were waiting for the go-ahead to hit the road.

"What the fuck are you lot waiting for? Go on; get moving!" Ken screamed.

Once again, there was silence. The sound of six wagons all firing up their engines could be heard throughout the factory. They left the depot in convoy to areas as far afield as Thurso, Belfast, Manchester, Birmingham, Newham, and Norwich. Each one of the drivers was only too happy to leave Ken behind.

"I'll be back in a few minutes," snapped Ken to his assistant. "There's something I have to do."

"Okay," the assistant replied meekly.

———————

Great, the sun's shining. I'd best get a move on before it decides to take the rest of the day off, Justin thought.

The warmth of the morning was welcoming. Sometimes winter threw up bright and crisp days, like this one, with enough warmth to feel comforted. This morning, Justin had decided to walk to the Clough by the main road. This route was steep, but halfway up its trajectory was an amazing vista, including a view of Blackpool Tower. The fells to the right were not like those of the Lake District. They were not feared. They were more pastoral, welcoming, and almost passive. They did not shout out danger when viewed. They had not claimed lives. As far as Justin knew, they had not been the cause of many tears.

There it is the tower of all towers.

This reminded him of the trips Nina and he had enjoyed as children. He remembered her comforting him after a visit to Madame Tussaud's waxwork museum. They had seen the House of Horrors, and the death on the motorway scene had given him a sudden shot of anxiety when he'd realised they had to travel home by car. *I really was a soft child,* thought Justin. *Nina toughened me up. That's for sure.*

Raising his binoculars to his eyes, Justin spotted a male blackbird strutting towards a large pile of cow dung. It looked ridiculously happy, as though it was entering the finest of restaurants. The bird nodded its head furiously, using its beak to obtain what Justin thought were dung beetles. Resuming the climb up the road, Justin thought of the time he and Nina had seen a flock of golden plover in the very same field. These days they were so much rarer. That day had been a good one. Nina had been about sixteen; Justin, fourteen.

"Here have a swig of that," she had said, handing Justin a half bottle of cheap scotch.

"Where did you get that from?" Justin had asked.

"Never mind where I got it from," Nina had replied. "Just be careful. Don't take too big of a gulp, or you'll regret it."

Following Justin's first taste of scotch, Nina's laughter had been so loud that the whole flock had taken flight, and plover after plover had bumped into one another trying to become air bound.

"I did warn you, Justin. I told you to be careful."

Walking rhythmically up the hill, Justin continued fondly remembering Nina. Whenever he thought of that particular day, he could still feel the scotch burning his mouth, then his throat, and finally his belly. He still wondered how on earth he had ever gotten the taste for whisky after that first encounter.

What a superb view, thought Justin as he adjusted his binoculars.

"Where is he?" demanded Ken.

"Where's who?" asked Tom's foreman.

"Don't fuck with me. You know exactly who I mean. I'll ask you again. Where is he?"

"Who?" repeated the foreman.

Ken grabbed the foreman by the throat and told him to warn Tom that he was looking for him. Shaking, the foreman said nothing, not wanting to incense Ken any further. Without saying another word, Ken turned and marched away.

"He's crazy," said the foreman. "I'm going to see the managing director about him."

While on his way, the foreman began to doubt whether this was a good idea. *If I grass Ken up, he's likely to follow me home. What if he attacks me? What should I do? I think I might just leave speaking to the managing director for a while, see if Ken calms down. I've my wife to think about.*

"That's amazing," said Justin. "What a sighting."

There in front of him, no more than fifty yards away, was a fox stamping the ground, vigorously digging into the soil. Without warning, the animal dragged a rabbit up and shook it so hard in its mouth that it died instantaneously. The fox then walked dispassionately towards the east side of the reservoir where its den lay.

The sight of the fox lifted Justin's mood a little, and he continued his walk. He wanted to immerse himself in nature. Yet the feeling of regret began scratching at him from the inside. The blind panic of sorrow was playing tricks in his mind, reminding him of his past.

Come on, Justin, remember, today is the day. Today is the only day."

Walking down towards the reservoir, he spotted another birdwatcher standing in the middle of the moors with his scope pointing towards the water. He wanted to ask the man if he was looking at anything specific, but Justin couldn't be bothered. He would have enough conversation over the weekend when he visited Tom. No, today he would spend in solitude fighting the sword of guilt alone. He planned to bombard his mind with positive affirmations and hoped these would hold back the cutting steel of non-forgiveness, the blade Justin felt slashing deep inside his heart, leaving it bleeding and fighting for rebirth.

As Justin reached the water's edge in front of the deciduous wood, he took a deep breath and said a silent prayer asking God to help him find the strength to forgive himself and also his friend Tom. Lifting his binoculars, Justin scanned the smaller of the two pieces of water. There were the usual suspects scattered across it. A raft of coots glided by, paying little attention to Justin's presence. They seemed oblivious to the five mallards that had to separate to allow them to continue moving forward. Justin spotted four tufted ducks that were feeding frenziedly, as though they had been told a famine was on the way. Now walking towards the bridle path end of the reservoir, Justin stopped to take in the view of Pendle Hill. Standing 1,827 feet above mean sea level, it looked formidable.

It's amazing. It can look a bit creepy when the mists descend, though. I wonder how many witches live there now.

Making his way from the water's edge, Justin leaned against a dry stone wall that had recently been rebuilt. For the past six months, he had wandered through the field that the wall now partitioned off. There he had seen jack snipes and even caught view of a polecat, a rarity in that they were mainly nocturnal creatures and not well distributed throughout the British Isles. However, they were now marching further north from Wales, their most inhabited area. Looking again towards Pendle Hill, Justin thought about how he and Nina had often walked up to the summit. Whenever Justin stopped and looked at Pendle Hill, he always imagined what George Fox must have felt upon reaching its peak. The last time Justin had walked it with Nina they had been university students. Both had spent a few weeks of their summer holidays staying with their parents. They had drunk a half bottle of rum, swigged at intervals in conjunction with sharing a cigarette.

"Tom, can I have a word?" said the foreman as he made his way towards Tom's bench.

"Sure, everything okay? You look a little shaken up."

"I feel a bit shaky. Listen, I don't want you to lose your temper. You need to be sensible ..."

"What is it?"

"Ken's been in asking for you. He was in a vile mood and really angry."

"Did he threaten you?" asked Tom. "Because if he did ..."

"Please Tom, listen to me. You'll get in trouble if you go after him"

"He's no right to threaten you. It's me he's after. I need to settle this once and for all. Have you spoken to the MD?"

"No, I don't want any trouble. I don't want Ken hounding me."

"This isn't okay. He's a bully and needs to be stopped. If you won't go, then I'll go for you. Ken makes my blood boil. I'm going to find him."

"Don't," pleaded the foreman.

"No. This needs sorting out right now."

"You'll lose your job," said the foreman.

"I don't care. What I need is for Ken to get out of my life for good. You stay there. Take a breather. I'll see you after," Tom said, quickly leaving the workshop.

There was much commotion when Tom entered the depot. Seemingly Ken had punched his assistant, leaving the man dazed and with a very sore mouth. Tom smiled when he looked at the aggrieved; thinking how much the poor sod now looked like Mick Jagger. *Stop it. Get yourself together,* thought Tom.

"Where's Ken?" asked Tom.

"After thumping me for no reason, he just walked out. I haven't seen him since," said the injured assistant. "I warned you about him, didn't I? I just didn't think I'd be his victim. The guy's crazy."

"How long ago was that then?" asked Tom.

"About fifteen minutes."

"You need to report Ken for this. Go and see the MD," said Tom.

"I'm not doing that. He'll batter me when he gets back to work," said the assistant.

"The chances are he'll get the sack for what he's done to you," replied Tom.

"Even if he did, could you imagine what he'd do to me? If he's just hit me for no reason, then what would he do if he found out I'd got him fired? No way will I do that," said the frightened assistant.

"Is there nobody around here that hasn't been intimidated by Ken? It seems you're all afraid of him. Well, I'm not. When you see him, if you see him again, then make sure to tell him that I'm now looking for him," Tom said, walking out of the depot. "Oh, and by the way, I hope your mouth isn't hurting too much."

Ken was outside the Brechin branch of the Clydesdale Bank. He was fighting back the urge to go into the building and demand to see Viv. Irritated, he kept looking at his watch as though this would somehow hasten time. *Come on. It must be your dinner break soon,* thought Ken.

Losing his patience Ken started to walk inside the bank, but saw Viv making her way from out the far counter. He stepped back outside and hid around the corner where he could spot which way she was heading.

Making her way into the newsagents, Viv picked up a copy of the *Dundee Evening Telegraph* to check out what was on at the cinema. She was looking forward to having a night out with Tom. She wondered whether they should use a taxi or whether to drive herself. She wasn't accustomed to drinking during the week.

Suddenly she felt someone grab her right arm from behind. Reflexively, she pulled forward making the person lose their balance and fall over.

"What did you do that for?" Ken shouted.

"What the hell are you doing grabbing my arm? Anyway, I didn't know it was you. More to the point, what are you doing here?" said an irritated Viv.

"I wanted to see you. I won't let you end our marriage. I demand you come home with me where you belong. Come on, Viv. It'll be like it was before," said Ken.

"Yes, and that's what I don't want. You're like a broken record. Just leave me alone," shouted Viv, aware that their interchange was attracting attention.

"That'll never happen. As long as I have a fart left in my arse, I will never let you go. Mine, mine, mine – yes, you're all mine. Get used to it," screamed Ken, who by now was shouting into Viv's ear.

Trying to ignore him, Viv started walking away quickly. The bastard wouldn't intimidate her. With senses on high alert, she went into the sandwich shop and ordered a chicken salad. She could see Ken loitering outside, flighty and dangerous. A malevolent energy seemed to be seeping out of his skin as he rapidly scratched his arms and torso as though trying to rid himself of an irritant.

He's becoming a bloody pest. I feel like he's a stalker. He won't listen to me. He's stuck in gear and can't move on. Hell, it was him that left me. What's changed?

"Well then, when will we move back in together?" Ken asked as soon as Viv walked out of the shop. "We don't want to leave it too long. I'm sure you'd like to get back into the routine of things. Shall I tell Riley, or will you?"

Stopping, Viv looked at Ken and shook her head. "Why are you doing this?"

"Come to think of it, I think I'm better telling Riley. There'll be less hassle," said Ken, completely ignoring Viv's question.

"You're not listening to me, again!" Viv screamed.

Thankfully, the bank was now in sight with about two hundred more yards to walk. Conscious that Ken was closing in on her personal space again, Viv remained alert. Her training and many battles in the ring were helping her focus on his movements. Though she was avoiding eye contact, she had enough peripheral vision to defend her position. As she had anticipated, Ken made a lunge at her. Stepping to one side, she quickly circled him and disappeared into the bank behind the counter, leaving him standing outside. Viv could see him staring in at her.

Standing outside the bank, Ken's mind was racing; his body, speeding. Rocking from side to side, he looked wired, tense, egotistical, and maniacal. His emotions were primitive, feeding on the raw feelings of hatred which were now constantly being stoked by his possessiveness and need to dominate. Staring hard into the Bank, Ken looked ever more the stalker, ready to wreak havoc on those that would defy him.

"It's not acceptable," said Tom to the managing director. "People are frightened to death of him. They won't report him to you because they're afraid of what he might do. He needs stopping."

"You're absolutely right. Where is he now?"

"I don't know," replied Tom.

"Leave it with me. I'll sort it out. I won't have my workforce intimidated. I can soon fill his vacancy," said the MD.

"Thanks," said Tom, leaving the office.

Reaching his workshop, Tom poured a cup of coffee from his flask. He needed to take a moment or two to get his composure so he could resume work. As he finished his coffee, his foreman entered the room.

"I've had a word with the MD. He's going to sort it out," Tom said.

"I hope you've done the right thing. What if Ken starts to intimidate me?" asked the foreman.

"Then you'll have to ring the police. Listen, he needs stopping. The sooner this happens, the better it'll be for all of us."

"Anyway, will you have a look at the canning machine? It's on the blink again," said the foreman.

"Yes, of course," replied Tom. "Stop worrying. Ken has to go, but you know that deep down, don't you?"

"Aye, you're right. I'm just worried about him hurting me."

"I know," said Tom. "You let me know if he starts."

"Okay," said the foreman, walking out of the room with his head bowed low.

He won't intimidate me. Even if he gives me a good hiding, he won't intimidate me, Tom thought as he collected his tools.

Arriving in the building with the broken canning machine, Tom could sense something in the air. A whirring sound of voices speaking in a low tone became louder as the workers watched him walk past them.

When Tom reached the machine, the chargehand greeted him. "Are you all right, Tom?"

"Yes, thanks. Why?"

"No reason," replied the chargehand.

"I think you're fishing." Tom smiled.

"Okay then, what's happened to Ken? Has he been sacked?"

"No idea," said Tom. "You know as much as me. But I hope so."

"He'll blame you if he has been," the chargehand said.

"I don't give a shit. You lot should have stood up to him. The lot of you know what he's like. Yet you've done nothing about him. You've all stood by and let him bully people for years," Tom said, not giving eye contact. Instead he focused his attention on dismantling the outer casing of the machine.

"It's easy for you to say," remarked the chargehand.

"Yes, you're right. It is easy for me to say. I'll say it again. People need to stand up to bullies," Tom retorted, by now feeling angry at his workmate's lack of courage.

"I'm going," said the chargehand walking away. "I can see you are annoyed"

"Are you sure you'll be all right?" Viv's boss asked.

"Yes, I'll be fine," said Viv.

"Go out the back way. He can't be in two places at once."

"That's a good idea; I'll do that. He keeps following me. He left me and now expects me to go back to him. I'm happy as I am. I don't want him in my life anymore," Viv said.

"I know what you mean. My husband left me for another woman. When he found out I was seeing somebody else, he was all over me like a rash. I didn't fall for it, though. What really annoyed me was him thinking he had a right to me. I couldn't forget what he had done. He really hurt me," Viv's manager said.

"To be honest, Ken's done me a favour. But like your husband, as soon as I've started seeing somebody else, he's demanding I go back to him," said Viv.

"You're seeing somebody else then, are you? Come on; let's have a cuppa, and you can tell me all about it."

On the hill to the south side of the Clough stood a wood made up of mainly conifer trees. Justin thought it looked denser than it actually was. He didn't really like going into it, as it tended to make him even more morose. It was as though there was a history that was hidden within its depths, a history that was more inglorious than glorious, a secret that needed to be shared but somehow had become lost in time.

Through his binoculars Justin spotted a pair of collared doves quickly disappearing into the conifers, their wings beating regularly while their movement remained synchronised. They were Holy Spirit–like, gentle and loving. Their proximity to each other seemed to expose their unity. *They might just bring some peace to the wood,* thought Justin.

Turning around, he walked down the path that ran parallel to the reservoir. Halfway along it he sat down and looked towards the smallest water. Staring out into it, his mind rested on Nina and yet more memories from their past. The Clough had been an escape for them during their teenage years. They had studied hard under their father's watchful eye, but they had also played hard. Their meanderings together on the moors and the many times spent with friends had been happy affairs. The Clough and its sheltering trees had been a perfect rendezvous for them all to meet. Few teenagers had owned a car in the seventies. Shanks's pony and, if one was lucky enough to own one, a pushbike had taken them to the moors.

Standing up, Justin continued to walk along the path towards the small deciduous wood where the broken wall lay. It was a place where he liked to stop and breathe and walk in-between the trees. They exhaled a positive energy. He recalled the many summer days from his youth when streams of light had burst through the trees as though they were lightning bolts sent down from the heavens. They had been spectacular. Justin stopped by the side of a large beech tree and ran his right hand along its damp trunk. Trees were important to him. They represented another time when the world was simpler. The Ribble Valley would have been one great forest thousands of years ago. The wildlife would have been different. These days he would spot roe deer as dusk approached or when dawn was breaking. They were a wondrous sight. With this thought in his mind Justin slowly made his way home.

———————

Uncharacteristically, Tom dropped his tools on his bench and stopped working. The cog he had been cleaning fell from his hands on to the floor.

I can do without this, he thought.

Sitting down, he began daydreaming about all the places he and Viv could visit together. She had brought meaning back to his life. Looking at his watch, Tom was relieved that there was less than an hour to go before clocking off.

I have to speak to Viv about the money. I just hope it doesn't drive a wedge between us. I could walk out from here and never return. But that would be unfair. The company has been good to me. I like the people. Given Ken's tricks, I'm tempted to up sticks and leave the area. I think we're best to skip the cinema tonight and sit down and talk about our future instead. I wonder whether Viv has ever thought about living in England.

———————

Fidgeting at her desk, Viv couldn't stop thinking about Ken. She was afraid that he was going to hurt Tom. She knew him. He certainly had the capability and the capacity to do so.

The sooner we're divorced the better. The thought helped her to focus more positively on her future, a future that included Tom. Her heart felt lighter when she thought of him. He was funny and thoughtful and above all treated her as an equal. He seemed secure in who he was and emotionally mature, unlike Ken. She was looking forward to seeing him later and believed that in ten years time she would still be looking forward to seeing him at the end of the day. What a difference the past few days had made to her life.

Imagine if Ken hadn't been unfaithful, she thought. This made her shudder. She also felt embarrassed, wondering what people must think about her. After all, some people judged others on the basis of knowing a partner. She had continued to live with him. She had been his wife, the woman who had cooked, cleaned, and washed his dirty underwear. She had had sex with him almost on a daily basis, not through choice but in order to fulfil his needs. Whenever she had refused, his moods had lasted until he'd finally had his way. Their sex had been unadventurous and orgasm-free. His grunting had defiled her ears, and his snoring had angered her sensibility.

Thank God he's gone from my bed, she thought.

A sense of disgust ran through her veins and came to an abrupt end in the pit of her stomach. Viv now knew she had a future. And it was a future that excited her. She would speak to Tom about moving in with him. She now knew this was what she wanted. There was no doubt in her mind. Ken could have the house – lock, stock, and barrel. She wanted nothing from him. If she had to start again from scratch, then that was what she would do.

After all, she thought, *what's money without happiness? Ken can't take that away from me. He will never own my heart nor possess my soul. He just needs to leave us alone.*

Driving towards Brechin, Ken was far too preoccupied to see that the traffic on the A90 was reasonably light. He was oblivious to his surroundings. His thoughts were taken up by Viv and their inevitable reunion. He intended to wait outside the bank and catch her on her way home. He would surprise her, and she would not be able to resist his charms. Their reunion would be finalised. Such was his state of mind.

"She's mine; she's mine," he repeated.

Ken took a right turn and left the A90, heading towards Brechin town centre. He parked to the side of the bank and sat in his car for a few minutes thinking about having sex with his wife. He would be satisfied again. She would do to him what he liked. Ken genuinely believed that Viv had enjoyed having sex with him. His stamina was legendary, or so he thought. Ten minutes before five he got out of his car and waited outside the door of the bank.

"Will you have a look for me and see if Ken's standing outside?" Viv asked her boss.

"Sure," her boss replied.

Making her way downstairs, Viv's boss was temporarily taken away from the task at hand to answer a quick enquiry from a cashier. Walking towards the front door, she spied Ken to the side of it. He seemed rooted to the spot but was swaying rapidly from side to side. *Irritated or what? He's too much unspent energy.*

Returning to Viv, she confirmed that Ken was indeed outside the bank and appeared somewhat irritated.

"I'll go out the back way tonight," said Viv.

"I don't blame you," said Viv's boss.

"I'll get going then."

"Okay," said her boss, watching as Viv made her way out from the back of the bank and swiftly walked towards her car.

"Have you seen Viv?" Ken asked Viv's boss as she walked out of the bank.

"She finished early," Viv's boss lied.

"What d'you mean she finished early? Where did she go?"

"No idea," she replied.

"A fat lot of good you've been. Thanks for nothing," Ken shouted as he stormed off.

"Good-looking, but nasty," said the boss under her breath, heading towards the car park.

Having returned home half an hour earlier, Justin had devoured a cheese sandwich and was now listening to Chopin's Piano Concerto No. 1. The 1947 recording by Arthur Rubinstein and the New York Philharmonic Orchestra had been his grandmother's favourite. They had listened to it many times, especially when she had been in a state of anxiety, something she had suffered from throughout her life. It had always befuddled him why Chopin had written only two piano concertos, given that both had breathed youthful exuberance. As far as Justin was concerned, Chopin certainly had the skill. Both concertos allowed Justin to leave his worries behind for a brief interlude. He would always close his eyes and feel each note reverberate through his tired mind and sick soul. It was a healing tour de force while it lasted, a sea of emotion that helped to soothe his exhausted body. Music made his life worth living. Music of all description allowed him to enter a world of fable, a world where he felt less tormented, a world of hope and beauty.

As usual Justin was spending the evening alone. Since moving north he had spent the majority of his time this way. At heart he was a gregarious person, but since that day he had become more and more insular. In the past, people had been important to him. These days they were meddlesome and complicated. He needed simplicity, a simplicity that afforded him time to re-establish his place in the cosmos – if, indeed, such a place existed.

If only I could be myself again, he thought. *I wasn't such a bad person. In fact I was okay. Yes, I was okay. Let's just say at the moment I'm not okay – and the world is not okay.*

Justin laughed. "Shut up, you prick," he said. "I think I'll have a whisky."

Viv was pleased she had accepted Tom's offer of a front-door key "Hello, Viv," Tom shouted as she walked into his house. Without speaking she quickly walked towards him, flung her arms around his neck, and gave him a firm kiss on his lips.

"I can do with more of those." Tom smiled.

"What a day," she said. "We need to talk, love, but not before we're settled and comfortable."

"Oh, that sounds ominous," said Tom.

"I hope not," responded Viv.

"Coffee?" Tom asked

"Why not," replied Viv.

Sitting down at the kitchen table, Viv removed his shoes. "I'm just going to get changed before we talk," she said.

"Ok, said Tom. "I'll put the kettle on."

Bastard Viv, she should have known I would be waiting for her when she finished work. She knows we need to talk about us getting back together.

Now heading back towards Forfar and ultimately to Tom's house, Ken kept up a constant conversation with himself. This was becoming more of a trend by the day.

Why didn't she wait for me? She needs me. She bloody needs me! Not that English prick. No, it's me she needs.

By now, he was almost hysterical, but he couldn't see this. As far as he was concerned, he was perfectly within his rights to demand his wife return to her rightful place next to him. She had married him and therefore belonged to him.

Before he knew it, he was turning off the A90 and heading towards Forfar.

I'll just nip into Gemma's flat and help myself to something to eat, thought Ken. *Hopefully, she'll still be at work. At least I bloody hope so. I don't want to have to look at her, never mind have a conversation.*

———————

Arriving home after a short taxi ride, Gemma was exhausted as she opened the door to her flat. Although the pub had been busy, Alistair had allowed her to finish early since she had worked an extra couple of hours the previous night. There were enough bar staff to cope. Alistair was good that way – since finding out she was expecting, he had made sure she wasn't over doing things. Ready to put her feet up, she thought about Ken. She was hoping not to see him, as she couldn't face an argument. Gemma started to put the shopping away, and then her heart began racing when she heard the door open and suddenly bang shut. Instantly, she knew that it was Ken. When he came into the kitchen, he seemed surprised to see her.

"I thought you'd still be at work," he said, not looking at her. "Why didn't you tell me?"

Why the hell should I?

"I was feeling tired. Alistair let me off a couple of hours early," she responded.

"Go and get changed; we'll go out for a couple of hours," he said.

This wasn't a genuine offer, as Ken didn't particularly want to spend any time with Gemma. His devious mind was working overtime. *If we're in the pub, then I can avoid answering any of her stupid questions. "Where've you been all day? Which friend were you with?" Christ, I can't be putting up with her bloody inquisition. Not tonight – in fact, not any night. I'm getting sick of her whining; all she'll do is drawl on about me taking responsibility.*

"I'm far too tired to go out," she told Ken. "Why don't you go and have a drink with the lads?"

Not expecting this response, Ken was knocked off balance. Gemma had played a blinder. If he did go out, she knew that she would have some peace, at least for a few hours.

He's bloody clueless. He has no idea that I'm sick to death with him. I now know how to play him, she thought, looking directly at Ken. *He's sly, that one. He likes to dominate by applying subtle pressure to get his way. He's patient, mind you; I'll give him that. He takes his time. His takeover is a slow ownership. One day you wake up and your life isn't your own. You're then his possession. Without thinking it becomes your will be done, O Ken.*

"Okay, I'll be off then," he snarled.

Aye, and don't bother coming back, thought Gemma. Out loud she replied, "Okay, I'll see you later. I'm likely to be in bed by the time you get back."

A huge sigh of relief overcame her when she heard the door slam shut. Turning on the TV, she wished that she had not been so stupid. She had forgotten everything about applying caution around certain types of men.

"Listen, love," said Viv, handing Tom a cup of coffee. "We need to talk."

"Go on then. I'm listening."

"You know you asked me to move in. Is the offer still there?"

"It certainly is," said Tom delighted. *Yes,* he thought. *Yes.*

"I don't know how to explain this, but I'll give it a go. You know my house – well, mine and Ken's – it'll be going on the market soon, but I've a feeling he isn't going to leave us alone. It's just a thought, and I need you to be honest with me. What do you think about giving it to him with a proviso that he leaves us alone? We can get it done legally. I know it's a lot of money, but I'd prefer our happiness to cash. It might make him go away. I could pay towards this house. I earn regular money. It isn't great, but neither is it a bad wage."

Listening to Viv reaffirmed to Tom that she had a beautiful soul. Viv had no idea how much he was worth, yet she was prepared to lose a substantial amount of money for their relationship, for their love. This touched him. *You're becoming more beautiful by the second,* he thought.

"Well, what do you think? Am I barmy or what?" Viv asked.

"You're bloody beautiful; that's what you are. As for the house, let Ken have it. I want us to work out, and I know we can be happy together. I don't care about the house. It's you I want."

"Okay, I'll make an appointment with the solicitor next week and discuss it with him. I hope it's not that grumpy old sod I got last time," said Viv.

"Quite," replied Tom.

"I just want Ken out of our lives for good," said Viv.

"Would you ever consider moving out of the area, say to England?" Tom asked.

"To be honest, I love living around here. I am a Scot after all. This is my country. Why? You don't want to move south, do you?"

"I'm not going anywhere without you. I was only wondering. Anyway, there's something else I need to speak to you about."

"Go on then. Please don't let it be bad news with the day I've had. I didn't tell you that Ken accosted me again. This time it was in the street during my dinner break. As usual, he was trying to get me back. That's why I thought of the house thing. Anyway, what did you want to say?"

"Maybe we should notify the police. Anymore and I will. As far as money is concerned, I've more than enough in the bank. In fact, I've over a million quid," said Tom.

"Get out of it," laughed Viv. "Yes, and I'm the Queen of Scotland."

"I mean it, Viv. I've not always been a manual worker. I used to travel the world with my job. I also had a small engineering firm for a time. Not only that, Chrissie's business sold for half a million, and I made a mint from the sale of our London house. You see, we have enough for the rest of our lives and more. I haven't invested any of it yet. It's just sitting there in the bank, and I want to share it with you."

"I don't know what to say. I didn't know you were rich. I hope you don't think I'm a gold-digger," said Viv.

"Quite the opposite," responded Tom. "You were the one who was willing to give up your house for me. And that I respect. In fact that's what I love about you. You're not particularly that materialistic. That's why it'll be interesting spending the money with you." Tom smiled.

"Well, I'm gobsmacked. And that's why I respect you. I would've had no idea without you telling me. At least you don't go around flaunting your wealth pretending to be the big man."

"Well, there you have it," said Tom. "We don't need to work, you know. I went back to work to keep my sanity after Chrissie passed away. And I'm glad I did. I'm also glad I moved to Scotland; otherwise I would never have met you. By the way, you know how we talked about you retraining? Well, there's plenty in the pot to follow that dream. You don't have to work."

"Thanks, love, but I'm not sure about that. I need a purpose. I like working. I'm still only thirty-four," replied Viv.

"Let's have a drink to celebrate you moving in here. You don't know how happy you've made me," said Tom.

"Do you fancy a glass of red wine or a beer?"

"Wine would be nice," said Tom.

"I think we'll give the cinema a miss tonight. Is that all right? I'm still in shock."

"That's absolutely fine. We'll spend tonight here celebrating," replied Tom.

Just as they were raising their glasses in celebration, they both heard Ken screeching Tom's name at the front door.

"Not again," said Tom. "I'm going to sort him out."

"Remember what I said about the house. Maybe I should just throw him the keys and tell him to go. It might work," said Viv.

"I doubt it, but you're welcome to give it a try."

Both Tom and Viv made their way to the front door. Opening it, they were ready for Ken. Stupidly he took a step backwards and made a charge for the door, so Tom quickly closed it, making Ken bang his head.

"You bastard, Tom, get out here," Ken screamed.

Tom and Viv were overcome with laughter. They couldn't help themselves. Tears streamed down their faces. Every time they looked at each other their laughter became louder. Ken's stupidity never ceased to amaze them.

"How dense can you get?" laughed Tom.

"That dense," replied Viv. "Let's try to ignore him. Leave him to burn out."

"Well, we'll leave it a minute or two, but I don't think I can leave it for too long," said Tom.

After a few moments, Tom opened the door again. Ken didn't make the same mistake. Instead, he stood back demanding to speak to Viv.

"What do you want?" she asked, leaning out past Tom.

"You know what I want," said Ken.

"Go back to Gemma. You've got her now and the baby," said Viv. "I'm sick of saying the same things to you, Ken. We're over."

"So are me and Gemma. I finished with her for you. I want you back. I demand you come back now!" Ken shouted. "And I mean now!"

"He's persistent; I'll give him that," whispered Tom.

"I'll never come back to you," she said, bored of repeating herself.

"You'll come back to me. You mark my words. You'll be mine again," said Ken. He turned and walked away towards his car.

At this, Tom and Viv made their way back into the house and locked the door.

Friday

"I wonder whether Ken will turn up for work today," said Viv.

"If he does, he's likely to get his marching orders," replied Tom.

"Everything's collapsing around him."

"Are you feeling sorry for him?"

"No, but don't forget I was married to him for seven years. I just wish he would sort himself out. I want to start my new life with you and not keep having to look over my shoulder."

"I know, love. We need to remain solid. Things will work out. We can always move from here. Find a place in the country."

"He'd find us. No, we have to somehow sort it out. How, I'm not sure. We still have the house to play with," said Viv. "Make sure you're alert today in case you bump into him."

"I will," promised Tom. "I have to go, or I'll be late."

Twenty minutes later as Tom pulled up in the works' car park he noticed Ken looking straight at him from the driver's side of the vehicle. Tom manoeuvred himself to the passenger side of his car and quickly got out.

"Frightened, are we, ready to piss our pants?"

Tom remained silent. There was no point in dialogue; it was lost on Ken. Instead he stood firm and stared at Ken.

"Cat got your tongue?" Ken mocked. "Or are you too scared to speak?"

Continuing to ignore the baiting, Tom remained silent.

"Oh, you're really scaring me with that stare," laughed Ken. "You listen and listen well: stay away from Viv. I'm giving you an ultimatum. Send her home to me, or you won't know what's hit you. Do you understand?"

"No, I don't understand. Viv is with me now. You left her, and you need to get used to it."

These words did not go down well with Ken. Tom could have sworn he saw froth leaking from the left side of Ken's mouth. He looked rabid. His eyes were frenzied and his body posture warrior-like. Danger was in the air. Tom wasn't sure whether to make a run for it or sit it out. Maybe Ken would eventually calm down or become bored with his game. There was enough space between them for Tom to remain out of Gucci Boy's reach – enough to ensure his safety.

"Are you all right, Tom?" shouted the managing director.

"Just about," replied Tom.

"Ah, it's you, Charles," said the director. "I want you off my property now, or I'll call the police. And by the way, you're fired. We'll send out what's owed to you. You have ten seconds to move; otherwise, I will call the police. Do I make myself clear?"

"Piss off," shouted Ken. "This is between me and gramps over there."

The managing director began dialling his mobile phone.

"This isn't over. You've cost me my marriage and now my job, which you'll pay for," shouted Ken over his shoulder as he walked towards his car.

"Oh, and don't think you'll get a reference from me," said the managing director.

"Get stuffed," shouted Ken.

"Tom, come and see me in my office at about ten thirty, will you? I want to know what the hell's been going on with Charles," said the managing director.

"Okay," replied Tom as he made his way to the workshop.

Confused and lonely, Justin resembled the fallen chick scrambling on the ground, unable to fly back to the comfort of its nest. Helpless and scared, its fate seemed sealed. The tears falling down his haggard cheeks stank of decay and tasted of death. Shaking his head, he managed a smile; it wasn't a happy smile but that of the gallows. The rain of Lancashire was pelting him as he walked towards the reservoir. After crossing it, he took shelter in the deciduous wood where the bailiff hid when searching for poachers. Justin looked a forlorn figure huddled under the tall and thin elm trees. His mind was running riot. Negative and unbending, his thoughts tore through his body, bringing much physical pain, a pain grounded in experience. It was so jagged an experience that the pain refused to leave him.

The rain continued to smash against the tops of the trees, cascading down in multiform. The life within the wood was now quiet other than the laugh of a solitary jay. Listening to the water flowing over the banks of the stream, Justin attempted to calm his thoughts. The rain was gushing through the hole in the wall onto the footpath and then down into the reservoir. Staring down, Justin saw a pool of water that had lost momentum and failed to make it down the bank. It was cut off from the ebb of life, echoing Justin Ivens' existence as a man on the periphery.

As Viv walked into her office, her boss said, "Ken's a nasty little thing, isn't he? Good-looking, I give you that, but he's got an edge to him."

"No doubt he was rude?"

"You could say that. Anyway, I told him you'd left early. He wasn't impressed."

"He's a nightmare. I'm sure he's mentally unstable. He's making mine and Tom's life a misery. Anyway, thanks for yesterday. I've got to go; I've a customer waiting to see me."

"No problem. I'll speak to you later." The boss headed towards her office.

"Now then, you look lost in thought," said a voice with authority.

"Oh, hello," replied a startled Justin. "How are you?"

"Fine, thanks, though the weather's crap," the sergeant major said. "Do you mind if I join you?"

"Not at all," replied Justin.

They stood in silence. It seemed that both men were deferring to the other.

"It's amazing here, isn't it?" said the sergeant major, breaking the quiet. "I love standing in this wood. Some days I swear I can hear its heartbeat."

"I know. It's as though it speaks to you. It helps me feel a little calmer when I stand among it," said Justin.

"Would you like a ciggie?"

"Cheers," replied Justin. "A Woodbine, hell, it's years since I've had a Woodbine. They were my granddad's favourite."

On lighting the cigarette the smell of it stirred memories of visits to his grandparents' house.

"Have you seen anything unusual today?" asked the sergeant major.

"There's some fieldfare across the road, a couple of cormorants, and a pair of great crested grebe on the reservoir. Oh, and I did see a tawny owl, believe it or not," Justin said.

"An owl with insomnia," laughed the soldier.

"Quite." Justin smiled.

Studying the soldier's face, he was compelled to engage him. This was unusual behaviour for Justin. He would normally bid good morning and then make excuses to move on. But today was different. There was something appealing about the soldier. He was kindly and seemed to convey a sense of peace that was charismatic.

"Do you miss the army?" asked Justin.

The soldier instantly became animated, answering Justin's question. What followed confirmed it.

"More than you'll ever know. It was my life. I'd still be there now if I could. It gave me an education, a purpose. It made me grow up quickly. I suddenly had to take responsibility for myself and of course for others. I had some great times and hold such fond memories. What about you? I hope you don't mind me asking, and you can tell me to sod off if you want. But why do you always seem so troubled?"

Not this one again, thought Justin. *Why do people always want to know more than what I want to share?*

Surprisingly, Justin refused to submit to the voice urging him to run and not to look back. Instead he shared a little about his life and his reasons for returning to Lancashire. Huddled together in the rain, Justin felt odd talking about his past with this man of war. But the soldier didn't seem perturbed. Justin sensed no judgement or disquiet from the sergeant major.

The soldier listened attentively until it felt right for him to comment on Justin's story. "Listen, after the Falklands Conflict some of my colleagues were frozen by terror and some with terrible shame. Soldiers are only people after all. Most of my men had joined the army as a job. They had no intentions of blowing people's brains out. They knew that this might happen, but it didn't obsess their thoughts. Nevertheless, when faced with life and death, they had to choose life and kill. Just as I had to."

"War is a terrible thing," remarked Justin.

"Yes, it is. Some people lose all hope after experiencing war," replied the ex-soldier. "For me, it made me realise that humanity is nothing without God. I will never forget the sound of the bullets I fired ripping apart a young Argentinean soldier. He was only a kid. It still haunts me and will until the day I die. I believe God knows people are frail and will continue to make mistakes throughout their lives, but thankfully, he is merciful and forgiving. People sell themselves short all the time. I reckon you're doing the same. What about St Peter? He denied Christ three times. Hell, according to the Good Book, Jesus already knew. You see, Justin, if God can forgive you, then you must forgive yourself."

Justin wanted so much to believe these words, to act upon them. They were common sense. But common sense could so often appear meaningless when the soul was damaged.

"You must take charge of yourself, and don't be afraid to walk tall in the world," said the sergeant major. "The law has dispensed its justice; the rest is your guilt. Only you can defeat that. Death is dreadful, but continuing to live it day after day is disrespectful to the dead. It's time for you to seek some peace. You can do nothing for the dead except to fondly remember them. As for the living, you owe it to them to give yourself in love, not sorrow. Take a tip from one who knows. Now is the time to move on. I have forgiven myself for killing that boy. It's still a nightmare, and I guess it always will be."

The rain was soaking both men, but neither noticed. They were two souls united in grief coming to terms with actions they would have preferred not to have undertaken. One man was further down the road of self-healing than the other. The soldier was still hurting, but he was also a pragmatist. There were now periods in his life which he could enjoy without the sinking feeling in the pit of his stomach that he had done something he wished he could revisit and change. This was the difference between the two. The soldier had learned to accept that this was impossible. Justin was still holding on to the very experience that had led him to the road of non-forgiveness.

———————

"Are you all right, Tom?" the managing director asked.

"I'm okay, thanks," Tom replied, taking a seat in the director's office.

"I'm not interested in your personal life, but I am about what happens in my factory. I had no idea that Charles was such a bully. Why didn't anybody come to me earlier about him?"

"Fear I guess," replied Tom.

"I pay my managers to ensure this sort of thing doesn't happen. I need to call a meeting with them. In fact, I'm going to do that now." Stepping outside his office, he asked his secretary to contact all the managers that were currently on shift. Turning back to Tom, he said, "I'd like you to stay, if you don't mind. I need you to tell them what's been going on. Then I'll call a brief meeting with all the employees. I need to stamp this sort of thing out. No one must be allowed to wage terror in my employment again. I won't tolerate such behaviour."

Within ten minutes the managing director was chairing a meeting with the managers. He didn't hold back in his disappointment at the way Ken's bullying had been allowed to continue over the years. Fear was no excuse. Those in charge needed to understand the issues that bullying brought not only to the workplace but also to those bullied in terms of esteem and production. They needed to understand their role in eradicating bullying from the workplace.

"As from today I want to be informed of any such behaviour on your shifts. If I find out there is bullying going on and you have failed to let me know, then there will be a consequence. Do you understand?"

There was silence. No one spoke a word, but a communal nod of heads confirmed that they understood. Everybody in the room was left with no doubt what that consequence would be.

———————

"Good morning," said Gemma tentatively.

"Good. Why is it good?" snapped Ken. "I thought you were due at work."

"I'm going," replied Gemma. She avoided eye contact, feeling intimidated.

"Well, go on then!" he screamed, scratching his head.

"Will I see you later?" asked Gemma, hoping that she wouldn't.

"Will I see you later?" he repeated mockingly. "How the fuck should I know? I'm helping a mate fix his car. I might pop in the pub afterwards if you're lucky."

Ken didn't wait for Gemma to leave. Instead, he left first and drove over to Tom's house where he sat staring at the front bedroom window. The image of Viv and Tom together, touching, necking, and screwing, filled him with enough anger to rip down a building, never mind an ageing Sassenach. The English bastard would soon know what Ken thought of him.

Crying, fearful, and humiliated, Gemma contacted Alistair and asked whether she could take some time off work. She told him that she would explain later. Alistair agreed. She then rang her parents' number.

"Mum, are you around if I pop over? Or can Dad bring you here? I need to speak to you both," said Gemma.

"Are you okay, love? You sound very upset," replied Gemma's mum.

"I am. That's why I need to speak to you."

"You stay there. We'll be over in the next hour."

"Thanks," said Gemma, already feeling a little safer.

Making a cup of tea, she started shaking. Grabbing her left hand with her right, she pressed her hands down hard onto the kitchen table to try and stop their involuntary movement. Sitting down, she dropped her head onto the table and began sobbing. A petite woman, Gemma wasn't particularly physically strong. Presently, she was emotionally wrecked and in a state of shock. She had lost weight recently and thought that her arms were beginning to look bony. Staring hard at them, she realised that she couldn't afford to lose any more. The intimidation she felt from Ken was to blame. She knew that. It was now time for it to stop. How she would manage to stop him was yet unclear to her. Nevertheless, Gemma was sure that the phone call to her parents was the first step in tackling this.

The old soldier bid Justin farewell and headed towards the stile leading to the field with the horses. Justin shouted his thanks, but the soldier did not look back. Instead he raised his right hand in acknowledgement.

What terrible things he has seen. I don't agree with war. But I don't understand it. How can I? I've never been, thank God. The intensity must be bloody awful, thought Justin, still standing under the trees.

Watching the sergeant major disappear through the fields, Justin acknowledged that his mind was his battlefield and his enemy was himself. His inner turmoil was his front line. The fear a soldier must experience before and during battle was incomprehensible to Justin. The fear he felt every day was of his own making, and that was unbearable.

He's right; I have to take control. I couldn't be a soldier. No way could I handle the pressures of battle.

As Justin continued to muse on the words of the sergeant major, he decided to make his way out of the wood. Looking up, he saw a heron flying awkwardly. Its right wing was overcompensating for a damaged left one. Being a birder, Justin knew that this injury could prove catastrophic for the big bird. It would now be prey for animals that were ready to feast. Foxes would try to sneak up on it and then pounce before it could ascend. He hoped the wing would heal but knew that nature would prevail. Some believed nature to be cruel, but Justin saw it as a cycle of life and death. Wild animals had to eat, and he knew the vulnerable would fail to survive. Always amazed by what he experienced when in the middle of the natural world, Justin continued making his way past the reservoir. The greyness of the great bird was soon lost against the background of a muffled sky.

"My God, you look terrible. What's happened to you?" asked Gemma's dad.

"I-I ... It's ..." stuttered Gemma in between bursts of tears.

"I'll make us all a cup of tea," he said, looking towards his wife in concern.

Gemma's mother gave her a long hug and reassured her that everything would be all right.

"Take your time, Gemma. We've got all day. Your dad's not at work until tonight."

"That's right," he confirmed. "Is it something to do with Ken?"

"Yes, he's not what I thought he was. He's horrible."

"He hasn't hit you, has he?" asked Gemma's father. "Because if he has—"

"Let's not start that," interrupted his wife.

"I'm just saying."

"Well don't. Can't you see Gemma's upset? Come on, love; tell us what the matter is."

"It's as if he's changed into a different person. Yesterday morning before he went to work he kicked the bedroom door really hard because we had no bread. He's barely ever around. It's like he's using my flat as a place to sleep. When I've asked him where he's been, he just shouts at me. My nerves are shot. I can't stand to look at him anymore."

"I presume he's got a key to get in," said her dad.

"He has," replied Gemma.

"Well, there's only one thing for it. I'm off to the DIY shop. I'm going to change the lock. I also suggest you pack a few things and stay with us over the weekend."

"Yes, that's a good idea," agreed her mum.

"Not just yet, Dad. I need to try to talk to him properly. I want him to tell me what his plans are. In fact, I need to tell him how I'm feeling. I can't do that if I've locked him out or if I'm staying at your place," said Gemma.

"Yes, but he sounds dangerous. You should come and stop with us as your dad's suggested," said her mum.

"I will, but not just now."

"I'm not happy about that," she said. "What if he hurts you?"

"I don't think he will. But I promise once I've had a chance to tell him how I'm feeling, I'll ask him to leave," said Gemma.

"No, Gemma. We've been here before, love," said her dad. "I don't want you getting hurt. I'm going to get a new lock and put it on now. That way he can't just walk in without you wanting him to. And you are coming home with us."

"I suppose so," replied Gemma passively. "I'll go and pack a bag. I'm working till late tonight, so I'll get a taxi to your house when I finish."

"Yes, that would be sensible," said Gemma's mum.

———

Like an injured animal Ken was licking his wounds. The humiliation of being fired in front of Tom was making him angrier. He imagined Tom laughing at him and playing the hero, telling everybody that he had won. But he hadn't, nor could he. Ken Charles was a hard man. Since the Sassenach had turned up in Scotland, things had changed. Ken had lost his wife and now his job. The English shit should be run out of the country. Vermin, that's what he was. He was a rat, a rat that had betrayed their friendship.

Ken pulled his car over onto the parking area on the A90 heading north from Dundee to Forfar. There were three things he could do. The first was to visit Viv at the bank and try again to get her back. The second, which would provide instant gratification, was to go back to the factory and give Tom the hiding he deserved. The third was to go to Gemma's flat, have a drink, and plan his next move. Ken wanted to make sure that he humiliated Tom the way he had felt humiliated earlier that morning by being fired.

I have to sort him out. I want to see the fear in his eyes. He knows he's inferior to me. He doesn't have the strength I have.

Ken started up the engine of his battered old car and headed into Forfar. He would go to Gemma's apartment. He knew that she would be going to work. At least he could think when alone. If she was still in when he got there, he would just tell her to fuck off and get to work. *What a weak woman. She isn't a patch on Viv.*

After drawing up outside her flat Ken used the first of the two keys Gemma had given him. Once inside he made his way to number three. In front of the door was a black refuse sack. Rummaging through it, Ken soon realised that the contents in it were his. There was no note with the bag explaining the reason for its presence. Ken was incensed that Gemma hadn't contacted him.

I bet she's changed the lock, thought Ken. Trying the key, his fears were realised.

"The bitch!" he shouted.

Hearing this, Gemma's elderly neighbour peered out from her door to see what all the commotion was about.

"What the fuck are you gawping at?" Ken screamed.

Without saying a word the old lady went back into her apartment and closed her door, leaving him to continue his profanities. After kicking Gemma's door a few times he eventually gave up and made his way with the black bin liner back to his car.

———————

"They're having a party in the depot. Or near as damn it." Tom's foreman smiled.

"Well, at least he's gone from here," said Tom.

"Aye, you're right there, although I think you'll have to be careful. Loose cannon, that's what he is. By the way, you need to have another look at the canning machine."

"Okay, I'll go and see what's wrong this time," laughed Tom.

The atmosphere around the factory was as bright and light as a street party. There was a sense of celebration in the air. Deciding to call in at the depot before working on the machine, Tom was greeted by a spontaneous round of applause from the warehouse staff when he entered the building. The assistant whom Ken had punched in the mouth was smiling. Not only had Ken gone for good, but the assistant had been put in temporary charge.

"Thanks, Tom," the assistant said, holding out his hand. "You did it. You did have the balls after all to see Ken off."

Maybe at work, but God knows what he's planning for me outside the factory, thought Tom. *I'll be glad to get home and talk to Viv about what's happened.*

"Let's hope we can start to enjoy work a bit more," replied Tom, shaking the assistant's hand.

The rest of the afternoon went by quickly without any incidents. Tom was feeling so much better. He could move around the factory like a free man, no longer a prisoner to Ken's presence. No longer did he need to keep alert. No longer while at work would he have that terrible sinking feeling every time he saw Ken or heard his voice. The factory was brimming with an energy not felt before. Laughter came from the depot. Work was now something to be enjoyed for the warehouse staff and drivers. Tom heard somebody whistling. It was bad whistling, but it sounded light and airy. The workers felt joyful. Stories of Ken's sexual advances towards some of the younger administration staff started to surface. Apparently, he liked to talk to the women through innuendoes. He would comment on how nice they looked and enquire as to whether their partners appreciated their sexiness. Tom could not believe that one person had affected so many people's lives. Ken had eroded their confidence. He'd played mind games by telling them they were stupid, and in some cases, he had physically bullied them. Life in the factory had now changed forever. The feeling in the air was that of hope.

The managing director has got to be happy, thought Tom.

"Hey, Tom," shouted one of the drivers, popping his head around the door. "How're you doing? I can't believe it. You actually did slay the dragon. Bloody hell, you'll go down in folklore for this. Seven years of punishment, that's what we've had. And you sorted him out in three."

"Funnily enough, if I hadn't started seeing Viv, I wouldn't have known what a nasty piece of work Ken is. How come none of you did anything about him?"

"We did try, but the managers above him were scared. Fear is a terrible feeling. He once grabbed me by the hair and kneed me in the balls. He said he would do my family if I said anything."

"I really can't believe what one man can do to so many people," said Tom.

"Anyway, have a good evening. And thanks," said the driver.

Sitting down at his bench, Tom wondered about his future and thought about investing some of his money in the company. It was doing well, and Tom clearly had collateral. There was no point just leaving it to stagnate in the bank. It would be something to discuss with the managing director. The time of day had arrived when Tom cleaned his tools if they needed it and then put them away. He always liked to brush under and around his bench whether dirty or not. It was a ritual he had picked up from his apprenticeship. Soon he would be home, and then he could tell Viv all about his day and what had happened to Ken.

The bank had been especially busy with Friday afternoon customers either drawing off their overdrafts or pleading for loans to help them become even more insolvent. Viv was unsettled. She had felt like this all day. Her thoughts were firmly on Ken. Although glad her marriage was over, she could not help but think he had lost his grip on reality.

She contemplated contacting his brother. The problem with this lay with them both being very similar characters. She feared that his brother would give her a mouthful of abuse and refuse to listen to what he considered to be her lies. She might not love Ken anymore, but she couldn't ignore his behaviour, as it was different from anything she had experienced from him in the past. This was something inhumane. This was cruel. And it was irrational.

I'll talk to Tom tonight; see what he thinks I should do. Ken's so spiteful; he's becoming dangerous. There doesn't seem to be any reasoning with him, thought Viv.

It had been one of those days that had gone slowly where time somehow seemed to be suspended. Tetchiness was beginning to take over her thoughts. It was like the old woollen jumper one felt compelled to wear when the aunt who had knitted it visited. Irritatingly itchy, no amount of distraction could ever take that uncomfortable feeling away. Even after removing the jumper the itchiness remained for a time, the brain completely convinced that the wool was still pressing hard onto the skin. It was the same with Ken. Whenever Viv consciously made an effort to stop thinking about him, she was soon reminded by her unconscious thoughts that he was there lurking in the recesses of her mind.

God, give me some peace, she thought.

Once again looking up at the clock, Viv hoped that she would arrive at Tom's house without incident. It would soon be time to leave work and with it the possibility of Ken lurking outside. She would leave by the back door as a matter of precaution.

"Thanks again, Alistair, for understanding and letting me have some time off," said Gemma.

"That's okay."

"By the way, we might be getting a visit from Ken at some point," Gemma said as she walked behind the bar.

"Why's that then?"

"The lock on my flat has been changed."

"Good for you," replied Alistair.

"My dad did it for me earlier."

"About time," said Alistair.

Almost before he could finish his sentence the pub door swung open.

"You bitch," shouted Ken. "You've locked me out. What have I done to deserve that? Do you want to know something? You're lucky I even looked at you, never mind fucked you."

"Right, that's enough," shouted Alistair from behind the bar. "I want you out, and while you're at it, you're barred."

"Come out from the bar and say that," screamed Ken. "Come on then!"

"Gemma, go into the back and ring the police," said Alistair.

"Don't bother with them," said one of the locals, standing up. "There are enough of us here to sort the little shit out. Ain't that the truth, lads?"

"Aye," said five of the locals in a collective voice. Standing up, they began making their way towards Ken.

Without any further utterances Ken turned quickly and made his way out into the night. A round of applause followed as the whole pub began celebrating.

"Good riddance," shouted Old Donald. "Alistair, get everyone a drink on me."

————————

Jumping into his car, Ken was fuming. Yet he still did not look to himself for answers to his woes. The world was conspiring against him, and he would never let it defeat him. Not knowing where to go, he put his car seat back and closed his eyes. This didn't help. The only thing he could see was Tom. He was there. His face was there whenever Ken closed his eyes.

Where the hell can I go? he thought.

Starting up the engine, he decided to drive to Dundee. He would book into a hotel for the night. He did think about going straight round to Tom's house, but he was tired. He would benefit from a good night's sleep. Tomorrow was another day. It would be a day when he made sure that the Sassenach knew there would be no let-up until Ken had his wife back.

"Thank God you're in," said Viv, hugging Tom after she walked into his house. "Let's have a drink, and I don't mean tea."

"Yeah, sure, how does a whisky sound?"

"Great, but make it a large one, will you? Thanks. I need a stiff drink," said Viv.

Sitting down at the kitchen table, Tom recounted his day. Viv looked horrified.

Will it never end?

"Tom, I'll understand if you want out. I don't know how much I can put up with Ken. Never mind what you have to put up with," said Viv, looking straight at him.

"I'm not letting you go. I owe my life to you, Viv. You've brought me joy. Whatever Ken throws at us we'll face together. Agreed?"

"He'll be worse than ever now. We'll have to be on our guard," said Viv, looking dejected.

"I know, love, but remember we've got each other."

Standing up, Viv opened the back door and strolled into the garden. The evening air was cold, but this didn't deter her from taking deep breaths. She walked slowly around the garden's edge, trying to see a way forward for both her and Tom. He watched from the kitchen window as she manoeuvred her legs and arms into a fighting position. She then punched out into the evening as though there was somebody in her line of vision. She continued to do this for a good three minutes, moving around the garden as though it was a ring. This was a fight she needed to have. It was a fight that would see her even more committed to the man that was watching her.

You will not win; you will never win, she repeated in her mind.

Her whole being was now focused on Ken. It was as though he was in the ring with her as she sent punches and kicks in combinations that would have done damage to the hardest of men. Tom did not interrupt; as he knew what was taking place was important for Viv. She was facing her demons, and from where Tom was standing it seemed she was easily defeating them.

Bloody hell, I wouldn't fancy being hit by Viv. Tom smiled. *I'd best not give her too much cheek.*

Tom took two pork chops from the fridge and then began preparing tea. Viv would return when ready. The weekend ahead seeped back into his mind. Ken would be the least of his problems when Justin arrived. Tom's life had taken a turn for the better when he'd met Viv. That much was true, but there was also much to fear. He was aware that Justin could ruin his newfound love if he really wanted to do so. He had ammunition that could prove fatal to a fledgling relationship. Then there was Ken, a presence that was nightmarish, a kind of dark spirit that was forever lurking in the shadows. One might not see him, but one knew that he was there. It reminded Tom of being afraid as a child when walking down the small lane at night near to his house. According to local legend a pact had been made with the Devil to save a local man from being declared a murderer. The man had committed the heinous act but had sought the help of local occultists to place the blame on a neighbour. It was said that the ghost of the innocent man would appear every night screaming like a banshee for mercy. Anybody passing at that time would have their souls stolen and then go straight to hell.

Viv walked back into the kitchen and broke Tom's thoughts. She looked red in the face but had a calmer manner about her.

"Feeling better?" asked Tom.

"A little," she replied.

"Sit yourself down. Tea won't be long."

Taking a glass from the cupboard, she turned on the cold water and filled it.

"Are you sure you want us to continue seeing each other?" Viv asked, sitting down.

"Yes, more than ever. After Justin's been, why don't we take a holiday? Get away from here for a while. A change of scenery would help us. We haven't spent time together without Ken being around. What do think?"

"I think it's a great idea. Where do you fancy going? I haven't done much travelling," said Viv.

"I don't know. I'll pick up some brochures from the travel agent."

"Okay," said Viv.

"Anyway, let's eat and forget about Ken. We could have an early night," said Tom.

"Why not," replied Viv.

The hours were passing by slowly. Back in his living room, Justin hadn't moved for most of the evening, as there was no reason to do so. Tomorrow he would walk the Clough before setting off for Scotland.

The weather report was fair with a slight drizzle expected mid-afternoon, by which time he would be on the road to Forfar. Decanting himself a scotch, he tried to find a positive spin on his upcoming time with Tom. Looking at the glass in his left hand, Justin acknowledged that he was drinking more than ever these days. It comforted him. Settling back down into his chair, he closed his eyes and could feel his heart beating heavily through his right hand that was now cupped around the side of his head. The evening ticked slowly away as he thought of nothing in particular. Flickering images from his past flashed through his mind with little intent other than to show that they had existed. Standing up, he thought he would take in the evening air. The rumble of a motorbike on the brow of the hill became more audible as it headed towards the village.

I'll bet he feels a sense of freedom, Justin thought. He then gave a wry smile as he remembered that the one time he had attempted to ride a motorbike the experience had lasted no more than thirty seconds. Though he'd tried hard to keep his balance, an attack of the wobbles had made him crash into his parents' garden, providing great amusement for the neighbours. After giving the bike back to its rightful owner Justin had sworn that he would never ride again, and to this day he had solemnly kept his promise. Once the nightrider had passed through the village, Justin was yet again alone with his hurting self. After taking one last peep at the stars he went back indoors, walked into the kitchen, washed his glass, and within ten minutes was in bed.

Saturday

The alarm went off; waking Viv, but Tom continued snoring. Oblivious to the sound of the radio and the splattering noise of the rain pelting against the window, he continued sleeping. This gave Viv the chance to have the first shower. She had a surprise for him, which she intended to give him after breakfast. Having dried herself, she made her way downstairs where she switched on the kettle and placed four slices of bread in the toaster. How different this felt after having begrudgingly made Ken's breakfast every day for the past seven years. *The lazy bastard,* she thought.

Everything felt so different with Tom – he was so much kinder, more loving, and certainly more engaging than Ken. These small gestures helped Viv feel worthwhile. Feeling invigorated, she was glad to have left Ken's world and knew there would be no turning back. His had been a world of monochrome, black and white, where people were judged on first impressions. Over the past few days, she had not heard Tom say a bad word against anybody, except of course for Ken and with good reason. Climbing the stairs, she walked into the bedroom. Tom was awake but looking tired.

"Morning," said Viv.

"Morning," he replied. "How come you're not at work?"

"Eat your breakfast, and I'll tell you," Viv said, handing over the breakfast tray.

Although continuing to make chit-chat, Tom couldn't help but feel some disquiet given that the day of reckoning had arrived. There could be no turning back; he had come too far down the road for that. To Tom's delight Viv slipped off her dressing gown and climbed back into bed.

Lost in his own world, Justin was sitting by the side of the reservoir. It was quiet except for a skein of Canada geese that had decided to halt flying and land on the opposite bank, making their presence known to all the residents of the water. The noise was loud enough to startle a feeding cormorant. Uncomfortable with their presence, it flapped its wings before flying across the reservoir in search of stillness. The sky was leaden like Justin's thoughts. The light of the morning was struggling to shine on a cold and dull day. Scanning the water with his binoculars, Justin had hoped to see something different, but it seemed he was out of luck. Moving on, he made his way towards the bridle track that took him down to a small feeder stream. An eel in self-preservation was slithering back into the water, disturbed by Justin's presence. The water was dark brown and looked dirty but surprisingly held much life. Lighting up a cigarette, Justin stared deeply into the stream to try to slow his thoughts down, which were now beginning to fixate on Tom. The day was here, and he was to travel to Scotland, but in search of what, he was still unsure. The weekend ahead was something he had been praying for yet, at the same time, something that he was fearful of.

I'm glad I've returned to these moors, thought Justin. The beauty of the Ribble Valley's landscape offered Justin comfort other places couldn't. At least it took him outside the four walls he had inhabited in London, the prison of his thoughts and the place of his wrongdoing. After walking a further fifteen minutes, all the while stopping to scan the fields and reservoir, he sat next to a dead tree. Twenty years previously the tree had been struck by lightning during a particularly harsh electrical storm, effectively killing it. It now stood alone, bare and as white as the hare's skeleton which was lying no more than two yards away. The tree was an outcast, no longer capable of providing shelter and camouflage for the birds and squirrels frequenting the nearby woods and fields. It was sad-looking, appearing unloved, lifeless, and lonely. Empathising with the tree, Justin stood up and circled it, touching its trunk. He recognised that it had done nothing to deserve its fate other than to be in the wrong place at the wrong time. It had no consciousness, it had no reason, and it could not make decisions – unlike Justin, whose actions had made him a criminal and who had suffered ridicule from the so-called enlightened and the morally incorruptible. They had harassed him. All of them had been incapable of expressing compassion other than for exchanges of pity and gestures that never felt genuine. He had sensed people's rejection, which had made him feel a renegade. He'd suffered their condemnation, their accusations of him being misguided, immoral, and egocentric; they had lectured him on ethics.

Making his way home by walking towards the field with the hawthorn tree, Justin asked God to help him during his upcoming time with Tom. The drive to Scotland now occupied his mind. Tom had told him that it could take anything from four to six hours. This preoccupation with logistics helped to take Justin's mind off the issues he would have to face over the next few days. Struggling over the stile that had lost its steps, he started down the small road leading to his house. On reaching it, he went straight into the bathroom and took a shower. After getting dressed, he packed his case.

"What're you doing? What about your work? I thought you had to go in for the morning or something," Tom said.

"Questions, questions," laughed Viv, snuggling up to him. "This is your surprise. I've been told I don't need to bother. Kate's doing it instead."

Kissing her, Tom moved his hands under the sheet to where she liked them. He loved her responsive moan which gave him confidence to continue exploring her body. The touch of her hand sent ripples of excitement throughout his body, making him grunt.

"I love you, Viv," he said without embarrassment.

"I know," she replied. "It's bizarre, don't you think? Here we are after a couple of days together as if we've been lovers for years."

"Hey, Viv, apparently when you get older, not only do your ears get bigger, but so does your cock," Tom laughed.

"There's hope then," she said, softly squeezing his balls.

Placing his head on her breasts, he closed his eyes, their curvature a perfect headrest. *It gets better and better,* he thought. *God, I'd forgotten how great love feels. She loves me. She bloody loves me.*

Viv climbed out of bed and put on her dressing gown. "Don't go anywhere," she said with a glint in her eye.

Still smiling, Tom couldn't believe his newfound flexibility. The thought of years of more discoveries was blowing his mind. The thing he loved about sex with Viv was how vocal she was in telling him what she liked and what she wanted.

What a prize pillock you are, Ken. No wonder you want her back.

Thanking the universe, God, and the stars for this new phase of life, Tom couldn't help but wonder what a lucky sod he was. What a difference Viv had made to him in such a short time. Last week he'd had no aspirations; now he was in love.

Getting back under the sheets, Viv laughed as Tom tickled her toes. Now lying silently next to Tom, Viv's mind began to wander, thinking about the day ahead. She would go and speak to Ken about the house and then do some tidying and washing. Tom pulled her towards him and kissed her breasts that had lain pert against his skin. Putting a finger on his mouth, she kissed his forehead before placing her mouth on his lips. They writhed with pleasure, the kiss seeming to last for an age until a knock on the front door interrupted them. Quickly getting out of bed, Viv looked out of the window.

"It's the postman," she said, looking at Tom who was now half dressed.

"Thank God for that. For a split second, I thought it might have been Ken. I'll go and see what he wants," he replied.

Watching, plotting, and ready to strike, Ken had seen Viv at the window and knew what she had been up to. *Wait while I get hold of the English bastard. I'll enjoy hurting him.*

Patience had never been Ken's best virtue, but he wasn't stupid. He knew that he wouldn't have any chance of persuading Viv to take him back if he alienated her too much. Through all the present turmoil, Ken gave no thought to the hurt and suffering caused by his behaviour, nor did he think about how Gemma might feel if she knew about his scheming. Ken didn't recognise that his affair with

Gemma was in any way to blame for the breakdown of his marriage. The blame belonged entirely to Tom.

"What time's your friend due to arrive?" asked Viv.

"I'm not too sure, probably around five. I need to be here all day just in case," replied Tom. "Maybe I should ring him."

Tom lifted up the receiver and dialled Justin's number. "Hi, Justin, it's Tom. I'm just wondering what time you're likely to be arriving,"

"Around five, five thirty. Is that okay?" replied Justin.

"Yeah, that's fine. I'll have some food ready," said Tom.

"Thanks," replied Justin. "See you later."

Tom's mind flitted from one thought to another, from a sense of fear to that of self justification. They were random as well as probing. *What have I done? Maybe I should have left things as they were. I don't want to lose Viv. What will she think of me when she finds out what I'm really like? I'll have to tell Justin about Viv. I hope he doesn't give me crap about it. Why should I worry? He's bloody lucky that I contacted him.*

Sensing his body tensing and his thoughts colliding, Tom made a conscious effort to stop dwelling on his anger. It was neither healthy nor useful.

"You're deep in thought; penny for them," said Viv.

"I'm thinking about Justin and what might happen," he replied.

"That sounds ominous," said Viv,

"Once Justin has left, I promise I'll tell you all about it," said Tom.

"Aye, okay," replied Viv.

As she applied her makeup and got ready for the day, her thoughts were coming thick and fast. *I wonder what's happened between those two. It wouldn't surprise me if they've fallen out over a woman. That's what men do. On second thought, Tom had been devoted to his wife; any fool could see that.*

Planning her day, she had no doubt that Ken would make contact with her today, as he needed to collect some clothes and personal things from the house. *He'll be staying with Gemma, poor woman. He can live on the moon for all I care.*

Viv had no guilt about being with Tom. Though seven years was a long time, she felt so different, so much more alive, now. What she was experiencing was a love built on respect, and it was liberating.

How many other women out there settle for complacency? How many men for that matter accept their lot without questioning their unhappiness? That's no longer me. Thank God.

The thought of seven more years with Ken made her feel physically sick. Only a few days ago she had been Mrs Charles going about her everyday, boring life. But now she felt free. Knowing what Ken was like, she pictured him telling everybody that his wife was having it away with his friend from work. This no longer bothered her; in fact, it was amusing, and quite frankly she no longer gave a damn. What mattered now were her new life and the many adventures that lay ahead with Tom.

———————————

Outside Tom's house Ken was still staring up at the bedroom window.

"I'll phone Viv soon and get her to meet me at the house. I'll carry on working on her. I can't wait to finish Tom off. Viv should be with me, not that doddering old shite. I'll get her back from that fat English bastard," he said.

Ken's thoughts were becoming ever darker. There seemed to be no let-up. Tom's time would come, and Ken would have his recompense; that was inevitable. Ken cared for nothing other than to right the wrong done to him. His id was growing by the minute, reminding him that he had taken out harder men than Tom.

He's nothing, absolutely nothing.

The fact that Tom had turned his wife's head was enough justification for Ken to wipe him out. Like a hunting dog he could smell blood. Memories of past conquests flooded his thoughts. They were all coming back, each barbaric victory.

God, I've missed the rush of violence. I will have my day. Tom will be under my foot. I can't wait. But for now I need to be patient. I'll start bullying him soon. I need to plan first; then I'll strike. Viv will be impressed with my power.

Although Viv had promised to call him, Ken decided to make the first move, as he didn't want to leave it to chance.

I'll play it friendly and appear reasonable. I'll lull her into thinking everything is fine. I know Viv. If it seems that I'm forcing her hand, she'll only become resistant. I'll charm her; she'll soon come back to me.

Ken called Viv. "Hi, Viv, it's Ken. Is there any chance of getting into the house? I'm outside it, and you're obviously not in," he lied, all the while staring up at Tom's bedroom window.

"You'll have to meet me there later. I'm tied up at the moment. Is two o'clock okay?"

"Aye, I'll see you then," said Ken.

Throwing her phone down on the bed, Viv screamed in frustration. "He's beginning to do my head in," she said.

"Mine's already done in," said Tom. "Be careful, won't you?"

"Of course, I'll be fine," she replied.

Noticing Tom sitting cross-legged on the bed looking anxious, she wondered if there was more to Tom than she realised. She hoped he wasn't hiding anything horrible from her. *Please don't let anything ruin our chances,* she thought. *Not now.* What she didn't need at this time was some heavy-duty situation exploding in her face. She decided against asking Tom for an explanation, thinking it was probably best to leave it for now. There was enough to think about.

I'll go back to the house, give it the once over, and wait for Ken, she thought.

Turning the key in the ignition, Ken parked his car round the corner with the intention of following Tom. He had an inclination that Tom would be going out soon. When he did, then Ken would surprise him with his presence.

I'll show Viv what Tom really is! That'll be fun. I feel like my old self again. Where've you been all this time?

"See you later love," said Viv.

"By the way, you're welcome to join us later this evening. That's if you want to," said Tom.

"Thanks, but I think it best you spend some time with your friend. It seems you've a lot to catch up on. I'll keep in touch with you and maybe see you at some point over the weekend," she replied.

"Yes, you're right," Tom said.

She kissed him and wished him well with Justin. Once again, Tom reassured her that he would explain all to her after his visit. Nodding affirmatively, Viv walked towards her car.

The Justin of old would have liked Viv, thought Tom. As for the Justin of today, Tom could only guess. Tom thought about his friend and his romantic liaisons. Justin had not been without girlfriends over the years, but he had never married. The reason for this was that the main love of his life, Poppy, had left him for a married man ten years her junior, which literally broke Justin's heart. After that he'd become consumed by his work and politics. Despite having many admirers he'd never felt able to engage anyone in the same way as he had Poppy. Recollecting evenings in the pub, Tom remembered Justin drifting into quiet melancholy whenever Poppy's name was mentioned. *I presume he's still single. I'll find out soon enough,* thought Tom

———————

It was an east-coast-of-Scotland type of day. Although it was drizzling, within the space of minutes there would be bright sunshine. This was often the misconception about Tayside. Of course it had its share of Britain's rainfall, but it was not as bad as some believed. Preoccupied with meeting Ken, Viv became more nervous as she drove towards their marital home.

I'll be polite but distant. The one thing I don't want is him thinking there's any chance of us getting back together again.

She couldn't believe how timid and blind she had become over the past seven years. Most people would never understand her present position. They would listen to and believe Ken, who would be playing the aggrieved husband. He was so egotistical. Turning up the radio, Viv pushed thoughts of Ken out of her mind.

Tom and Justin had been best friends for well over twenty years until the day which had split them apart. Not only academically bright, Justin was also a deep thinker. His friend Tom was less so and on this occasion was still not sure how to approach his old friend. The time they were to spend together was likely to be uncomfortable and difficult. Despite his blossoming relationship with Viv, Tom felt guilty. Having made his way into the dining room, he removed his wedding photo from the sideboard. Chrissie looked beautiful. Seeing the huge beam on her face made him smile. What a joker she had been, forever playing tricks on him.

"Mad woman," he laughed as he looked deep into the face of his dead wife. How alive she had looked on their wedding day. *What a beautiful woman you were.*

He took the letter she had left him from the sideboard drawer and placed it in his shirt pocket so that he could read it later. With thoughts of Justin intermittently hitting his brain, Tom decided that it would be best to be open and frank with Justin. Although he wouldn't hide his relationship with Viv, he did think it best to show a modicum of sensitivity towards Justin. Moving into the kitchen, Tom took two painkillers and drank a glass of water.

Having arrived at her house, which no longer felt like home, Viv looked at Ken's clothes in the wardrobe and had no appetite to cut them up or to play the wounded wife in any way whatsoever. In fact, she felt nothing. It was all rather ironic and almost comical. If Ken had not strayed, then she would still be with him and none the wiser that a better life and deeper relationship was waiting for her around the corner. Until recently, she had never really thought about providence; it had all seemed a little too much like Hollywood to her. Yet here she was on the threshold of new beginnings, and she wanted it. Exasperated by Ken's antics, she was growing ever more concerned about his callous side. She knew he was playing the long game. Fearing the worst, she wondered how much more sabotage was going to come from him. She could see Ken had returned to his old ways and knew there was nothing he wasn't capable of doing. Playing out such scenarios in her head seemed to help her, as it provided a sense of perspective and reminded her never to let her guard down when around him.

Unless Justin has taken the pledge, whisky should be a good starting point, thought Tom as he walked into the supermarket.

Placing two bottles in the trolley, he moved along to the beer shelf, where he picked up twenty-four cans of lager. It was likely to be a boozy weekend even with its seriousness if their past friendship was a guide. Turning into the next aisle, Tom was immediately disturbed by an unwelcome voice.

"Hey, granddad, how would you like some hospital food? You just keep an eye on that back of yours," shouted Ken.

Refusing to be drawn into his game, Tom continued shopping without giving Ken any eye contact. Ken's malevolent presence seemed to be everywhere. Ken was so close that Tom could feel his breath on the back of his neck, which made him nervous. It was disconcerting knowing that Ken could easily attack him from behind.

Don't let the bastard grind you down, Tom thought. *Keep moving.*

Continuing towards the till without looking back, Tom felt relieved when in the corner of his eye he saw Ken walking towards the exit. After paying the cashier, Tom made his way to the car park, looking tentatively around for Ken. He didn't have to wait long. There he was looking menacing with bad intent in his eyes.

"Hey, there's that randy old fucker again, everybody!" shouted Ken, pointing his finger at Tom. "Look, everyone. There he goes. Make sure you buy a chastity belt for your women. Keep the key well away from him. He steals people's wives."

"You've got what you wanted; you've got an audience. Now go on; piss off, and leave me alone," replied Tom.

"That's never going to happen, fat boy. I'm here to make your life hell. I'm the evil spirit that'll haunt you till you give me back what's mine," replied Ken, now laughing manically.

Having put his shopping in the boot, Tom jumped into his car and drove away, leaving Ken to make his way to meet Viv at their house. Ken wasn't concentrating on the road, and his vengefulness clouded his road sense, so his driving was now dangerously erratic.

Ha ha. I enjoyed putting the shits up Tom. What a twat. And there's so much more to come.

Turning left off the main road; he slowed down and parked his car. Here he was – home, where he and his wife should be. He didn't bother knocking; why should he? It was his house, and he saw no reason why he should. Spying Viv in the kitchen, he decided to sneak up behind her and put his arms around her waist. After startling her he laughed.

"Sorry about that," said Ken.

"It's not funny; you could've given me a heart attack," replied Viv, shaking

"Well, my lover, how are you?" Ken asked.

"We need to talk settlement," Viv replied curtly.

The bitch, she's not playing. I'll have to work harder on her, Ken thought as he entered the bedroom to gather his belongings. The bitterness he was feeling towards Tom was so powerful that it took all his effort to stop himself from smashing his fist through the wardrobe door. In all their time together he had never hit Viv, but now he had an overriding urge to smash her in the face and demand she have him back. It didn't feel right having to move out. Here he was filling his bags with clothing that belonged at this address.

It's my house, my bedroom, and most of all, it's my wife downstairs.

"I've made you a coffee," shouted Viv as he made his way down the stairs.

This hit Ken hard as he realised that this might be the last cup Viv would ever make for him.

"Have you got what you need?" she asked.

"Aye, for now," he replied, knowing that what he needed was the woman who was speaking to him.

"About the house," she said. "Do you want to buy it?"

"I'm not sure yet; everything has happened so quickly," he said.

"Will you think about it and let me know?"

"What about lover boy? Aren't you moving in with him?"

"I'm not here to talk about Tom. I need to know what your intentions are." She sighed, refusing to fall for his taunts.

"I want to be with you," he said. "Let's try again."

"I've already told you that's not an option. It's over. You now have Gemma. Why don't you start a new life with her?"

"But I don't want Gemma. I want you. Let's start again; come on, love. Deep down you know you want to," he said.

He just won't listen. He's so presumptuous. As if I'd have him back, she thought. Then she said, "Ken, what bit of no don't you understand? All I want is for you to leave me alone."

"I won't let you go. I don't care about you being with Tom. I'll accept your apology, and then we can start again," he stated.

"You self-righteous bastard," shouted Viv. "Not once have you mentioned your part in the break-up. You're nothing but poison. How could I ever think you were ok? You're nothing but a nasty little man that's showing his true colours."

"Come back to me, Viv. You don't stop loving somebody after all this time. Tom's not the one for you. I know you better than he does. Come on; what do you say?" Ken said not having heard a word Viv had just said.

Go fuck yourself, thought Viv. Thankfully she was able to resist shouting this out. It was not worth fighting him. That was what he wanted.

"It's over Ken," she said.

"I know you still love me," Ken said. "I'll keep asking you till you're back with me."

"Go home, Ken."

"This is my home, you stupid cow. I'll never give you a divorce. You'll have to wait for years. You will come back to me. Do you fucking hear me? You will come back! I'll be in touch," he screamed, banging the front door on leaving the house.

———————

The hatred that had spewed from Ken's mouth was making Viv flinch. She had seen his vitriol directed at others years ago when in Glasgow but never at her. It was disgusting. He was disgusting. Taking a deep breath Viv sat down at the kitchen table. She was shaking not out of fear but out of a deep thankfulness that Ken had left. The atmosphere in the house was now overcome with oppression. Ken's malicious presence had been so noxious it felt as if it was oozing out of the walls. The house had been tainted forever. Even if it didn't work out with Tom, Viv wouldn't want to live in the house anymore. Drinking her lukewarm coffee she thought about the countless women in the world experiencing the monotony of a partner that cared for no one but himself or herself. They probably lived their lives fantasising about another world, engrossed for the majority of time watching TV and responding only on command. Viv had freed herself from this scenario. Even if her relationship with Tom didn't work out, at least he had helped her find enough confidence to know she never wanted Ken again. For that she would be eternally grateful. When Viv thought about getting old, she knew that if she had stayed with Ken her life would have been one of unimagined bitterness. Now she had no reason to live with his small brain, lack of subtlety, and, worst of all, his vanity. She could not thank him enough for letting his cock rule his life

I need to get away. I'll drive to Jedburgh and stay overnight with my mother.

Gemma was awake and feeling refreshed. She had just experienced her first full night's sleep in weeks. There was no fear in her or any concerns for her and the baby's safety. How she felt liberated. Ken was gone. Although Gemma was wise enough to know that he would try to harass her in the future, for now she felt well and was not suffering acute anxiety. The world looked and felt a different place. She could look forward instead of worrying about what Ken was going to do next. She was confident enough to know that her father wouldn't take any nonsense from him. He might not be able to deal with Ken physically, but he would have little constraint in contacting the police or taking out a restraining order.

Lying comfortably in bed, she wanted to experience freedom for a little bit longer. *Thank God he's gone*, she thought.

There was a gentle knock on her bedroom door. It was familiar, comforting, and welcomed. Gemma's mother had made a cup of tea and two slices of toast with marmalade, which she laid down on the bedside table.

"You're looking better, dear," said her mother.

"I feel better. Thanks for everything. I don't know where I'd be without you and Dad."

"It's what we're here for. You stay as long as you need. It's lovely having you back home. I can fuss over you."

At this, Gemma began sobbing tears of relief, of love, and, most accordingly, of hope.

Justin was heading up the M6 towards Carlisle. A full hour had passed since he had hit the road. As with all long journeys, it was boring. The motorway was busy with a huge array of trucks from across all areas of Europe.

"It must be a really stressful job. I couldn't be a lorry driver," he said to himself.

Being a GP had brought its own pressures, but to pound the tarmac for a living and dodge other people's mistakes were not for him. Trying his best not to think too much about the weekend ahead, he started singing along to the CD that was playing. Unfortunately, this failed to take his mind off the upcoming times with Tom.

God, I hope things work out. I need to be leaving with some kind of resolution.

It was a long journey, and for now The Waterboys would help soften his anxiety.

Tom was feeling the pressure from Ken. He was nervous and worried. A sharp pain was shooting through his stomach born of apprehension.

"Is it all worth it?" he asked himself. Yet the alternative was unthinkable. "It would mean losing Viv, which I won't allow."

Stay grounded. You've to hold yourself together even when Ken harasses you. You mustn't let him get to you, he thought.

Arriving back home, he unloaded the shopping out of his car. Though feeling on edge, he would not capitulate to Gucci Boy's intimidations. He hoped Viv was okay and wished that she was by his side. "All the more to look forward to when she is," he said to himself.

In less than three hours he would see his oldest friend who had for many years been closer than kin. There could be no more pretence as to the reasons their lives had come to this. Both had to reach out, listen to each other, and see if there was anything worth salvaging from the wreckage of their friendship. Tom wanted Justin's permission for his new relationship with Viv. But it had been three years since they had last seen each other, and Tom knew that he had no right to demand anything, let alone expect Justin to give his blessing to Tom's new love. It would take time for both to say their piece, and Tom wanted to listen without criticism. He knew this had to begin with him acknowledging the pain Justin was suffering. When they'd spoken on the telephone the other night, Tom had realised the magnitude that day had had upon Justin's life. This was reinforced by Justin's frank admission that he had not been able to work since. The voice that had spoken back to Tom hadn't sounded like Justin; it was cracked and old, lacking energy, and monotonous. The time was fast approaching when Tom could say he was sorry and mean it. They had gone their separate ways after that day, both engulfed in remorse. For Tom, this remorse was decreasing to a level where he could face its destructive force, more so since meeting Viv. She had given him hope and something to live for.

Back in front of Tom's house, Ken was getting himself ready to begin yet another period of surveillance. Fighting hard to contain himself, he really wanted to act on impulse and break Tom's legs. His life in Forfar had been relatively trouble-free until the bastard in the house in front of him had decided to stick his nose in his affairs. *Maybe it's worth doing time,* thought Ken.

If he could not have Viv, then nobody could. He would see to that. These were dangerous times for Tom. Ken did not have any thought for Gemma or the child she was carrying. His professed longing for children was ostensibly lost in the bitterness he was feeling. Anyway she had made her views clear to him. The fact he was mulling over whether it was worth spending time at Her Majesty's pleasure to exact his revenge indicated his thoughts were no longer rational. Brooding was potent. Being a product of his ego, he was that person who turned to the crowd after a monologue of self-praise and said in all sincerity, "That's enough about me. What about me?"

The telephone rang. Half expecting it to be Justin, Tom was surprised to hear Viv's voice.

"Hi, love," she said. "I'm just letting you know that I'm going to stay with my mother tonight."

"Okay, Viv. Hopefully I'll see you at some point tomorrow. Have a good time," he replied.

"Have a safe journey, and I'll see you tomorrow. I love you."

"And you," she replied. "I hope things go okay with Justin. Bye."

Returning to the kitchen, he thought it wise to start preparing the chilli for later.

The sign for Hamilton told Justin that Glasgow was not too far away. Deciding to take a break and grab a cup of coffee at the next service station, he moved into the inside lane. He had surprised himself by volunteering to visit Tom in Scotland. He'd made the decision on instinct. If things didn't go well, Justin would find a hotel or, depending on the time, drive back to Lancashire. Feeling a little stronger, he hoped that this visit might prove to be the beginnings of a new life. Looking to the left, he spotted a sign telling him that the service station was another two miles down the motorway. He was ready for a rest.

Already well on the way to seeing her mother, Viv would decide when she got there whether to tell her about Tom or not. Even though she had lived with her father after her parents' divorce, she'd remained close to her mother. Looking back at her parents' relationship, she was well aware that they had had little in common. Her mother, numbed by the dross of life, had been able to realise her potential for happiness after starting an affair with the local gamekeeper. Life with him offered her more than serving a man she barely spoke to or even cared for. In retrospect, this seemed to mirror Viv's marriage, and therefore comparisons between her relationship with Ken and that of her parents were highly appropriate. The difference was that although her father was boring to live with, at heart he was a good man and never vindictive like Ken. Still happy in her decision, Viv's mother held no regrets about her divorce except for hurting her first husband. Seeing Ken earlier had only reinforced Viv's resolve to keep away from him. She too was hoping for a second chance at love. Parking the car, Viv took a second to gather her thoughts. She was looking forward to catching up with both her mother and stepfather, George.

After drinking a cup of coffee and eating a scone Justin felt much lighter in his pocket. Spending money at service stations always riled him. He told himself that it was the principle, as these places couldn't lose. They had the motorist every which way. Yet he had only himself to blame. If he hadn't have been so lazy, then he might have prepared a flask beforehand. It was the same for those sitting around him. The thing they all had in common were lighter pockets from when they'd first begun their journey. Listening to himself, he realised he was sounding like a really grumpy old sod. Forcing his mind to think of something positive, he was peering around the diner when he saw a young man slip and drop his tray on the floor. People began laughing, some from the pits of their stomachs. Justin found himself laughing, an act that was not normally a part of his daily routine. It felt good. Maybe this was to be a good day after all. Thankfully, the youth was not hurt. Standing under a cloud of embarrassment, the young man could do nothing else but pretend it hadn't happened.

Making his way towards Forfar centre, Ken wasn't sure where to go. He was no longer welcome at the Boar. Being deceitful, he thought it best to speak to Gemma over the weekend and try to keep her on board until Viv was back with him. *She may as well be useful for now.*

In addition to his scheming he had also been thinking about the different scenarios his life might take. There was no doubt Gemma needed placating. He thought that in time he could persuade her to let the child move in with him and Viv once they were back together again. But for this to happen he needed Gemma on board. These thoughts highlighted Ken's brittle mental state. Parts of his life with Viv were quickly being rewritten in his mind as untruths became his new reality. Refusing to acknowledge that Viv didn't want a child of her own, never mind one that was his by another woman, was one such example. Grandiosity was clouding his judgement and giving way to a world based in fiction.

She knows she has to apologise for sleeping with Tom. But she also knows I want her back, he thought. *She understands.*

Ken now believed people were laughing at him behind his back, and this laughter was becoming more audible in a mind without social boundaries. The unchecked excesses of distorted emotion were now driving his actions. It was if there was a voice inside him screaming out for vengeance. The voice had become his master. He could no longer deny its command.

Alistair asked Gemma if she was ok. Preferring to keep her feelings to herself, she told him that everything was fine. She didn't want sympathy.

I could kick myself. I thought I was wiser for my past mistakes. But I've done it again. What is it with me and men?

Married for a short period in her early twenties, her husband Jed had been a real character, good-looking, huge in physical stature, but after a few drinks, a monster. Lashing out, he would use words that could be described only as pure filth. At the beginning of their relationship he had seemed gentle and caring. Thinking him a charmer, many had fallen for his charisma. Not only had he kissed the blarney stone, he had managed to swallow it whole.

Standing behind the bar perusing her surroundings, Gemma was annoyed at her lack of caution when beginning her affair with Ken. He'd seemed to be popular with the other regulars and had always had good manners when talking to her. These all had combined to lull Gemma into a sense of false security, and she'd dropped her guard. The time she'd spent alone with him had left her feeling excited and wanting more. When he'd explained how he'd like to have children but his wife had always resisted, she had felt sorry for him, thinking Ken would make a perfect father. Hindsight now revealed that he was deceitful and completely self-absorbed. After the breakdown of her marriage Gemma had vowed never to be deceived again and had done a good job until Ken had entered her life. She had been dazzled by an ignoble light.

Gemma was thirty-eight years old, and the child growing inside her would be her firstborn. She'd believed that the opportunity to be a mother had all but gone. In a relationship or not, Gemma had all intentions of keeping the baby. Many would think she had planned to get pregnant, but this was far from the truth. She had taken the necessary precautions. Typically, Ken had not, reliant on her to be the sensible one. The coil she had worn was obviously not as secure as first thought. Blaming her for not taking safeguards, Ken refused to acknowledge his role in her pregnancy. His excuse that it didn't feel natural wearing a condom had been immature and irresponsible. Yet Gemma had continued believing his deceit, although it was hard to forget his reaction when she'd told him she was pregnant. The look of horror on his face had taken her by surprise. And the prickly silence that had followed his long rant about having to tell Viv had baffled her, especially since he had constantly denigrated his marriage. Later that evening he had reassured her that things would work out for them. He'd kissed her cheek and told her that he was happy and just needed some time to adjust to the news. They had lain on the bed in each other's arms discussing whether the baby would be a boy or girl. Both had said they didn't care as long it was healthy. They had laughed about future times together and the happiness they would share as a family.

Now Gemma would have to cope without him. This was well within her capabilities, and she was adamant that Ken would not bully her. At least she could turn to her parents for support. They had been delighted at the news of her pregnancy and promised to do what they could to help. Her brother, Robert, would also lend a hand. His wife, Elly, had already kindly offered to look after the child on Gemma's return to work. Staring into space, rubbing her stomach in a circular motion, she knew that within a few weeks the whole world would see that Gemma Atkins was expecting a baby.

After a five-hour drive from Lancashire, Justin had finally arrived in Forfar. As he sat in his car outside Tom's house, the nervousness in the pit of his stomach transferred to every nook and cranny in his body. This did nothing for his health. Swallowing hard, he could feel sweat oozing out of his hands as his knees began to twitch.

Fuck was the first word that felt appropriate. *Fuck* was the second too.

Breathlessness overcame him, his bowels moving like a slow landslide, his insides gurgling like a blocked drain. These physical feelings reflected Justin's inner fears of rejection, hatred, non-forgiveness, violence, and, above all, himself. Feeling immobile and rigid in the car, a prisoner of circumstance and a victim of his own decision-making, he needed a few minutes to compile himself.

I can't just walk in as though the past three years haven't existed, he thought.

The last hour of the journey had not been conducive to positive thinking. Working himself into a frenzy of doubt by repeating the many questions that needed answering had done nothing for him other than to wear down his already overworked brain. The crushing feeling he had outside Tom's house was one of pure terror. His nervousness was so intense his heart was physically hurting. It was beating as fast as an express train, and he knew any attempt to stand would fail. Spending the next few minutes breathing in deeply, endeavouring to calm down and not fill his trousers, Justin seriously thought about turning his car around and heading back down south. Such was the weakness of his whole body and the uncertainty of his brittle mind. Holding firm to the steering wheel in an attempt to stop shaking, he realised that anybody watching would think he had been drinking or had some neurological difficulties. The day he'd longed for was now finally here, but the future didn't seem bright, just terrifying. Filled with dread, his mind replayed scenes from the past three years. It felt as if an infestation of negativity had suddenly possessed him. He held his hands against his ears, trying to force these thoughts out the top of his head. He let out a loud scream demanding they leave him alone, as though performing his own exorcism. Wiping the tears from his eyes, he shouted that he needed some peace. But he knew that he could no longer put off contact with Tom. The reason for him having travelled over three hundred miles was to find out what Tom wanted. Not knowing was terrorizing him. Justin could only guess what was in store. He would soon find out.

———————

Parked opposite Tom's house, Ken was once again watching for any activity. If Tom spotted him hanging around, then he would drive away. The intimidation Tom would feel knowing that he was being watched would be satisfaction enough. This was beginning to feel like fun, the sort of fun he had left behind on the streets of Glasgow but had never managed to eradicate from his psyche.

Looking along the street, he thought he could see Tom. *It can't be him. It's not his car, unless he's bought a new one in the past few hours. I doubt that.* Taking another look, he noticed the man making his way to Tom's house. *It's not Tom. He's knocking on the door. I wonder who he is. If he's a friend of Tom, then he's likely to be a real prat.*

———————

Standing up on hearing a knock at the door, Tom looked at his watch. It was just past five thirty. *It'll be Justin,* thoughtTom.

Over the past couple of days Viv's presence had helped Tom from becoming too anxious about the forthcoming time with Justin. But now he was nervous, especially with Justin standing at his front door waiting for an invitation to step inside.

What shall I say? How do I handle this? His heart was telling him that if Justin had made the effort, then so should he. Opening the door, he beckoned Justin in. The figure standing in front of Tom looked older and much thinner than the last time they had met. Tom was surprised by this, although Justin had never been a heavy person. He had been muscular and wiry. His hair had gone silver in parts, displaying small areas of dark that had once been the envy of many a balding man. His hair was still thick but now seemed lifeless.

"Good journey?" asked Tom to break the ice. He took Justin's coat and hung it at the side of the front door. He placed Justin's suitcase at the bottom of the stairs so as to be ready for when Justin was shown to his room.

"Yes, fine," Justin replied.

"Fancy a drink?" asked Tom. "Whisky or a brew?

"Whisky will do thanks. I had a coffee on the way. I stopped at Glasgow," replied Justin.

"Sit down; make yourself at home," said Tom, feeling apprehensive and not really knowing what to say to help Justin relax. "Here goes." Tom handed over a glass of whisky that would be best described as a liberal measure.

"Nice house," said Justin, attempting to break the silence.

"Yeah, I like it," replied Tom, realising Justin was very uneasy.

Noticing Justin's eyes were rapidly darting from side to side, Tom wasn't sure whether to tell him to breathe and relax. In the past he would have done this. These days he wasn't sure whether Justin would take it from him. Remaining quiet, Tom was offering the opportunity for Justin to reconfigure himself, hoping they would be able to connect later. Sipping from his glass, Tom asked Justin to excuse him while he checked on the chilli in the oven, giving them both a little time to readjust to the situation.

There was a sudden knocking at the door which Tom opened.

"Come outside, and I'll kick the fuck out of you. Come on then, you soft bastard."

"Piss off," replied Tom. "I've better things to do with my time."

"You're nothing. Absolutely nothing. I won't tell you again. Stay away from my wife!" screamed Ken.

Quickly shutting the door, Tom made his way back into the living room. The man was screaming through the letter box that he would have his revenge.

"Are you okay, Tom?" called Justin.

"Yeah, I'm fine, nothing to worry yourself about," he replied. "He's just a dickhead. I'll explain all later."

———————

After Tom had rejoined Justin he poured them both another whisky. Justin could see that Tom's hand was shaking. Inspecting Tom's face for signs of intent, still suspicious as to the reason for making contact again, Justin was feeling uneasy. After all, the last time they'd met had been in a courtroom.

Both men sat in silence. It had already crossed Justin's mind that Tom had found another woman. It seemed he had been right after all. He was surprised that she was married. Justin had always been led to believe that Tom had clear boundaries regarding his relationships with women. Before he had married, Tom would preach about the virtue of not being the one to wreck people's lives. Affairs with married women had always been anathema to him. Trying to understand Tom's actions, Justin could only measure them against his old friend's past position. It seemed things had changed. In truth, Justin was feeling exhausted with his life and really didn't give a shit whether Tom had a harem of married women, although he couldn't dismiss fully the feeling of disloyalty Tom was showing to his wife's memory. All that Justin wanted was release from his own nightmare.

Justin took a large swig of whisky. It was a good medicine. Since his twenties, he had always had a couple of glasses a day. As a GP, he had enthusiastically argued in support of its healing properties. These days there was more caution from the medical world about the merits of alcohol, as there was with smoking. Refusing to become overcautious regarding these two vices, he would not bow to overenthusiastic health freaks afraid of their own mortality. Acknowledging that he wasn't a very good role model or GP in many people's eyes, Justin thought life too short to allow interference from ideologically lacking politicians spouting an agenda of social control amid their own personal corruption. These meandering thoughts made Justin realise that in the moment he had nothing to say to Tom. He wondered if it had been a mistake driving to Scotland. They could sit here for the next hour attempting small talk, but Justin knew that with not having spoken to many people over the past three years conversation could prove difficult. When he had engaged others, dialogue had barely gone beyond the surface of social convention.

Justin found himself staring at Tom. They had once held a deep love for one another, sharing comfortableness that was rarely found among people. They had once forged a tie they believed to be unbreakable. It had seen them support each other throughout life's traumas. Their friendship had seemed unshakable by distance or situational change. It had existed outside time and space. People said that if you kicked one you kicked the other. That was until that day. And now sat together for the first time in three years both felt the gulf. And it was equal only to the distance between the earth and Mars. They no longer anticipated having a laugh and spending time together debating the meaning of life or the latest albums they had purchased. This was sorrow. This was uncertainty. This was painful.

Justin could see that Tom had his own troubles. He didn't know what to say or what to do, although he told himself that he needed to give Tom a chance to explain. And it was Tom that broke the silence by asking Justin if he was okay. Justin replied that he was.

"Tom?" asked Justin. "What am I doing here?" Sweat was now dripping from Justin's brow.

"You tell me?" replied Tom, not fully engaging with Justin.

Justin felt angry at Tom's curt reply, although, he understood that part of Tom was still with the Scottish guy that had earlier been shouting the odds. Justin also wondered whether Tom was thinking about his new woman. This thought was soon to be proven right.

"Do you mind if I make a phone call?" asked Tom.

"Actually I do. Tell me why you've asked me here. Ever since I arrived you've been evasive and have had very little to say to me," said Justin, looking directly at Tom.

"I really need to make that call," said Tom. "Let me ring, and then I'll speak to you."

"Ringing your new girlfriend, wondering if her husband is with her, jealous are we? My God, you're such a hypocritical bastard," said Justin.

"Yeah, okay, but not now. I need to speak to Viv, make sure she's all right."

"You mean check up on her!" shouted Justin.

"You know nothing about this, so just keep it shut, eh?" replied Tom.

————

Making his way to the kitchen, Tom dialled Viv's mobile. It was on answer machine, so he left a message asking her to call him. *I need to know if she's ok. I have to keep her safe.*

Remembering Viv's words that Ken wasn't violent towards women did nothing to allay his concerns for her safety. The notion of honour among criminals had always seemed a myth to Tom, a misrepresentation by those prone to violence. It was an illusion created to make people think criminals still had an ounce of humanity in their diseased bodies. *Viv might trust Ken not to hurt her, but I don't,* he mused.

The one person he had allowed into his heart since the death of his wife was Viv, and he would do anything to protect her. Her sensitivity had moved him. She was now his future, the one who had shaken him to the core by challenging him to look outside his own frailties and faults.

If Justin wants to know the reasons for the invitation, then I'll tell him. But first, I need to make it clear that Viv was not a part of my life when I first invited him to stay. I need Justin to understand me. He has to know that I want to put things right between us. Plus he needs to know that this has nothing to do with Viv. Tom missed Justin they had once been great friends. Even through their nightmare they had never declared themselves enemies. Yet here they were driven apart by each man's mistake, by each man's lack of self-forgiveness, by each man's fear of the future.

―――――――――

Waiting for Tom to return, Justin's anger was still pouring out from him. Its negative energy was bouncing throughout his body and the blood vessels in his head were now close to bursting. *I need to tell Tom that he's ruined my life and that his abandonment that day placed too great a burden on me. He also needs to know that I never expected him to stab me in the back.*

Prior to the day in question an understanding had been reached which would see them help each other, but this had never materialised. Unlike Tom, subsequently Justin had not been able to lift himself out of the slough of despondency. All of Justin's spiritual beliefs had dissipated in those few moments in time. This was what Tom needed to understand. If this was the only thing Tom was able to take on board, then Justin would feel he had made a small step forward. The ringing of the telephone broke Justin's thoughts.

"Thank God you've rang. Are you okay?" Tom said before recounting his latest encounter with Ken.

What's he playing at? Justin thought.

"I'll speak to you tomorrow. At least I know you're safe. Love you," said Tom before placing down the receiver.

Those last two words sent a wave of anger throughout Justin's being. *How dare he throw this woman in my face?*

"Justin, about the earlier incident with Ken, you must believe me that Viv's marriage was over before I started seeing her."

"If you say so," replied Justin dismissively. His heart was still firmly nailed to the cross of introspection and weighed down with an overwhelming sense of betrayal and jealousy.

———————

Walking in the large garden to the rear of the house, Viv and her mother were talking about Ken.

"I've started divorce proceedings," said Viv.

"You don't know how relieved I am to hear you say that," her mother replied. "I never understood why you put up with him for so long, ghastly man. He's like a ticking time bomb"

"Well he's out of my life now," said Viv.

"Good, but promise me you'll be careful. I can't see him taking too kindly to you leaving," Viv's mother said. "Have you found somebody else?"

"No, what makes you think that? Anyway, it's a bit hypocritical of you. Double standards or what," replied an exasperated Viv.

"There's no judgement, dear. All I've ever wanted is for my girl to be happy. I only hope he's kinder than Ken and more suited to you. Remember you can fool all the people some of the time, and some of the people all the time, but you can never fool your mother any of the time. Come on, Vivienne; tell me his name."

"What are you like? I wasn't going to say anything. I can't get anything past you, can I? He's called Tom."

"I hope he has a bit more about him than Ken. Let's face it, love: Ken's hardly Einstein."

"Well, you're certainly not wrong there," Viv replied, reciprocating the laughter.

"So who is he then? Can he read?"

"He certainly can. You'd like him, Mum. He's lovely. Very thoughtful and, you'll be pleased to know, kind. Tom's a widower by the way. He's older than me."

"Do you know something, my love? For the first time since you were a teenager you're inwardly smiling. Your eyes are sparkling.

That's all I've ever wanted for you. Ken's held you back for years, and I thought he might have trapped you forever. Thank God you're free of him. Come on; let's crack open a bottle to celebrate the great escape. He's different, this Tom; I can tell by your body language. Good for you." Viv's mother embraced her daughter.

"I'm pleased that you now know," said Viv.

"I knew something was different as soon as you walked through the door."

Both lifted their glasses and toasted the future. Viv continued talking about Tom, which made her mother happy. They both agreed that Ken could be somewhat obsessive.

"Have you seen the way he hangs up his clothes and lays out his shoes?" said Viv.

Viv's mother shuddered at the thought of him. "No, dear, take it from one who's tried. You're always better with a bit of rough. He was always too smartly dressed to be trusted," she said.

This made them laugh even more.

Finishing his whisky, Justin accepted the offer of a top-up. Being together brought back memories of the many nights they had spent drinking and talking about their ambitions. Losing his position as a GP had been devastating for Justin, especially as he'd had to experience this alone without the support of his friend. Never in a million years had Justin expected Tom to display such treachery; he had been the one person Justin thought would have supported him. Instead, Tom had stepped to one side and then launched a fierce assault that had effectively sealed Justin's fate. The judge had thanked Tom for his contribution, praising his honesty. The walk from the dock to the prison van had been a lonely one for Justin, especially after Tom had turned his head away and started talking to the solicitor next to him. Justin had felt this disloyalty throughout his two-year incarceration. There had been no letters or any kind of correspondence, let alone visits, from Tom. Scores of Journalists eager for a story had attempted to contact Justin while he served his time. Justin had quickly dismissed these, as with all enquiries from the media. The many letters from sympathisers never provided comfort, nor did they bring light to the dark night of his soul. The pain Justin had felt was indescribable. Nobody could understand. The time in prison had done nothing for him, as he'd spent it idling under a course of antidepressants that had had no constructive effect on his guilt. Showing little understanding of Justin's remorse, his cellmates soon had become bored with his self-persecution, crowning him, 'King of the Jaws.' Mocking him, they'd made him a saint and started calling him St Moaner of the Order of Fucking Moaners. They had been merciless when taking the piss out of his beliefs.

"You need to tell me what you're thinking, Justin. I'm not a mind reader," said Tom, interrupting Justin from his reminiscences.

"You're not a very good friend either," chided Justin. "I come all the way here, and you act as though there is nothing wrong between us. What the hell do you want from me? What do you want me to say? That you're a complete and utter bastard for what you did to me? And that you left me to take the rap for everything? There, I've said it. Am I angry? Damn right I am. Can I forgive you? I'm not sure. What were you thinking leaving me to do the work that you promised to do? It's screwed me up, Tom."

Having been drinking heavily in Forfar, Ken was indiscriminately threatening to punch people's lights out. Nobody in the Boar had expected him to walk through the door, but standing there just inside the pub, he screamed obscenities. Before he could be removed, a man in his mid-forties and of slight build walked through the door hoping to see familiar faces and play a game of pool. The poor man was not ready for what was to happen next.

"What're you looking at?" shouted Ken as his double punch landed on the nose then mouth of the new drinker, laying the man on his back with his hands over his mouth. Without a second thought, Alistair rang the police, but by the time they had arrived, Ken had long gone. The victim's mouth was now swelling and starting to turn black and blue. Even this couldn't persuade the new drinker to go to hospital.

"Give me a double whisky. That'll help. There ain't any way I'm going to hospital," he stated firmly. "I'm not waiting around."

Other drinkers that had converged around him were now laughing at the poor man's expense. Coming to a little, the new drinker began joining in their piss-take, even laughing when Old Donald mockingly called him Rocky. The police asked the victim for his name, to which he replied through hurting gums, "Tim Balls."

"More like got no balls," interrupted Old Donald, at which point the whole pub erupted with laughter. Even PC Evans was finding it difficult not to laugh.

"Settle down," he said, trying his best to control himself.

Attempting to provide a description of Ken, the victim could only describe the shape and size of his fist. "I wasn't able to get a good look at him. Everything happened too quickly," replied the injured man.

Like everybody else in the pub he knew his assailant was Ken, but as with them, he was also too frightened to say so publicly. The attack had outraged Alistair, though, and he walked outside and stopped PC Evans to give him Ken's particulars. He was glad that it was Gemma's night off and she hadn't had to witness Ken's senseless behaviour.

The police finally caught up with Ken as he staggered along Peter Street threatening anybody within his sight. They approached him from a distance, asking him if he was Ken Charles. Predictably, Ken refused to answer and threatened both police officers. After avoiding two punches they managed to handcuff and then throw him into the back of the meat wagon. There he came face-to-face with three other drunkards who were also going to spend the night in the cells. Ken started shouting obscenities at the largest of the three, calling him lard-arse. Without warning the smallest of the trio, although still larger than Ken, stood up, moved towards Ken, and head-butted him flush on the nose. Blood poured down Ken's shirt.

"I'll smash your face in for that," Ken threatened.

"Sit down, old timer, and keep your mouth shut. That's if you don't want another battering. Next time I might just split your head open. How's that sound, old man?"

Silence prevailed, and Ken didn't utter another word until reaching the police station where he complained about having been attacked. This was denied by all three men.

"He hit his face on the side of the van when trying to stand up," said Lard-Arse.

The police, knowing this to be unlikely, told Ken they couldn't do anything without any evidence.

"It's your word against them," said the desk sergeant. One of the officers standing by was smirking.

"You're lucky to only have a split nose. You need to be more careful in future. It's probably best you don't go upsetting young Knuckle Johnson. He's a nasty piece of work. I think you've met your match there."

"Oh yeah, just wait till the next time I meet him. He'll be the one that's fucking hurting," shouted Ken.

"We'll have less of that," said the desk sergeant.

"I'll kill the fucker," continued Ken.

"I've just told you to button it. Anymore and you'll be sharing a cell with those three bozos," threatened the sergeant.

Ken complied.

"I'll look after him for the night and make sure he comes to no harm," said Knuckle. All three were now goading Ken.

"Come on, lads; you've had your fun. It's time to be quiet and start sleeping off the night." Looking at the pathetic figure that was Ken, the sergeant took pity on him and placed him in a cell some distance from the three head-the-balls.

For the best part of two hours, Knuckle Johnson continued winding Ken up, telling him he knew where he lived and would visit his house someday soon.

"Oh, and by the way, fat boy might be a lard-arse, but only his mates can call him that. Do you understand me, you prick?"

"I'll catch you by yourself one day. You won't be laughing then, dick face," replied Ken.

"Hey, Knuckle, I bet you're shitting yourself," derided Lard-Arse.

"Hell yeah, I'm quaking in my boots," he replied.

Once again, there were derisions of laughter.

Getting sick of their verbal abuse, Ken switched his thoughts to Tom. Sitting on the side of the so-called bed, he contemplated the most efficient way of exacting his revenge on Tom. There had to be pleasure with it. The game had to satisfy his need for retribution. The split nose had done nothing to ease his sinister thoughts. Rather than making him come to his senses or take a more reasonable approach, it served only to bring back those feelings of enjoyment so often experienced in Glasgow when stalking his victims. The pain he suffered tonight was nothing to what he had in store for Tom. Now on the edge of reason, feeling euphoric, he jumped off the bed and sent out punch after punch, simulating hitting Tom in all the places that hurt.

Tomorrow's a day nearer to the English bastard's end. With a bit of luck and an apology the filth might just give me a caution.

Lying back down on the bed life was again starting to feel good even though his nose was hurting like hell.

In Tom's house, the opportunity for spiritual renewal and release from his emotional prison was confronting Justin. As Justin got ready to strip bare in front of his greatest friend, the hideous voice of resentment was keeping his heart from rebirth. Looking around Tom's kitchen, Justin tried to focus on something that might take his mind away from the slow burn of resentment that would soon spew out over his friend. Anger was potent. Unresolved anger was dangerous. His attempts at praying were failing to lead him away from his vulnerability.

"I need some air. I'm going to take a walk. I'll see you after," said Justin.

"Yes, no worries," replied Tom. "I'm not going anywhere."

Tom poured himself yet another scotch and moved into the living room, where he sat looking at a photo of his wife. The physical change Chrissie had endured towards the end of her life had been shocking. It had reminded him of images of Holocaust survivors. Like them, she had been nothing but skin and bone, barely resembling a human being. The day he had found his love on the floor lying confused and in pain would be forever etched in his consciousness. His first thought had been that she'd been drinking and had fallen over. This wouldn't have been too out of character. Chrissie had always liked a drink, and he'd laughed when first lifting her up into his arms. Then her continued moans started alarm bells ringing. He immediately called for an ambulance. By the time this arrived Chrissie had come to a little and was asking Tom to stop fussing. After settling her in at the hospital and being reassured that she was stable, he made his way home. They hadn't been able to tell him what the problem was and insisted they would know more after the completion of tests. At home Tom telephoned Justin, who reassured him that if there were any complications, then Viv was in the best place possible. Sensing some hesitancy in Tom's voice, as though he had omitted some information, Justin asked Tom to be honest with him. Justin then reinforced that it was too early to tell.

The look on the nurse's face when Tom walked on the ward the next morning was a mixture of apprehension and pity. Immediately upon seeing Chrissie he knew that things weren't as they should be. Holding his hand, she encouraged him to be brave and listen to what the consultant had to say, for her sake.

"You need to hear the diagnosis, love, and, more importantly, the prognosis," Chrissie said.

The words from the medic, Mr Davey, soon left him shell-shocked. Finding it too difficult to understand the medical terms, he was not able to take everything on board. All he heard was that Chrissie had a brain tumour. He chastised himself, wondering why he hadn't made her go to the doctor's earlier. Chrissie interrupted him, asking him to be quiet for a while and listen to what the consultant was saying.

"Yes, but you'd had the headaches for weeks. I should have insisted that you go to the doctors," he repeated. "I should have known, been more aware of your suffering."

The consultant explained that he had undertaken a routine neurological examination, which had consisted of tests measuring the effectiveness of Chrissie's nervous system, including her physical and mental alertness. Her responses had not been considered normal, and so he'd wanted to undergo further examinations before making a decision on which treatment to follow. This had meant having a brain scan. Feeling sick at this news, Tom cried. He squeezed Chrissie's hand, not wanting her to die. She was brave enough to ask for a prognosis if the treatment failed to work. Mr Davey could not say, as he needed to clarify the extent of the tumour's development and malignancy. Deep down, Tom and Chrissie knew the truth.

The day was grey outside but was considerably darker on the ward after Mr Davey spent time explaining the intricacies of brain tumours. This information would be forever stored in Tom's brain. Such facts were vivid; ependymal cells formed the lining of the brain and were described as ependymomas when cancerous or anaplastic ependymomas if they ever became aggressive. Chrissie asked the consultant whether this type of brain tumour was common and if a cure had been found. Mr Davey stated that ependymomas were actually uncommon in adults and constituted only about 5 per cent of primary brain tumours. They could occur either in the brain or the spinal cord. In Chrissie's case, it had been the brain. It seemed to Tom that the consultant tried to put a positive spin on the situation by claiming that they were slow growing.

Treatment consisted of surgically removing those parts of the tumour that were visible. If successful, then a series of MRI scans would then be undertaken. These would provide images of Chrissie's brain, showing whether the cancer had spread or not. Chrissie asked what would happen if surgery failed and whether there was any other way of treating the growth. Mr Davey made it clear that surgery would be the best option, but if that failed, then they could always try radiation therapy. Frank in his honesty, he explained that this intervention only reduced the size of the tumour and didn't actually remove it. After delivering such bad news, he suggested they remain positive and said it would be best to wait to see whether an operation was necessary before discussing options. These words made Tom shout out that Chrissie had done nothing wrong to deserve such a deal. She was kind and loving. Why had it to be her? Thinking about all the bastards in the world, he asked why they never seemed to get ill. There was no fairness. Chrissie kissed his hand and smiled at him, starting Tom crying. That kiss of reassurance relayed the message that they would fight this thing together. He smiled back, but inwardly his heart flooded with sorrow. Mr Davey asked them whether they had any questions for him. Both agreed that they couldn't think of any at that time. Suffering from an acute attack of uncertainty, Chrissie and Tom were stunned. Before leaving the room, the consultant informed them that the surgeon would visit later, and if need be, an operation would take place the following day. Tom would never forget the excruciating silence that followed Mr Davey's departure. It was only seconds but felt like an eternity. His and Chrissie's life together flashed in front of his eyes as he battled with the thought of eternal separation from the woman he so dearly loved.

"You can't leave me. You mustn't leave me, love. Please don't leave me. You have to fight for your life. Stay for my sake. I won't be able to cope without you," he said to Chrissie.

"Who knows, love, the surgery might yet be successful," she said.

In typical Chrissie style she placed a finger on his lips, shushing him to be still. Forever giving, she stroked his hair and kissed his brow. Needing some peace and time to digest the information Mr Davey had provided, Chrissie then asked Tom to remain quiet for a while.

The surgeon arrived towards the end of the afternoon and spoke openly about the procedure. Introducing himself as Mr McKinnon or Joe, he tried to put both of them at ease. Tom was initially uncomfortable being on first-name terms with the surgeon who was responsible for the care of his wife. But on Chrissie's insistence he didn't make a fuss. The surgeon told them about the role of surgery, stressing that it was the first-line therapy for patients with primary brain tumours, and both Chrissie and Tom began to understand a little more of what they had to face.

"It's those bloody ependymomas, isn't it?" Tom asked.

"Please be quiet, love; let Joe explain things," Chrissie replied.

"Yes, I'm afraid so," Joe stated. "But they are the type of tumours that respond to surgery, and therefore we're hopeful that we can remove the entire tumour."

For a brief moment everything seemed straightforward, until Joe made it clear that removing the whole tumour was no guarantee of success.

"Like with anything, they could grow back at any time. We also have some concerns that there may be other small ones developing. Obviously, we will know more once you are in surgery."

That specific moment of elation and subsequent deflation would follow Tom to his grave. It was as though he had won an Olympic gold only to have it snatched off him by a technicality.

Joe stressed the importance of follow-up meetings with Mr Davey. "Any recurrence needs detecting early," Joe stated.

His words were plainly delivered, something for which Tom and Viv were grateful.

"There is increasing evidence showing that the complete removal of the tumour, as long as it is safe to do so, is the best option. If this isn't possible, then the operation might still be beneficial alongside other treatments."

"What d'you mean by that?" Tom asked.

"Radiation and chemotherapy," Joe replied. "But I have to warn you. There are possible side effects from surgery, including infections, blood clots, and neurological deficits. These are possible rather than probable, but I have to stress that all surgery, no matter on which part of the body, carries some risk."

Chrissie and Tom thanked Joe, and he left the room, leaving Chrissie and Tom holding hands. They didn't speak too much about consequences for the rest of the day. Instead Chrissie asked Tom to read her snippets from the newspaper, hoping this would bring some light relief. They laughed at a story of a man who had lost the bottom half of his false teeth only to find them eighteen months later lying at the bottom of his washing machine. Both wondered how he had never heard them clattering. There was a photograph of the man, gummy and smiling, holding them up for the camera. Chrissie joked that this gave a completely new meaning to cleaning one's teeth. They both laughed. When the time came for Tom to say good night, he was reluctant to leave her.

"I'm going to stay with you," he said.

"No, love, you must go home and get some rest. There's nothing you can do for me. I'll see you tomorrow," she insisted.

Early the next morning Tom phoned the ward. Having been restless, tossing and turning all night, he found it difficult to calm his nerves. The ward sister informed him that Chrissie would be undergoing a premedical that morning and if all went well surgery in the afternoon.

"Can I visit her before surgery?" Tom asked.

"I think it might be best after she has had the surgery. She needs to rest. I'll give you the direct number to the ward so that you can keep in touch. It will save you having to go through the switchboard," the sister replied.

"Please pass on my love to her," Tom said.

"Of course," she replied. "I'll speak to you later."

Tom lay down and tried to rest. He shut his eyes but could only see Chrissie undergoing surgery. It made him feel useless. Of course, Justin telephoned asking if Tom needed anything. They made arrangements to meet at the hospital later in the day. Then the staff nurse who was looking after Chrissie rang to say that surgery seemed to have gone well. Tom felt ecstatic.

When Tom reached the ward, Joe immediately suggested that he be patient.

"Your wife needs constant observation. The following twenty-four hours are critical in knowing whether the operation has been a success," Joe said.

According to Justin tumours could come back at any time even if the operation proved successful. He also advised patience. Both Tom and Justin sat by Chrissie's bed until the end of visiting time. Heavily sedated, she had not moved a muscle since returning from surgery. Helping to calm Tom's anxieties regarding pain relief, Justin explained the positive side of opiates and their part in the recovery process. Justin also informed him of their side effects, such as depression.

"She will have to adapt to new routines and might not be able to work for a long time, if at all. The constant visits to hospital and the expected sickness from therapy will all be factors in her depression. I only hope she can adapt quickly to the new regime. Depression can became a problem and in some cases refuses to disappear. Tears will inevitably be shed. Don't forget that she could lose her sexual desire. On top of that there's the chance of increased anger and irritability. You'll have to work with these circumstances if you're to support her."

"I'll do anything. I just want her home," Tom said.

"Well, her GP will prescribe the relevant antidepressants and put her in touch with talking therapies, including various support groups. If that's what she wants."

"I'm not sure if she'd want any therapy," Tom replied.

Along with explaining the importance of chemotherapy, Justin also explained how it worked and made Tom aware of some problems that might arise from it. "You need to know that the drugs used in chemotherapy could cause harm to healthy cells. These could also affect her hair. However, side effects are likely to improve or even disappear once chemotherapy has finished. Don't forget as well that another positive effect of chemotherapy is that it keeps the spread of cancer at bay by shrinking the tumours that cause pain, thus relieving pressure on the brain," Justin continued.

These had been difficult lessons for Tom. After that first day when Mr Davey had informed him and Chrissie about the possibility of her having a brain tumour, he had taken on the mantle of student, making it his job to know as much as possible about the disease.

"You need to remain positive, Tom. That's the most important thing of all. Don't become overanxious about rashes that might appear on her body. These are commonplace for cancer sufferers; just inform her GP or consultant so that they can stop any medication causing the problem. They will then prescribe antihistamines or some form of steroid. If the rashes fail to heal after stopping the medication, then she must contact her GP as soon as possible, as this could mean other complications."

Chrissie had never needed to take any medication in her life until her admission to hospital. She had been the epitome of health. This was what made the situation difficult for Tom. There had been no warning signs. Yes, she had complained about headaches but only relatively recently. Confirming that this was often the case, Justin once again asked Tom to be patient. Assuring Justin that this was his intention, Tom also made a promise to assimilate as much knowledge as possible for when Chrissie eventually returned home. But his wife never did go home. Instead, she'd taken a backward step. After the operation it had proved difficult to stabilise her. First she'd contracted a virus, then her heart had needed monitoring, and then to cap it all she'd contracted a serious case of diarrhoea. Twenty-five days after the operation, having found more tumours, little ones that had proved to be insidious and nasty; the coffin door had been opened wide. Mr Davey had stressed that it was unusual for tumours to return that quickly, but as Tom had known, there had been nothing usual about Chrissie.

Hearing the front door open, Tom returned his thoughts to the present moment, quickly got to his feet, and met Justin in the kitchen. "Have you enjoyed your walk?" he asked.

"It was okay," replied Justin. "I needed some air; I was beginning to feel stifled."

I know the feeling, thought Tom, holding back his tongue, still breathing the memories of that awful day in hospital. *I don't think the walk's done you that much good. I can feel the tension in you. I'm starting to feel tired.*

"Would you like a drink?" asked Tom.

"I'll have a beer if you've got any," Justin replied.

"Coming up; I've got some in the fridge."

The tension in the house was almost touchable. It felt as if it had a life of its own and was looking to possess those within its proximity. *What should I do next? What can I do next?* Tom mused.

Returning to the living room with a beer for Justin, he soon had his answer. Without provocation, Justin began an outburst of colossal proportion, taking the wind out of Tom.

"Nina was my sister and your wife!" Justin screamed. "She kept asking me, and I kept refusing. She knew it was against my beliefs. She knew I couldn't sanction the act. Yet she kept pushing me. Where were you, eh?"

Tom remained silent. There was nothing he could say. The question was hard hitting and had left him feeling like he was drowning in a bath of paranoia. He already knew that at some point over the weekend he would have to face this very question. Yet no amount of rehearsing such a scenario provided him with the tools to deal with the reality of being asked this directly by Justin.

"I was a doctor. My job was to preserve life not to take it. Before killing my sister, I loved my life. Nina meant the world to me and I loved her deeply. You must remember me advising her about taking the right medication and telling her that the pain could be managed, but no, Nina insisted that medication could never take away the ignominy of her loss.

"I remember," interjected Tom.

"She said that she was a prisoner to her condition and argued that her quality of life had degenerated to the point where she no longer held a thought for more than a few seconds."

"That's right," stated Tom

"She asked me for empathy, not sympathy. She wanted me to understand the absolute indignity she was suffering on a daily basis, having to rely on others to undertake basic tasks such as toileting, washing, and feeding."

"I know Justin. I was there remember?"

Justin ignored the question and continued, "Every time I visited her, Nina demanded an end to her misery. I would never have contemplated pumping a pleading, helpless patient with a cocktail that ended their life. Yet this is what I did to my own sister."

"I know, Justin; it must have been hell. I don't know what to say," said Tom.

"I effectively split my inner self that day. My faith disappeared into a black hole. I surrendered my moral certitude to the pleading voice of my sister. In that moment, I turned my back on all that I believed in, and for this I'm finding it difficult to forgive myself. Night after night, I wake up soaked to the skin, having replayed in my dreams the moment when the liquid began seeping through her veins," cried Justin.

"That must have been terrible for you," said Tom.

"Seconds earlier, Nina had kissed my hand and told me she loved me. She thanked me and even asked me to forgive you for not being there at her moment of death.

"You should have been there. You should have been there," repeated Justin.

"I injected her with seven grams of Nembutal. I could feel it percolating through her body, and I watched Nina close her eyes for the very last time. Within a few seconds, her heart had stopped. She was a wonderful light in the world and she was dispelled by my own hand. I could see that Nina was free from her physical suffering, but the realisation of what I had done hit me as I fell to my knees. The sorrow I felt took away my breath," shouted Justin. "Do you understand, Tom? Have you any idea how I feel?"

"I'm trying to, Justin," he replied.

"I didn't even know that I'd dropped the syringe on the floor. I was sobbing so much; I thought that I would choke to death. What happened next is a blur. I think the nurses heard my crying," said Justin.

The nurse in charge had instinctively known that something other than the passing away of Dr Ivens' sister had taken place. After entering the room she had soon spotted the evidence on the floor. Her professionalism had been such that she'd ordered all patients back to their beds. Then bending down to Justin's level, she'd gently put her hand on his right shoulder and asked him to go with her into the office. Fully complying with this instruction Justin had then taken a seat and waited.

"I remember my whole body trembling. A nurse placed a blanket around my shoulders and left me with a cup of tea. I think the sister quietly asked a staff member to contact the police. After that I can recall very little until a few hours later when a solicitor arrived at the police station. Apparently, the detective informed him that his client had admitted killing his sister."

Nina had been a bold force in the world, a tremendous personality with a sharp intellect, someone that had held her own with the greatest of thinkers. From a very young age she had insisted that her name was Chrissie, except for Justin, who had been allowed to call her Nina. Only her parents called her Christina. A moment of moral vandalism had seen him kill his own sister, leaving his career in tatters and giving him a jail sentence that did nothing to repair the damage he had not only caused Nina but also himself.

"You bastard, you still haven't told me why you didn't turn up at Nina's bedside. What were you doing? It was you and Nina that planned the damn thing!"

Nina had always been able to coax Justin into doing her will. Since her death many had tried to support him by encouraging him to start afresh. Some had even offered him work. Universities had enquired as to his availability to present lectures on assisted suicide, not only to medical students but also to those studying philosophy. Never sure whether these people perceived him as a freak to be wheeled out for the public to stare at, Justin had refused their enquiries. Intellectually open to new ideas, Justin accepted that society was changing and that assisted suicide was creeping onto the political agenda. This made no difference to him. He still felt nothing but contempt for himself and for those who talked about taking life as if it were a mere pressing of the syringe. The majority of those who shouted the loudest about the right of others to choose when to die would fold when confronted with pushing the needle into the skin of the person they loved. They would strangely pass that responsibility on to those that are asked to save lives.

"During my visits to see Nina she always managed to turn the conversation to the subject of ending her life," Justin said.

The diatribe pouring from Justin was like an exploding Vesuvius. Before that day, Justin's patients had experienced his care and love with some believing him to be a godly figure. Many times in the past Tom had taken the piss out of him because of this. To many, he had been a humanitarian, a healer, a helper, somebody who could feel their pain. He was a liberator.

———————

Tom was stunned. The consequences of his non action that day were plain for all to see. He could not believe the man standing over him was the same person. Not only was he gaunt, as if he had injected large amounts of smack over a long period, but psychologically he was fucked. Tom wanted to ask this impostor where his old friend Justin had gone but thought better of it. There was darkness in Justin's eyes where once there had been joy. For much of the time during their friendship they had laughed together. Now the burning heats of rage and hurt were discharging all over Tom.

I have to try to change the future for Justin's sake. Christ, look at the state of him. Though, now is not the time to interrupt him or to ask for forgiveness.

All that Tom could breathe was Justin's volatility. Staring at him, Tom was trying to process Justin's emotional explosion. He thought about how Vesuvius had changed the world around it forever as the Sarno River had redirected its great flow away from the decay and death of a burning city. Justin had failed to do the same with his anger, his life. His darkest hour had effectively kept hold of his breaking heart, keeping it vice-like within that moment when his sister had died.

"You need to know, Tom. I didn't assist Nina to die. I killed her. I was no liberator. Her constant pleading broke me. It subverted my beliefs, making me deaf to that inner voice that some in the world see as weakness – my conscience."

The veins in Justin's neck were ready to burst, yet there was still more to come.

"You're like Judas; you betrayed me! At least he had the decency to do something about it. Whereas you! Parading your new woman around makes me feel like you're fucking rubbing my nose in it. Have you no bloody loyalty to Nina? And as for this Viv, her husband wants to break your legs. I can't say I blame him. He obviously knows what you're like."

Tom tried to interrupt but without success.

"Why the hell have you contacted me? I keep asking, but you never seem to answer me."

That's because I can't get a word in.

"Are you so insensitive, to think I want to see you living a new life as if nothing's happened?"

"Trying to answer your questions is a waste of time. You keep cutting me off!" shouted Tom.

Three years of emotional repression were blasting out from Justin. Knowing that he wouldn't be able to have his say until Justin had burnt himself out, Tom decided that he would sit and wait for that time.

Pacing up and down the room, Justin pointed his finger at Tom. "You still haven't told me why you left me to do the dirty work. Nina needed you, you bastard. She wanted you to be there. But no, you wimped out like you always did. You not only broke the pact we made but also her heart."

I know why I wasn't there, and you will once I have the chance to tell you, thought Tom.

Such an opportunity was some time off, as Justin would still not let him speak. For Tom the thought of losing Chrissie had been too much to bear. He had lain in bed, his head under the pillow with a breaking heart. The letter Chrissie had left him had provided some comfort over the past three years. It expressed her love for Tom, telling him that their life together had been all she had wished for and thanking him for the years they had spent together. In typical Chrissie fashion she had made sure that he realised they would never meet again. Written in her own hand that was barely legible given her condition were the words 'As you know, my love, there is no heaven or any form of afterlife.' This had cut deep into Tom even though he hadn't been religious, but he understood the sentiment with her having been an avowed atheist.

I really need Justin to read the letter. I'm sure it would help him. I'll show it to him when the time's right. Then he'll know that I've also suffered.

As Tom returned from his thoughts, Justin was still shouting.

"Do you know what prison's like? Of course you don't; you've never been there, have you? You're a complete bastard for doing what you did in court. I thought we were friends."

Once again, Tom tried to interrupt, this time by waving the letter his wife had left him. "Listen to me, Justin. This letter clearly told the court that Chrissie wanted to die but needed help to do so. The judge took that into account."

"Don't interrupt me," screamed Justin. "You've not lost everything; you don't wake up during the night with a sickening feeling running through your body. Who the fuck, do you think you are?"

Wanting to shout, "I'm Tom," he thought better of it. Although beginning to feel frustration at not being given the chance to speak, Tom continued holding his tongue.

"You're alright, you're still earning a living. Me, I have nothing. I can't work. I can't sleep. I can't get what I did out of my head. If you had been a friend, you'd have tried persuading me from killing your wife. Instead, what did you do? Sweet, fuck all, other than lie in bed sucking your dummy!"

I also live with guilt. I'm trying to come to terms with my passivity. I miss Chrissie every moment of my life. Do you not think I have to get up every morning and face myself? You're not the only one who's suffered. "Listen, Justin, do you think I haven't—"

"Don't interrupt; I haven't finished yet!" screamed Justin.

———————

Gemma had worked the afternoon shift. Exhausted at the end of it, she had spent a little time talking to her parents before they'd advised her to get an early night as she looked worn out. She'd drifted into a deep sleep and now awoke with a start. Confused, she thought she was in her flat. She had dreamed about Ken. They had been on holiday. Where this might have been she couldn't tell. She only knew it was somewhere abroad. The sun had been sweltering. They had been walking with a young toddler, a girl, and had been laughing. Putting on her dressing gown, she went downstairs and switched the kettle on. Sitting alone, she wondered what Ken was doing. Although Gemma no longer wanted to be with him, she still felt upset at what might have been.

He'll be with Viv. She's welcome to keep him. He's been awful. It's as though he's been living in another world of late, which doesn't include me or the baby, thought Gemma.

Her hands were shaking. Her mind was hurting, and her heart was heavy. *I need to try to keep positive. I can't stay with my parents for too long. I'll contact the housing association about a bigger place.*

One thing Gemma didn't want was her child growing up in an unhappy household. Returning to bed, she made an effort to stop thinking about the situation and especially Ken. She knew that it was important that she slept well.

Slumped on the settee, Justin was far too exhausted to speak. Tiredness had taken over his body, paralysing his thoughts. His throat was tender, and the drop in his body temperature made him shiver as though stranded in the midst of a winter freeze. Aching both physically and emotionally, he asked Tom to show him to the bedroom so that he could have a lie-down.

Returning to the living room with his head mashed, Tom poured a large whisky. Having been close to losing his temper with Justin, he was now thankful that he had shown restraint. Taking a large swallow from the glass, he closed his eyes, but instead of thinking about Chrissie and Justin, his mind settled on Viv.

I wish you were her, he thought.

When in her presence the troubles of the world passed him by. Renewed by her, his life now had a purpose. *How I wished Justin could find some purpose.*

Inevitably, his mind wandered back to the day of the court case and his replies to the barrister who had cross-examined him. Every day for the past three years, he had lived with the knowledge that he had abandoned both his wife and best friend. No amount of whisky could numb the feelings of regret. Every time Tom relived the trial in his mind he became tearful. The moment he pointed the finger of culpability at Justin for Chrissie's death would live with him forever.

Taking another large mouthful of whisky, Tom thought about Justin's life. *He can no longer practice as a GP. If only I'd pressed the syringe. I'd have probably still got a job in industry. What have I done?*

That day not only ended Chrissie's life but also Justin's. Justin was the embodiment of the living dead. Tom felt ashamed of himself. *I want to help you, Justin, but I'm not sure how I can,* thought Tom.

The physical state of Justin had shocked Tom. On opening the door to him, Tom's initial response had been to recoil at what he'd seen. The man in front of him had looked more like a character from the Soviet Gulag who had suffered the most appalling neglect, not his old friend Justin. Memories of their time together began to lighten Tom's mood as he remembered going with Justin to the Labour Party meetings. Justin's political zeal and commitment had never really rubbed off on Tom. Tom's refusal to become a party member was a clear example that he had been content to earn his money and spend it in the pursuit of happiness with his wife and child – unlike Justin, who had never married and had not shown any inclination to do so after Poppy had walked out of his life. Instead he had devoted himself to his work alongside various political and spiritual quests.

Coming out of his memories, Tom had an overwhelming wish to speak to Viv. Thankfully she answered her mobile.

"Hi, Tom," she said. "How are you and your friend getting along?"

"Okay," he lied. "I'm missing you."

"I'll be back tomorrow. Have you been partying with Justin?"

"No, I wish I could say I have," replied Tom. "It's been somewhat emotional. I'll tell you all about it soon. I promise."

"That's okay; all in good time. Listen, Tom, I'll have to go. My meal has arrived. George is treating Mum and me. I'll speak to you tomorrow."

"Okay. I look forward to that; take care, love," said Tom.

"I will," she replied.

————————

Justin lay in bed wide awake, his thoughts refusing to abate. They were tsunami-like, engulfing his breath and sweeping away all coherent thought. He tossed and turned, sweat trickling down every inch of his body and wetting him through as though he had pissed his bed. Thoughts of suicide once again entered his weary mind, but he dismissed these – one death had been enough. He sat bolt upright, and his breathing began to return to normal. No matter where he went the ghosts of his past were there to greet him. Thinking about Nina and that day, he could no longer dismiss her selfishness when insisting he end her life. Yet, having looked into her eyes, he had read her heart. Death was her prize; she had wanted to die. It held no fears or preconceptions for her. The God he believed in was a forgiving one, and therefore, according to Nina, Justin would have plenty of time for contrition once she had gone. This had done nothing to ease his conscience; it had wounded him, leaving him with the feeling that she was belittling his faith. And taking him for granted. It was the same when she suggested that if there was eternal condemnation, it would be she and not he that would suffer. Being close to a sibling always brought its problems. The cry of a loved one was difficult to ignore. Images of Nina's physical and mental state before her passing would haunt Justin to the end of his days. Lying in bed helpless, she was wretched, thin, and dying, nothing more than a breathing corpse. The whisper of her muted voice weakened by the tumours was almost inaudible. Stripped of all dignity, with a high risk of choking, she had eaten pureed food. Lying in bed all day, nurses she did not know had fed her. Giving her life-sustaining medication, washing her, and dressing her, they had had little to say other than what they had done the previous night. Being totally reliant on the nurses for toileting and, worse still, wiping her arse baby style had done nothing for her mental state. Nina could find no enjoyment in hearing their stories or any freedom in her condition. The fact of the matter was that it had made her more intransigent in her wish to die.

"I have no life, Justin. Look at me. I have no life. Please help me. Don't let me carry on like this," she had repeated.

Here he was in Tom's house, sitting motionless in bed doing what he had been doing for the past three years – thinking. He was pissed off with this; it was the one thing he did too much of. No wonder he had no friends. His inability to deal with his grief had worn them down, alienating all from his life. Alone in the world, imprisoned in time, he was the personification of Billy No-Mates. Like Nina, he also had sought liberation, although he knew this would not be found by taking his own life. He'd spoken to countless priests, ministers, and charlatans and all had told him that God was a forgiving being. Yet these words had not comforted him; they had not helped him change. Rationally, he sought justification for his actions by telling himself that he had ceased Nina's suffering. Yet when he examined his heart, he couldn't help but feel that this smacked of arrogance, an arrogance that if not checked could become a charter for those who did not value life. Justin still felt sick when he thought of his actions, even though he understood the argument that he had helped to cease his sister's suffering.

If people like me that proclaim to live by a spiritual truth can take a life, then how much easier might it be for those with none?

Fearing the entrepreneurs, Justin could imagine them queuing up for a good business opportunity. He envisaged a SOHO-style area where assisted suicide and mercy killings were commonplace. Big lights would advertise a cut-price killing. Alongside pubs, clinics might be found on every street corner carrying trading names such as 'Rent a Syringe' or 'This Syringe for Hire'.

I'm a bloody hypocrite. I know that.

His actions that day had been a reaction to the desperation of his only sibling and the most important person in his life. There had been so many times in his life when she had been there for him, too many to count. Whenever his relationships had ended, Nina always had been the first to ensure he was coping, either by staying with him or inviting him down to spend time with her, Tom, and his nephew, Mark. They had never missed the opportunity to come together, celebrating birthdays, going on holidays, or just visiting each other. Justin used to take his nephew birding or to the cinema. When their team Blackburn Rovers played in London, they would always go together and watch them. Harrowed by seeing his mother wasting away, Mark had thrown himself into his studies, which had helped him to cope.

Breaking from his thoughts, Justin spied a large crack in the wall where the plaster was hanging on for dear life. This was a simile for his life. As he slowly lowered himself down into the bed, the damp duvet clung to his body. A small smile broke out over his face as he remembered the day he and Nina had played a trick on Tom. Tom had been for a job interview, and Nina had suggested they wind him up. She'd contacted one of her employees and asked him to ring Tom pretending to be from Forsyth's engineering firm.

"What?" Tom had screamed. "You can offer me a job as a semi-skilled operative? You know what you can do. You can piss right off?"

As they had made their way back to Tom with tea and biscuits, Justin and Nina had been able to hear him talking to himself. It had been a soliloquy of immense proportions, making it impossible for them to hold back their laughter. He'd asked them what was going on, but they hadn't been able to answer him. At first, he'd thought they were taking the piss. Then the penny had dropped. They had been.

"You two had something to do with that phone call, didn't you?" Tom had shouted.

"Us?" Justin and Nina had said together.

"Yes, you," he'd retorted, beginning to calm down.

"The look on your face when you were offered a semi-skilled job, priceless, absolutely bloody priceless," Nina had laughed. "You're a snob."

As he felt himself being pulled into a deep sleep, Justin was beginning to smile again, and it felt good.

Back in the kitchen, Tom was helping himself to some of the chilli he had made earlier that day. There was no mindfulness in his actions; he simply heard his mother's voice reassuring him that he needed to eat to keep his strength up. He took another mouthful and dropped the fork onto his plate. Bowing his head, he began to cry. He didn't know what to do and didn't know where to turn. Whether the situation with Justin would ever be resolved he couldn't say. What he wouldn't give to go back to that day, relieve Chrissie of her pain, and tell her that he loved her. This he knew could never happen. His performance in court had hurt Justin very deeply. The shame Tom was feeling reinforced his revulsion at abandoning two of the people he had most cherished in life. With his head slumped down, he continued crying. The tears rolled down his cheeks, dropping onto the table.

"Chrissie, oh, Chrissie," he whispered. "Forgive me."

As for Viv, he vowed that he would tell her all about Chrissie, his own cowardice, and his abandonment of his best friend. After all, she had a right to know what kind of a yellow-bellied shit he was. For the past three years, he had deceived himself by constantly making Justin a scapegoat ... Now he was looking beyond his own suffering. The stirring in his heart over the past few weeks was still present. For the first time in his adult life, he transcended himself and began to pray.

God, I don't know if you exist, and I'm not asking for proof. What I am asking for is the strength to face Justin with truth and honesty.

———————

Once again Justin had woken in a sweat. Since that day it had happened whenever he slept. The nightmare he had just awakened from had found him alone in a desert weakened without water. Every time Justin had tried to stand the sand would separate, leaving him drowning in it. A hand always helped him out, pulling him loose, though he was never able to identify its owner. The hand might well be that of God, but even with his help Justin still failed to put his past behind him. Even though he had been saved, he was never left feeling happy or liberated. He was still thirsty. Justin knew the dream symbolised his inability to move on. Now pushing his face down into the pillow, he tried to force out any negative images from his tired brain. This didn't work.

Turning on the bedside lamp, he noticed the clock and couldn't believe that it was midnight. Searching in his bag for a smoke, he remembered they were in his coat, which was hanging by the front door. At times like these, a cigarette helped to steady his nerves. As a medic, he knew that physically they had no value in helping a person to relax, but psychologically, he believed they helped stabilise him in the short term. Making his way downstairs, trying not to make a noise, he put his coat on and took out his cigarettes. Stepping out into a cold night, he decided to take a short walk in order to keep warm. There was a lack of stars as the clouds hid them from view. On finishing his cigarette, he headed back towards Tom's house. Stopping outside for one last look, he noticed a figure sat in a car directly opposite. Justin nodded to the figure, but there was no response. Shutting the door behind him, Justin made his way towards the kitchen to get a glass of water. Then he would try to sleep again. On entering the kitchen, he could hear loud snoring. There was Tom fast asleep with his head on the table and leaning heavily to his right-hand side. His precarious position meant he was close to falling off the chair. Justin smiled, remembering the countless tricks they had played on each other over the years. In the past, Tom would have been frightened half to death by now with Justin shouting in his ear, laughing hysterically.

After having made them both a cup of tea, Justin woke Tom by gently prodding his right shoulder.

"I didn't put sugar in it. I expect you still don't use it," said Justin, passing Tom a cup.

"That's right," replied Tom. "What time is it?"

"It's half past twelve," Justin said.

Both sat in silence concentrating on drinking their tea. They didn't feel as awkward as four hours previously. Neither had the strength nor inclination to start tackling the issues of that day, at least not for tonight.

"Did you manage to sleep?" asked Tom.

"On and off," he replied.

"Do you fancy a nightcap?"

"I reckon that's a very good idea," replied Justin.

Both began sharing memories of their times together where scotch had been the fuel for the night. It had always been an icebreaker, a kind of cleansing agent for them. Although best friends they had never been sentimental. Many a time they had argued, sometimes fiercely, yet they had always managed to settle their differences, usually around a bottle of scotch. Continuing to sit in silence, both were remembering days they had spent together.

Holding out his glass towards Justin, Tom wished him good health. "Let's hope we can find closure over the next day or two," he said.

Wanting to tell him where to go, Justin refrained from doing so. "Yes, let's hope we do," he replied.

As he raised his glass back in recognition, Justin had an overwhelming urge to ask Tom about his new girlfriend. The way he was feeling he wanted to tell Tom that he was abandoning his wife's memory. He once again refrained from opening his mouth. Justin was glad that he didn't have a partner, as it would only be one more added pressure. Anyway, no woman in her right mind would go within a thousand miles of such a miserable bastard. Justin managed a dry smile.

Tom noticed this and asked, "What's amusing you?"

"Oh, nothing," replied Justin.

"It didn't look like nothing," said Tom.

Sensing Tom's insecurity, Justin said, "I was thinking that if I had a girlfriend then the poor woman would have to be extremely desperate or classified insane to take me on."

It was now Tom's turn to smile. Deciding to risk the moment, he began telling Justin a little about Viv. His vibrancy was plain to see. Talking about her made him much more animated. There was genuine feeling in his words. It had been the same when Nina was alive.

"I hope in time you can accept her as a friend," said Tom.

Working hard at holding back his anger, Justin privately conceded that Viv was likely to be a good person. But at this time, Justin couldn't look too far into the future; he was having enough problems dealing with the present. Not wanting to either confirm or dismiss Tom's hopes, Justin changed the subject by asking him about his work. According to Tom, it was a refreshing change to be on the shop floor fixing things instead of managing products and people. The money was less than he had become accustomed to, but this didn't bother him, having made a large profit on the sale of his house in London and Chrissie's business. He could afford not to work. Ever since being a child, Tom had always taken things apart and enjoyed rebuilding them. This reminded Justin of the time his friend had managed to acquire an old blue disabled car and turned it into a very efficient go-kart. They were now both laughing together for the first time in three years. Quietness descended as they sipped their whisky, slowly savouring its flavour. Words had deserted them for the moment. It was late, maybe time to say goodnight and resume their journey in the morning, hopefully in good heart. After finishing their nightcap, Tom suggested that they try to get some sleep. Wanting another cigarette before he retired, Justin made his way to the front of the house.

"You can smoke inside," said Tom.

"Thanks, but I'd like to grab some air," replied Justin.

Both smiled, agreeing that it was somewhat ironic that Justin was filling his lungs with toxic fumes at the same time as wanting some fresh air.

"Good night. I'll see you in the morning. I hope you sleep well," Tom said as he climbed the stairs.

"Thanks, you too," replied Justin, who was taking the latch off the front door ready to step outside.

Finishing his smoke, he locked the door, went to the bathroom, cleaned his teeth, and then climbed back into bed.

Sunday

"Sign here. You're in court on January 14," said the desk sergeant, handing Ken his belongings.

Ken grabbed hold of his possessions and walked out of Dundee Police Station. He took a taxi to Forfar and asked the driver to drop him at the house where he and Viv had spent the last seven years. Once again he would try to get her to see things his way.

She must be able to see how much I love her. Tom needs to understand that he's nothing but a distraction for Viv.

That was it. He would make sure Viv listened to him, and he would not leave until she admitted that the thing with Tom was only a fling, like it was with him and Gemma. Ken's thoughts were burning a hole in his head. It was as though he had been baptised by a hateful energy that was telling him his actions were good and that in time Viv would recognise this. Banging hard on the door of his house, he shouted Viv's name, calling her to open the door as they needed to talk. After two minutes he realised that she wasn't there.

Tom, the bastard, he thought, while walking away to collect his car from the hotel car park.

Rather than go straight to Tom's house he parked up and walked into the Dog Inn. He ordered a pint of lager and proceeded to take large gulps. The beer was soon finished. He ordered another and quickly downed it all the while obsessing about Tom. His life was now defined by how and where he should confront Tom. There were no other concerns. Sitting upright, he rigorously tapped his feet. The beat was not musical; there was no timing, just the pounding of irritation mirroring his agitated mind. Laughing loudly, the type that always brought attention, Ken licked his lips, trying to rid himself of a dry mouth. Oblivious to his surroundings, he wrung his hands together as though holding back energy that if let loose would blow away all in its path. The sad thing was that Ken didn't care – he was not able to care. Some people would think that he was insane. Whatever the diagnosis, Ken was a ticking bomb that had lost all perspective, a callous bastard that seemingly enjoyed hurting people. A deep feeling of loathing was leading him to a place of no return. This made him dangerous. Revenge was not only sweet; it was a necessity for him. It seemed nothing and no one could stop him seeking revenge and harvesting his crop. The only thing occupying his thoughts was Tom's shouts of mercy that would surely come when he eventually made his move.

Even a night in the cells couldn't dampen his hatred of Tom. His life was falling apart, but he didn't connect this with his own malevolence. There were two ways of dealing with those who got in his way, hurt or hurt them harder.

Leaving the pub, Ken made his way to his car and began driving. Making a right turn, he manoeuvred his car along Castle Street. It was there that he spotted the meathead who had given him a bloody nose the previous night walking alone no more than twenty yards away. The opportunity had arrived. Ken felt a surge of elation running through his body. The physical pain he had suffered from the earlier beating seemed to disappear. It was as though he had suddenly been injected with a large dose of morphine. Nothing mattered more to Ken than revenge.

He's by himself. Perfect. I'll have him now, Ken thought.

Pulling over, Ken watched Johnson turn left onto Queen Street, a long, thin, quiet road populated by small businesses and residential houses. Ken was following on foot at a distance when the Knuckle suddenly stopped outside the tavern on the corner of Canmore Street as though he was thinking about going in. Instead, he continued to walk slowly on and then took a left onto Green Street. Ken was now euphoric. He quickened his step as he did not want to lose his prey. As he turned onto Green Street, he was taken by surprise and knocked off his stride. The Knuckle was ready and waiting for him. Johnson lifted Ken off his feet and threw him to the ground. The Knuckle then put his right foot across Ken's throat, which immediately rendered Ken incapable.

"Now then, what've we got here? I think it might be a maggot! What shall I do with it? Maybe I should crush it. No, I'm in a generous mood today. Take this as a warning. If I catch you within a hundred yards of me again, you will be eating hospital food for a very long time, and it'll be pureed because you'll have no fucking teeth left. Do I make myself clear?"

The Knuckle released his foot a little off Ken's throat.

"Yes," gasped Ken.

At this, Johnson pressed his foot down even harder into Ken's throat. Close to passing out, Ken provided no struggle. He couldn't move. He could only suffer the humiliation of once again being outmuscled by a much younger and much stronger man.

"Now fuck off back to your nursing home before I really lose my temper," shouted Johnson, releasing his foot.

Lying there disgraced, Ken couldn't stop coughing. He gasped for air, his stomach aching so much that he was close to retching. It seemed to take an age before he started feeling normal again. A passer-by enquired as to whether he was all right. Instead of thanking her for her concern, Ken looked through steely eyes and gave an unfriendly growl. Looking up, he saw Johnson take a right turn into Wellbraehead.

"Bastard!" Ken kept repeating. He wanted to shout it out, but his larynx was too sore. Holding his throat, he began the lonely walk back to his car. It felt to him like the walk of shame. There were no tears just a mind full of hatred and spite.

"You look terrible," said Alistair. "Have you been crying?"

"I'm okay," Gemma said, struggling to hold back her tears.

Knowing from the beginning that only heartache would come from her liaison with Ken, Alistair was worrying about her. No stranger to such things, sadly he had seen it all before. Having worked in the pub business for years, he had observed the highs and lows of human existence, recognising the good from the bad, the kind from the unkind, and the humane from the inhumane. Always wary of Ken, Alistair had thought him bad, unkind, and downright spiteful. Not that he would necessarily relay this to him. Although Alistair was no mug when it came to using fists, he sensed something dark about Ken, a darkness that had no compassion. It would not surprise him if Ken finished up behind bars for a long time.

I did try to warn Gemma, but she fell in love. She was taken in by his charm, smarmy bastard.

Looking over at Alistair, Gemma smiled. *I'm so lucky having a good boss. He always looks out for me.*

Calling her over to him, he reached out and gave her a strong hug.

"If you ever need to talk you know where I am," said Alistair.

"Thanks," she replied.

Busy pulling pints at the other side of the bar when Knuckle Johnson walked into the Boar with his two mates in tow, Gemma initially didn't take much notice of them. It was only when they started laughing and joking about some tit of a Glaswegian that Knuckle had hammered the night before and earlier that afternoon that she started paying attention. She could see that Alistair was trying to placate them. He knew Knuckle well, having served in the Grenadier Guards with the boy's father. Many had also feared the father. Thankfully, Alistair had always managed to keep on his good side.

"You seem pleased with yourself," said Alistair.

"Aye," laughed Knuckle, "I am. We finished up in the cells again last night. We were completely wasted. It took six of the filth to arrest us."

The two heavies with him began laughing.

"What about that idiot from Glasgow, the one you head- butted. He was lucky not to suffer even more. Pillock," laughed Lard-Arse. "We taunted him throughout the night. He had to be put in a cell away from us."

"Who might that be?" asked Alistair, thinking it sounded like Ken.

"I've seen him in here before," said the third thug whose name Alistair didn't know.

"That's why we're here," said Knuckle. "We feel like a bit of sport."

"Not in here, lads, if you don't mind. If he does walk in, I don't want any trouble. I've a business to run," said Alistair.

"It sounds like you know him," said Lard-Arse.

"I'm just saying I don't want any trouble. Your dad and me go back a long way," said Alistair, looking directly at Knuckle.

"Aye, okay, but I want to know if he comes in here," he replied. "Come on, lads; let's finish our pints and go."

Once they had left the pub, Alistair began breathing again. In some ways, he hoped the three of them did find Ken and give him a good kicking.

Although she had been at the other end of the bar, Gemma had heard the conversation. Like Alistair, she surmised they must have been talking about Ken.

"How're you feeling?" asked Alistair. "You never know; it might be somebody else those meatheads were describing."

"I doubt it," said Gemma. "What have I done wrong, Alistair?"

Shaking his head, Alistair wished she had never met Ken.

"Now you listen to me. You're not the first to fall for the old story about how the lover's wife didn't understand him. There are probably thousands if not millions of women throughout the world that have questioned themselves as to what it was they did that turned their lover against them. It's times like these that I'm ashamed to be a man. I blame myself for not telling you to stay away from him in the beginning. I think he's mentally ill. I may as well tell you now. Last night he punched a fella here in the pub. You need to keep your wits about you."

"Do you think he's gone back to Viv?" asked Gemma passively.

"I don't know, but it's unlikely. I may as well say it. I really don't know what Viv or you see in him. He has a violent past from what I gather."

"It's the same old story. At first he was good fun, but now I don't even like him."

"You've enough to think about," said Alistair, pointing at Gemma's stomach.

———————

Gemma stopped talking when she heard a couple of customers walk in to the pub.

"What would you like she asked

"Two pints," said the taller of the two pointing to the cask ale.

Not being able to stop thoughts of Ken flooding her mind she hoped his wife would take him back. That way he would be sure to leave her alone.

It was ghastly to feel imprisoned. Living in Forfar had been good until Ken had entered her life. The majority of her friends lived close by, but these days she hardly ever saw them. The nights out she'd enjoyed with them had suddenly stopped until she was spending all her spare time with Ken or waiting to see him. It was only recently that she'd realised he had changed her. She hadn't felt guilty about starting a relationship with him, especially after being fed stories about Viv not understanding him and her blatant nastiness when it came to children. Reassessing this position, Gemma now wondered how Viv had managed to stay with him all those years. At the time of meeting him, Gemma couldn't believe that a good-looking, seemingly thoughtful man had wanted her. Loneliness had interfered with her judgement, and soon she had been powerless to stop her longing for him. After her experience with Ken she could empathise with the many mistresses throughout the world who were feeling exposed and used by their lover's lies. In the beginning, he had seemed full of life and made Gemma laugh. If she could have a penny for all those times women had fallen for such deception this year alone, then she would be a very wealthy woman. What a bloody fool she had been.

Ken was staring at Tom's house. Earlier he'd wanted to knock on the door but hadn't been sure about the person currently staying with Tom. Part of him didn't care, as he felt confident that he could see them both off. His ego was telling him that he was impregnable. Not acknowledging that he was getting older, Ken failed to see that he was living on his past reputation and victories. But no matter what he thought, he was getting older and slowing down, weakening physically. The episode with Knuckle Johnson was a case in point. Egotists never recognised their own demise. They failed to sense danger, as witnessed in Ken's dismissal of what he saw as the two idiots in the house opposite. How could Ken know Justin's fighting capabilities? Many men had been left hurt and embarrassed by such poor judgement.

The night was turning very cold, not that Ken noticed. Outside of his car, the temperature dropped to below freezing. Nothing entered his mind these days other than his loathing for Tom. Tapping his fingers on the dashboard, opposite his nemesis, he became ever more excited at the prospect of victory.

I wonder what Tom's doing. Viv's car isn't here. Should I knock on his door again and offer him out? Ken thought.

Sitting cobra-like in silence, holding perfectly still, he was ready to strike. Although getting older, he was still dangerous, an avenging angel that was fortified and, in his mind, morally justified. In Ken's eyes this was a righteous crusade. His confidence was growing by the second. There was nobody capable of stopping him. By getting rid of Tom, Viv would in time appreciate his actions and understand them for what they were – an act of love. Falling at his feet, she would beg forgiveness for her infidelity with fat boy. Any boundaries of human decency left in Ken had by now been dismantled, smashed down by his possessed mind. He gave no thought as to whether he had gone too far. He had no awareness of the way his eyes were scurrying from left to right. The dice had been well and truly cast. Time no longer existed in Ken's world. Sitting in the same position for many hours, he was living within the confines of his obsessions. Only when he saw the lights go out in Tom's house did he become aware of his surroundings.

Where can I go now? If only I had a key to my house, I could crash out there. Why have I been so soft and allowed Viv to walk all over me? It's not as though Viv's staying there much. She's usually here at Tom's house. I need to sort this out.

Like an admonished child, he had placidly handed over his key when Viv initially had turned up at Tom's house. He hated himself for that.

Have I not been a good husband? Did I not support her at kick-boxing competitions? Have I not shown my loyalty? This is the thanks I receive for all the miles I've driven.

Now shivering through a combination of rage and cold, he would have to make a move soon. He thought about going home. If Viv wasn't there, he would break in. The filth wouldn't arrest him for this; it was his house, and they wouldn't know that Viv had thrown him out. If they turned up, then he would apologise for the disturbance, telling them that he had lost his key. It was either smash the back-door window at his house or go to the hotel again. That was the nearest, but it wasn't ideal. If Gemma hadn't changed the locks, he could have gone there. Mind you, she got on his nerves in every possible way. She was always tired. She was a whiner. She had also wrecked his marriage. Between them, Gemma and Tom had ruined his life.

What the hell does Viv see in Tom? He doesn't have my looks or physique.

In truth, Ken might feel a little less humiliated if she had gone off with a younger version of him, maybe somebody from the kick-boxing club. At least it would have shown the world that she had wanted a real man with strength and power. Instead, not only had she dishonoured him by having an affair, she had picked Tom, a middle-aged, ugly, fat bastard. Ken didn't deserve the aggravation Tom was causing him.

Ken had to make a decision as to where he would stay tonight. He could remain where he was, but it was getting colder as the night passed. If he was to stay, he could knock on Tom's door in the morning and see if he wanted to play out. That sounded appealing. Finding this thought amusing, he sniggered out loud, his eyes still rapidly darting from side to side. He was becoming more excited at the thought of breaking into Tom's house and wondered about waiting in the kitchen where he would greet him in the morning. That would definitely make Tom edgy. Ken got out of his car and walked to the back of Tom's house. He climbed over the wall and made a beeline for the door. He was out of luck. Even Tom was not stupid enough to leave it unlocked. It was the same with the kitchen window and the downstairs back room. Not having any success, Ken felt deflated. His adrenaline began to subside, giving way to the bitter cold of the night.

There's nothing else for it. I'll have to go to the hotel, he thought.

Walking back to his car, he took one last look around. The disappointment was acute as he was beginning to like the idea of hiding in Tom's house. What fun he could have had.

———

Once again Gemma woke up. This time she had experienced a sudden sinking feeling in the pit of her stomach after having once more dreamt about Ken. The dream had reminded her of the good times – the fun times, the planning ahead, and the laughter. Thankfully she brought herself out from these thoughts.

What's that about? she thought.

Remembering the way Ken had been treating her recently soon made her come to her senses. The thought of him near her now made her skin crawl. How things had changed. Gemma winced with fear when she recalled the times Ken had rummaged through her fridge. In the near future, she was hoping to move, having put her name forward for one of the social housing schemes on the north side of Forfar. Her first choice was for a house, but wasn't sure whether she would be allocated one. The scheme was likely to offer her a two-bedroom flat, which of course she would accept. Neither career minded nor a high earner, Gemma hadn't obtained any qualifications throughout her life. She had been a barmaid for the majority of her employment, a job which she still loved. It didn't pay well, so her options for moving would be limited. Her savings were very little.

She shuddered when remembering one of her last encounters with Ken. Lying in bed, she had been able to hear him banging around in the living room. She'd feared that he would turn nasty. He had been talking to himself, but it had seemed unintelligible, more a type of noise than words. The thought of him in her flat had been unbearable. Pulling the duvet over her head, she had attempted to block out the noise. She'd touched her stomach, worrying for her unborn baby, and had vowed that she would keep the maniac away from her child. Gemma hoped that in time he would refuse to have anything to do with the baby.

Justin woke with a start, again having experienced one of the four recurring nightmares. The black dog had visited him again. He'd named these night-by-night visitations after reading about Winston Churchill's battle with bipolar disorder. Though Justin didn't have such a devastating illness, at times his sickness seemed just as debilitating. The nightmares seemed to feed his darkened mood. One such nightmare would see him paralysed and unable to move. There was nobody else near him, only a presence that was malevolent. Justin knew it was there, though it had no shape, no form, and made no noise. The nightmare always saw him gasping for breath when he awoke. Medical professionals explained this as a form of sleep dysfunction, suggesting stress as its root cause. For Justin, experiencing the same nightmares seemed to him symptomatic of his life. Wringing wet, his body was covered from head to toe with sweat. Having failed in his attempt to go back to sleep, he decided to take a shower. Before doing so, he looked in the wardrobe and found some clean sheets. The duvet was too damp to use again. Fortunately, tucked away in the bottom drawer were two blankets. After this nightly visitation, Justin prayed that he wouldn't be disturbed again. Various professionals within the fields of psychiatry and spirituality had spoken at length with him, providing logical answers to his troubles. Unfortunately, up to now, all attempts at helping him to stop these visitations had failed. There was no doubt they related directly to his killing of Nina. If he and Tom could work through their distress, then maybe his nights could once again become his own. He was desperate and would do almost anything if it meant sleeping soundly through the night. It was now nearly four in the morning. These nightly showers helped shift his mind away from the nightmares. It was bad enough that Justin had to suffer one of them; he certainly didn't want to dwell on it.

Waiting for the water to warm, Justin's thoughts shifted to the other female love of his life, Poppy.

I wouldn't have done what I did if you'd still been with me. You brought common sense to my impulses. You pulled me back when I was stupid. I still love you.

The day Poppy had broken the news of an affair with her economics lecturer had come out of the blue. Their liaison had been so secretive that none of his or her friends and family had had any notion that it was taking place. It had been going on for twelve months. Twelve months where Poppy had been able to fool him. Justin had felt stupid. He couldn't understand how the affair had eluded him. She hadn't been distant. They had continued living as normal. The moment when she'd told him still felt as if it was only yesterday. Such had been the shock. The breathlessness of truth had left him silent as she'd walked out of his life forever.

Standing outside the shower cubicle in his brother-in-law's bathroom, Justin wasn't sure whether these memories of Poppy were cathartic or heartbreaking. Once Poppy had left, he had withdrawn his romantic heart from the world, refusing the love of women that he had known or of those he would meet in the future. The many evenings he had spent with Nina and Tom and one of their eligible female friends were too numerous to count. According to Nina some of these women had been perfect and had shown clear feelings towards him, feelings he had ignored to the bemusement of his sister.

"You're a stubborn one, Justin. What's wrong with you? Don't you think it's time to move on? Poppy has gone, and she's never coming back," she had so often told him.

No matter how much Nina had encouraged him to find another girlfriend, the loss of Poppy could never be extricated from his heart.

"One day you'll wake up to find you are a lonely old man with a life that is almost over," she had said.

This had amused Justin at the time. He had tried to explain to Nina and Tom that his work and faith would become his new lover. "It's like the girl during wartime whose sweetheart is serving overseas, and she receives news that he has been killed. She makes the decision never to become engaged or to marry. Is she wasting her life?"

"But Poppy's not dead," Nina had said.

"I know, but if I can't have Poppy I don't want anybody. She took my heart, and I can't give it to another. Please leave me alone. I don't want to be with somebody I can't give myself fully to. I don't think that's wrong. I would call it sensible. Why would I give somebody false hope?" he had replied.

His faith had seen him through the heartache with Poppy, and being a bachelor hadn't been all that bad. He had been able to throw himself into his work. His life had been full and his work fulfilling. Five years down the line he still felt the same for her, although he knew she had gone. He didn't live his life pining for her. Poppy was still alive, living somewhere near Oxford, but was dead to him in that he would never again share her tears, hear her breath, or hold her tight. She hadn't even bothered writing to him during his time in prison or sought to find out how he was. He still wanted her. If she turned up out of the blue, he would be there with open arms. Yet Justin knew that life wasn't black and white. His experience as a GP had taught him that much at least. There was more chance of Nina being resurrected from the dead than Poppy ever knocking on his door. Poppy had gone. But it was different with his sister; he still hadn't learned to let her go.

Stepping into the shower cubicle, Justin's thoughts shifted to Nina. Although his love for her was infinite, her disdain for his beliefs still cut deep into his soul. By the time he'd been studying medicine at Cardiff University she had been entering her final year at the University of Sussex. Growing up, both had attended mass, but her three years as an undergraduate had changed her view of the universe. This included refuting religion as nothing more than superstition. For her, it had been both subjective and incompatible with development and change. It had become her task to expose the myths of religion by pointing out to those who had ears that as a paradigm it was dying. The heavy burden of history was catching up with all its lies and deceit. Religion had been exposed and debunked as primarily a tool to enslave individuality.

"That's hardly an original thought," Justin had countered. "It's easy to point the finger. If you want to play that game, what about you scientists working for the pharmaceutical companies making drugs that are useless? As Dylan said, dealing drugs that will never cure your ills. It's that old chestnut again. Religion equals corruption. You can swap religion for any other individual or institution in the world and get the same results."

"That might be the case, but at least science doesn't claim to be pure," Nina had said.

"No, but it still claims to hold truth. Anyway, you know I agree that religion is, in itself, unhealthy. Faith is different."

Until that awful day three years previously, Justin had regularly studied the scriptures, and his inflections had led him to believe that the person of Jesus was God and certainly had a few things to say that were still relevant to the world. No matter how much Nina had tried to persuade him that faith wasn't rational, Justin continued to search for meaning through his Christian faith.

Soaping his body and feeling the freshness of running water, he remembered arguing vehemently with Nina that the one they called Christ offered something different for the world. The simplicity of Christ's message had been missed on her, and no amount of Justin's explaining had made her look afresh at spirituality and faith.

"You don't need religion to have a moral code," she had said.

"No, you don't," Justin had agreed. "But the expectation that Christ has of his followers is to be brave enough to start again and leave behind learned prejudices and predilection in judging others. Now science doesn't ask you to search deep within yourself to make oneself a better person so that you can then help to create a better world, a better mindset. The world of the scientist is external."

"What you've just said is shite, and you know it," she had replied.

"Well, the world is such a safer place with scientists at its helm," Justin had said exasperated. "We've got bombs built by scientists pointing at each other just waiting to obliterate the world. That's real nice work, isn't it?"

From an early age, Justin had been interested in spiritual disciplines, having read books on all the major religions. He felt an affinity to the Dali Lama's questioning of why a westerner would wish to become a Buddhist. The holy one had suggested that the individual might want to study and embrace the faith that had informed his or her own society. This view fascinated Justin, encouraging him to examine scripture and the lives of the saints. For him, the spiritual history of the church offered a unique diversity ranging from the contemplative to the charismatic.

"You never understood my beliefs, did you, Nina?" said Justin under his breath.

Spitting out the running water from his mouth, Justin remembered Nina's words.

"How can somebody as intelligent as you support an institution that has caused havoc and hurt throughout the world? At least science is trying to build a better world."

"You mean like nerve gas."

"No, I mean like medical breakthroughs. If it was left to the church, we'd still be using dock leaves to heal scabs," she had said.

"That's your problem, sis. All your grievances are around the role of religion in the history of the world. I know the havoc caused by religion across the globe, not only culturally but also on an individual level. Christian institutions can no longer defend their actions as can corrupt scientific institutions. I agree with you. I'm no apologist for sickening crimes perpetrated by religion in the name of God. Their ungodly acts are now biting it well and truly on the backside, and their sins are there for all to see."

"Sin, sin, sin. That's another bit of bullshit. It serves no purpose other than to either turn people off or to frighten them."

"Before you say it, no, I can't quantify sin. But what I can say is it is that place in the heart which needs revising. Sin is the action that hurts people and that part of the personality which is malicious. Jesus can bring change. He is change."

"Here we go again," Nina had said. "It's worse than psychobabble. There's no credence to your argument."

His knowledge of scripture had helped him to point out many passages in the New Testament where Jesus had rebuked those passing judgement.

"See, you're just as bad. You're always passing judgement on my beliefs," Justin had argued. "No matter what you say about my beliefs, I like the idea that God in the person of Jesus was prepared to live among the depths of depravity while also experiencing the heights of human joyfulness. The gospels are testimony to this. You know, sis, no amount of suffering is lost on God, and no amount of laughter could ever be too loud. God is interested in the smallness of humanity, the happy, the sad, those with direction, and those that have lost their way. He's interested in everyone, including you!"

A smile came across Justin's face. He could feel it. It lifted his spirit. He remembered the look Nina had given him. She had nodded her head in frustration and asked him if he had wanted to go to the pub. Of course he had, and for the rest of the evening they had discussed family matters.

"Sweet Nina," Justin said as he felt the water roll down his chest and towards his legs.

His mind shifted from memory to memory. The last day Justin had spent at the seminary was now firmly in the forefront of his mind. It had been an emotional day. Central to Justin's spiritual formation had been Fr Hennessey. On that last day, Fr Hennessey had taken Justin aside and presented him with a copy of the Divine Office, reiterating the importance of exegesis.

"Remember, Justin, reading the Bible without reflection or the aid of scholarly interpretation is tantamount to a crime. And interpreting the text literally will always provide a backdrop for misunderstanding leading to a lack of love. And that, my son, is the polar opposite of Christian teaching. Don't ever forget that love brings with it much pain. Spirituality is not for the faint-hearted. It is a tough journey calling for the submission of self to the will of God. I wish you well in your new venture. You'll make a great doctor. Oh, and keep your mind on God."

The water had now washed away any semblance of soap from Justin's body.

"You were a quality person," Justin said, thinking about Fr Hennessey. "I wish I could speak to you now."

Re-soaping his body, Justin was feeling warm under the water. Mentally, he was battling the feeling of anger towards Tom. Washing the soap out of his eyes with the running water, his mind turned to the day he'd taken his sister's life.

How many others who have lost a loved one have lost their faith? I certainly have. How many have found faith? Some certainly have. How many individuals continue to say their prayers, all the while remaining angry that God has taken their loved ones? Probably too many to count, thought Justin.

Thrusting his face under the water, feeling it rhythmically fall down from his forehead, invading his eyes, nose, and mouth, did nothing to wash his pain away. People still couldn't grasp that when talking about going against his beliefs he meant going against his very nature, the stuff that made Justin Ivens the unique individual that he was. No matter how much he tried to resurrect himself, Justin was no longer that person of faith and hope; he remained dead, as dead as his treasured Nina. It disturbed him that the term 'assisted suicide' was just another brand name that sanitised the act of killing. Justin never wanted another person to have to go through the turmoil he had suffered.

Spitting out water from his mouth, Justin was feeling sad and tearful. The general public's lack of engagement in defining the direction of a nation worried him. Their manipulation would be easy by presenting opinion polls as a true reflection of a nation's thoughts. In effect, the nation might be handing over power to those who really didn't give a fuck. Or to those that had business interests in death.

Shaking the water from his head, he turned his back to the tap. Sighing loudly, he was once again concerned about society's acceptance of state killing. *The eugenics movement is as active as ever and claiming support across all the political divides. They'll continue to knock on the door of public policy, and without a strong opposition there could be a move towards the extreme. Who will be the next to die, the disabled, the old, the unemployed? History is just another process from which the human race has learned absolutely nothing.*

Switching off the shower, Justin instantly felt the coldness of the air. His biggest regret was that he could never eradicate the 19th of March 1999 from the record. If Justin had refused Nina's request, she would have continued loving him. Although he would have had to witness the slow awful death of his beautiful sister, he needn't have had to live with this guilt, and undoubtedly, his friendship with Tom would still be intact.

I would still be looking after my patients, he thought.

A feeling of nausea overcame Justin as he recalled the moments before helping Nina escape the humiliation of her inevitable death. It was ironic that twenty minutes earlier he had been attending to a patient. Prior to taking Nina's life, spiritual discipline had been self-explanatory to Justin. Yet on the day of her death, he had stopped seeking the presence of God and abandoned any attempt at prayer. This had resulted in him hearing only the one voice, that of his sister. Even after three years, her cries for deliverance still left Justin unable to justify his actions that day, either as a medic or as a professed Christian. It hurt him that she had dismissed his pleas to abandon her wish; instead, she had continued to ask him to take her life until his resolve had folded.

Justin pulled a towel tight around his body. He acknowledged that it was his responsibility to reconnect with God. God hadn't gone away; Justin's guilt had created the separation, and only he could fix it. He now understood the situation to be like a friend knocking on the door. If Justin kept on refusing to open it, then the friend may become lost forever. Before Nina's passing, Justin had always set aside time for contemplation. Now wishing to resurrect this practice, he would have to start reaching out not only to God but also to others. This would begin by examining his mistrust of people that had developed over the past three years.

Making his way back to the bedroom, he threw himself onto the bed. It was 4.40 in the morning. *There's still time to save myself. There might yet be time to transform into a new Justin Ivens.* Hopefully, this would be an altogether wiser and more compassionate human being. Thankful that Tom had allowed him to release his anger and hurt, Justin was now ready to listen to his friend's story. *How have*

I become so inept at connecting to my problems? Here in the early hours of the morning at his old friend's house, he was now beginning to gain strength. This strength would hopefully help focus him on the issues that he would inevitably face during the second day of his stay with Tom. Not only had Justin lost his raison d'être for engaging in a spiritual life, he had also lost his trust in humanity. Prior to Nina's death these had been the two areas of his life that had kept him positively engaged with the world.

Why have I been so blind?

There was no hiding from it. Justin had lost sight of his God who would demand he forgive his old friend. Over the past three years, he had ingested the darkness of antipathy and the poison of anger. He was now able to see what such poison was doing to him. And it was time to spew this out and begin afresh.

Wide awake, having been disturbed by Justin taking a shower, Tom began thinking about the complexity of his life. Ever since Ken had started to threaten him, he had found it difficult to sleep through the night. Putting a brave face on Ken's shenanigans, Tom tried reassuring himself with the thought that, in time, Ken would disappear into another life. But a creeping feeling remained in Tom's mind that Ken was plotting something. Increasing anxiety was beginning to unsettle him. Negative thoughts attacked his confidence, leading him to think he was about to lose Viv – that she might return to Ken. After all, Tom hardly knew her, and people went back to their partners for many different reasons. Maybe she was using him to get back at Ken for his infidelities.

How many couples over the years have been unfaithful and then gone back to each other?

Tom thought about Chrissie. His need for her had been so great that he would have taken her back if she had been disloyal. There was nothing to say that Viv wouldn't go back to Ken as a way of putting two fingers up at Gemma. Yet the tenderness she'd shown and the fun they'd enjoyed together seemed genuine. If this was not the case, then Viv deserved an Oscar or should be crowned queen of the stage as her performance over the past few days would befit the greatest of actors. If Viv didn't come back, Tom would feel that he was once again bereaved. Wishing it was later in the day with Viv by his side, Tom acknowledged just how needy he was. This was not new; he had always been the same. Early in his relationship with Chrissie she had rightly berated him and refused to accept his hints of jealousy.

"You either sort yourself out or piss off," she had so eloquently said.

Naturally, he'd known he wouldn't be choosing the latter. Trust, according to Chrissie, was a positive pronouncement and not one to be feared. Such insights from her had made him examine his pettiness and over time become a better person.

"Remember," she had said, "the energy jealousy generates not only exhausts the body but also damages the mind."

"You were a genius, Chrissie, a bloody genius." He smiled.

The lessons he'd learned from her were too many to count. What he did know was suffocating the one you love was nothing but a false love.

Lying back down in bed, he closed his eyes but couldn't get back to sleep. Feeling glad that Justin had visited, he told himself that today would be a day where they could help each other. Whether they would actually say what they needed to say, Tom didn't know. What he was hoping for was honesty, although he didn't particularly want a repeat of the previous day when Justin had launched into a tirade of anger. Tom began preparing himself just in case.

I know, he thought. *I'll suggest we go out, maybe visit the Loch of the Lowes.* This was about a twenty-mile drive from Forfar, which would take them past Glamis Castle towards Pittlocry, where the Queen Mother had grown up. In summer, a pair of nesting ospreys lived and bred on the side of its shore. At this time of year any amount of waders could be seen. Knowing how much Justin loved birding, Tom thought this was a good idea. It also made him remember Chrissie, as she had also been a bird lover. When living in London they had spent as much time as possible driving out to the South Downs walking and birdwatching. If Justin didn't feel up to birding, Tom could take him to a local distillery at Fettercairn on the way to Glen Esk where they could enjoy a wee dram. They may as well be outdoors rather than feeling stifled and claustrophobic in the house. He would see what Justin wanted to do.

It seemed pointless to stay in bed now that he couldn't get back to sleep, so Tom got up. It was only five thirty in the morning, but his mind was far too active to rest, so instead of brooding, he made his way downstairs.

It was seven thirty when Ken began stirring. After taking a quick shower he left the hotel room and booked out. He walked into the chill of a November day.

I need to speak to Viv and tell her I want to keep the house. I can't continue living like this. Anyway, we'll need the house when she comes back to me, he thought as he headed towards his car.

Feeling like a refugee, Ken cursed the fact that he had nowhere to go. *What has my life become?* Normally at this time on a Sunday morning he would still be warm, hung-over, and lying next to his wife. *What am I left with now, absolutely nothing? And it isn't my fault.*

Walking into the kitchen, Justin saw Tom sitting at the table. The radio was playing. This made Justin smile, helping him remember happier times. A fan of the radio, he preferred it to the television. On seeing Justin, Tom bid him good morning and offered him a cup of tea. After relaying his plans for the day, Tom asked Justin if he had any objections or preferences. Justin had none. The likelihood of it raining heavily at some point during the day was very high, so Tom advised packing waterproofs.

"I'll drive. I know the roads and of course where we are going," said Tom.

"Thanks. I'll nip to the car and get what I need," replied Justin.

On his way back from the car, Justin heard the sound of a speeding car. As he turned to look, the driver greeted him with a one fingered salute. Puzzled as to the reasons for this, Justin walked into the house and relayed it back to Tom.

"What type of car was it? Was it blue?" asked Tom.

"Yes, a Vauxhall I think," replied Justin.

"It's that idiot Ken." Tom shook his head in exasperation. "He obviously thought you were me."

"I'm not sure why. I'm far too good-looking," laughed Justin. "He definitely has a problem with you, though. I saw him sitting in his car when you went to bed last night. Do you remember, I said I was going out for a smoke? It was a bit disconcerting, as though he was staring at me. I reckon he's dangerous. You want to be careful. I'm not being rude, Tom, but what's this Viv like? Are you sure she's all right? It does leave me wondering, especially being married to an idiot like him."

"Yeah, I can understand your concerns. But trust me she's nothing like him. I can't understand why she was ever with Ken. She really is lovely," reassured Tom.

"I hope she's worth all the aggro," said Justin, relieved that he didn't have to deal with such an unpredictable character.

What a state of affairs. Tom does seem to have genuine feelings for her. I won't raise any more concerns. We've enough with our issues, thought Justin.

"It doesn't mean I've stopped loving Chrissie," Tom suddenly said. "She was my first love and still lives in my heart. I will always love her. That's what's amazing about Viv. She never wants me to forget Chrissie."

"Does she know the situation with you and me?" he asked.

"No, though she knows something hasn't been right between us for the past three years. I wanted to see you first and try to resolve our issues before telling her."

"She might change her mind when she finds out the truth," said Justin.

"That's what's worrying me," Tom replied. "I can only hope she understands."

"We need to do that, understand our own position I mean, and then each other," said Justin.

Both knew that the possibilities of closure and of renewal rested with them seizing the initiative during their time together. Each had his story to tell; each was living his life within distinct intensities of pain. For three years, they had been living with the knowledge that given the opportunity again their choices would be different on the nineteenth day of March 1999.

"I'll tell you, Justin. I contacted you because I was having random thoughts about life and death. Stuff, as you know, I always told you to stop worrying about. Honestly, I've lived the last three years as if Chrissie was still by my side. I keep looking at myself and the way I behaved on that day. It all keeps pressing on my mind. Chrissie is dead, and I've denied her rest. Letting go has proved really difficult for me. That's why I wrote to you. After meeting Viv, which, by the way, was only a few days ago, something began to change inside me. I could taste the sweetness of hope. The more I began thinking about that day, the more you entered into my thoughts. I reached the point where I could no longer avoid responsibility for the damage I'd caused. I needed to tell you how sorry I was for deserting you."

It was taking all of Justin's energy to listen and not retaliate. "Tom, I know I have to forgive you. I too had an epiphany last night while lying in bed. I have to tell you that I've held bitterness towards you and Nina for giving me all the responsibility on that day. It seemed neither of you had given a damn about me, my feelings, my future; all you were bothered about were yourselves. It feels like you and Nina never loved me. Why else would you dump such heavy shit on me?"

"I'm so sorry, Justin. I never really looked at it that way before. I thought if I didn't turn up you would just abandon the plan."

"Come off it Tom, you know what Nina was like. When did she ever take no for an answer? Anyway, you should have tried to stop me. You could have told me what you were thinking. It felt like you were looking after your own arse."

"Honestly, it wasn't like that," said Tom. "I was traumatised. I couldn't move."

"You bottled it. You let me kill your wife. It ain't an excuse thinking I wouldn't carry it out."

Sensing another avalanche of emotion building in Justin, Tom suggested they get ready to go out.

Knuckle Johnson and his two accomplices were having a party that evening to celebrate Lard-Arse's twenty-third birthday before hitting a club in Dundee. They were going to buy some supplies from the supermarket in Forfar. Turning down the aisle marked beers, they started sniggering. There was Ken, and he was a sitting target. Looking at each other, the three thugs knew exactly what they were about to do. Before Ken could defend himself, they had him surrounded.

"Surprise, surprise," shouted Knuckle as he smashed his right fist into the side of Ken's face. "I warned you to stay away."

Staggering backwards, Ken was not able to retaliate as all three began landing kicks all over his body. Shielding his head, he rolled himself into the shape of a threatened hedgehog. After a few more seconds, the beating stopped, leaving him concussed. He was bleeding from his right ear, nose, and mouth, and pain was raging throughout his body. Every time he tried to inhale, a sharp pain stabbed him around his ribcage. Managing to stumble back to his car, Ken refused all help from staff and concerned passers-by. Even the beating he had just taken taught him nothing; he didn't question the dreadfulness of violence or the senselessness and brutality of it. Instead, he was already devising ways to deal with his assailants after he had sorted Tom out. Manoeuvring his car seat, he lay back for twenty minutes contemplating whether he should go to hospital. There was nowhere else to go. Driving would be sore but not impossible, although his ribs were still sore and the pain in his ear was making him flinch. Walking into the Ninewells accident and emergency department, he counted seven people that were already waiting for treatment. After providing his details he made his way to a seat. Closing his eyes, he resigned himself to a long wait.

———————

As he turned onto the A90 heading northwards, Tom was thinking about all the great advantages of living in Scotland.

"I love the scenery around here. They've got good ale as well. But the best of all is the lack of traffic," said Tom.

"Do you remember London? It was a nightmare trying to get across the city," said Justin.

By accident Tom pressed his foot on the accelerator a little too heavily, making Justin jolt forward.

"Sorry about that," apologised Tom. "So tell me, Justin, what do you do if you're not working?"

For a second Justin felt defensive. *What a stupid question. I'm surviving, you idiot, no thanks to you.*

Rather than answering the question, Justin explained how life without his beloved medicine seemed futile. The loss of his vocation was like an extra bereavement. Being a doctor was more than treating ailments; he had become involved in problem-solving with his patients and had learned to listen. Often the best medicine had been encouraging patients to express themselves. He had loved his job and now missed it beyond comprehension.

"Can you imagine how I feel no longer being able to practice?" asked Justin.

"Knowing you well, I believe I can."

Driving further along, surrounded by the beauty of a Scottish landscape, they were beginning to rebuild their friendship, albeit slowly. They knew it. They sensed it.

"I couldn't sleep last night," remarked Tom. "I kept thinking about that day, questioning whether assisted suicide is wrong. I still don't think it is, Justin. What was wrong was my selfishness in wanting to keep Chrissie alive. I couldn't bear the thought of her never being there for me. The mess I've caused. How has it come to this? We were so close me and you, closer than brothers. It would be laughable if it wasn't so tragic. One death has affected so much. It's time to drive out that day and banish its sinister influence over us forever."

"You're not wrong there, my mate," replied Justin.

After an evening and a few hours of a new day they were talking to each other again in a deeper way. The anger was still within them and the feelings of loss for both men still sharp enough to cut deeply, but together they were confronting their demons. It didn't go unnoticed by Tom that Justin had just called him mate.

"What I did was wrong," Justin said. "I still believe that. I know you have the opposite view. I said it yesterday; you should have helped Nina die, not me."

"I know," admitted Tom.

Conversation became sporadic, but at least they had started to express themselves through admitting their failings and discussing the distress each had inflicted on the other.

"Do you think you might find some work?" enquired Tom.

"I'm going to need a job at some point. I can't work in medicine or the caring services, but I have been offered some lecturing hours at University College London. The trouble is I don't particularly want to move back down south. I was approached by a publishing house while in prison, but I told them where to go. There's nothing to celebrate in what I did, and in no way do I want to sensationalise or trivialise it. I won't make money out of people's misery."

"I was approached about writing a book too. I used stronger language than you, though," remarked Tom.

Continuing to talk both stated they would never forget Christina, although they confessed that their lives had reached the point where they wanted to lose the pain caused by that day.

"What do you fancy doing, walking in the Cairngorms or visiting a distillery?" asked Tom.

"Do you really need to ask?"

"Is there anything I can do to help you in the future?" asked Tom sincerely.

"Seeing as you and Nina ruined my life, maybe get me a new one. Failing that, how about getting my job back for me?" replied Justin sarcastically suddenly switching back into his angry self.

Continuing to drive, Tom remained quiet, allowing Justin time to calm down.

After several minutes of silence, Tom turned to Justin and said, "You have to believe you can be reborn; otherwise you may as well give up and go back to Lancashire. Hell, Justin, you're the one that used to talk about faith."

"It's okay for you. You're not a killer," he retorted.

"Why do you keep saying you've killed Chrissie? You helped her to move on. Killing suggests something sinister, dark, and calculating. Many would believe you to be a rescuer, not a murderer. Can't you see that helping Chrissie was an act of bravery on your part? It was a selfless act. It helped the most important person in your life to be free from humiliation and self-disgust," pleaded Tom.

"Yes, but at what price? I've suffered for what I did ever since. Anyway, no matter how much you try to present it, I did kill her. It's as simple as that. I stuck a needle in her arm and pressed down the syringe," replied Justin. "If that's not killing, then I don't know what is. Don't keep trying to dress it up as some kind of great humanitarian act. I didn't save Chrissie; I took her life."

"Not in the way you think. Stop saying it like that. You helped her pass on," Tom said.

"I killed her!" shouted Justin.

"For God's sake, Justin, stop persecuting yourself," pleaded Tom.

Tom swerved suddenly to avoid knocking down a pheasant that was staring up at him in mortal fear. Thankfully, his turn of the wheel prevented such a needless end.

"Shit, that was close!" shouted Tom.

"You're not joking. They're not the brightest cookies, are they?" said Justin.

Tom didn't reply, waiting for his breath to come back.

"Anyway," Justin said, "no matter what you say, I killed your wife, my sister."

"We're going round in circles," said Tom.

"Where else is there to go?" replied Justin.

As Tom indicated right into the Fettercairn distillery, both were hoping they might be able to purchase some food and then go on the tour. Removing the car keys from the ignition, Tom could sense Justin's discomfort. Once more there was a period of silence. Tom could smell Justin's breath; it reeked of stale tobacco.

"Why did you betray me, Tom?"

Tom wanted to deflect the question as he thought he'd already given his answer. Yet inside, he knew that he had to expand on the reasons he'd already given. After all, this was the reason why he had invited Justin in the first place. The truth would out at any cost. It therefore needed deconstructing before answers could be sought.

"As I've already explained Justin, I was scared and angry that Chrissie was no longer with me. I felt confused and needed to blame somebody for her death. You have to accept what I'm saying. I didn't initially intend throwing you to the wolves. It's just that as the court case proceeded, I became more heartbroken and wanted to see you pay." Holding his head down, Tom couldn't look at the man he had betrayed.

Staring intently at him, Justin was not sure whether he could forgive Tom for such disloyalty. But he knew he had to. God was asking him to search his heart; he also knew that Chrissie was demanding it. And in truth, Justin missed Tom deeply. With these thoughts attacking his consciousness, Justin walked away from the car, asking Tom not to follow him. He took slow, measured footsteps towards the grassy area. For now he couldn't bear to look at Tom.

Frozen to his seat, Tom was speechless. Throughout his friendship with Justin he had been fiercely loyal to his friend. Yet on the day he needed to show this, self-preservation had seen him undertake an act which had not only been harmful to Justin but also to himself. After all, Tom had only needed to give support to his friend and to tell the truth about him. This he had failed to do. His disloyalty was there for all to see. He, like Justin, could never be the same person again.

Still waiting to be seen by a doctor, Ken was falling in and out of sleep, his discomfort making it difficult to drift off for any sustained period.

"Ken Charles," shouted the nurse.

Raising his hand, he slowly made his way towards her.

"You're in a bad way," she said. "Been in a fight?"

"I was attacked by three thugs," he replied. "It was unprovoked."

"Have you informed the police?" she asked.

"No, and I'm not going to neither. I'd rather sort it out myself," he informed her.

He was led into a small booth separated by curtains. He could hear the cry of a young boy who had fallen and broken his hands. Ken was feeling awful. The worst pain was in his right ear, where he'd taken the force of the first few kicks.

"Where are you experiencing pain?" asked the nurse.

"Here," replied Ken, pointing to his ear. "Also here in my ribs. Can you give me some painkillers?"

"The doctor will need to examine you first. Sorry, you'll just have to put up with it for now," she said.

"That's just bloody brilliant," said Ken irritably. "How long's he going to be?"

"Twenty minutes to half an hour."

Becoming more and more irritated, Ken just wanted the doctor to patch him up so he could get on with his day. This of course meant visiting Tom. He also wanted to see Viv and get the key back to their house. If she refused, then he would break in. The house would be his again.

––––––––

Continuing his walk around the grounds of the distillery, Justin began to pray. What else could he do? The rush of anger he was experiencing towards Tom wasn't helping him. Emotionally blown, he asked God for direction. Kneeling down on the grass, Justin looked deep into his soul, knowing that he needed help.

How do I forgive him? What should I say? These were only two of the questions bombarding Justin. *I have to forgive. I have to.*

The problem with non-forgiveness, as Justin well knew, was its festering tendency towards bitterness and its capability to permeate every part of a person's life. If he did not make an effort to forgive Tom's betrayal and Nina's manipulation, then he may as well accept that there was no transforming power in the universe and that God was effectively dead. Still kneeling, Justin thought of all the people throughout the ages who had spoken about being transformed by a higher power. According to cynics these people had flaws in their character and lacked courage. Justin thought the opposite. It took bravery to believe in a personal God, to stand up and be counted in an increasingly secular world. Fr Hennessey's face came into Justin's mind. This made him smile.

He would have known what to do. Lifting his head, Justin brushed his hair with the fingers of his right hand. The man of faith would have advised him to set in motion the act of forgiveness. The Priest would have asked Justin to examine his heart, demanding that he die to self by submitting his rampaging id to a higher power. If not, then the base instincts of anger, hatred, and jealousy would continue to eat away at him, and there would be no change. Forgiveness was a healing process in which Justin had to make the first move.

Standing with his eyes closed, he sensed not only external stillness but also a quietness of soul. There was no sound other than his breath, which for the first time in three years was slow and reassuring.

"I can't make the move alone," he whispered to himself. *You know what to do, Justin,* a voice from inside his heart said.

Walking in a large circle, Justin continued asking God to soften his heart. He implored the divine to give him the grace to forgive the shit that was presently sat in the car. Turning around, he saw Tom climb out and start walking towards him. Within a few seconds they were facing each other. Without warning, Justin pulled his arm back and smashed his right fist into Tom's nose. The release of tension from Justin was immediate, as was the blood that burst from Tom's nostrils. Completely taken aback and in a state of shock, Tom could do nothing except nurse a throbbing nose. There was no need to ask why Justin had thumped him. That was obvious. If the price to pay for abandoning his friend was a sore nose, then he'd got off lightly. It was a very small price to pay.

"Bloody hell, my hand!" shouted Justin. "I think I've broken it."

At that moment the miracle started taking hold. They laughed so loudly they couldn't stop. Every time they tried, the laughter began again.

––––––––––––

"Mr Charles," said the doctor, "I would like to run some tests on your ear. I think you might have a burst eardrum."

"Will it mend itself?" asked Ken, by now fed up of waiting.

"Probably," replied the doctor. "But to be on the safe side, I think it best to—"

"Just give me some pain relief," demanded Ken. "I'm a busy man."

"But—" the doctor said.

"No buts," said Ken.

"If you insist," replied the doctor, infuriated. "The rest of you will be fine. Your ribs are not broken, but they will be sore for some time. They're heavily bruised."

Leaving the hospital, Ken was already feeling better.

At least my ribs aren't broken. It'd take more than those three animals to keep me down. I'll pick them off one by one. Don't they know who I am?

––––––––––––

"One step at a time," said Tom after they eventually stopped laughing.

"Yeah, I suppose you're right," replied Justin. "My hand's beginning to swell."

"What about my nose? It really hurts. There's blood still dripping from it."

"That's because it's enormous."

"There's no need for projection," replied Tom.

"Sod off," laughed Justin.

They decided not to go on the tour of the distillery given the state of Tom's nose and the swelling to Justin's hand. Instead, they made their way to the entrance to buy a couple of bottles of scotch.

"What do you fancy doing now?" asked Tom.

"All this forgiving business has made me hungry," cracked Justin.

"Let's go to Edzell; it's got a great chip shop," said Tom.

"That sounds about right," replied Justin. "Come on then; make haste."

On reaching Edzell, Tom parked directly outside the chip shop. Unfastening their seat belts, they got out of the car. Justin took a few steps towards the door of the shop and asked, "What do you recommend then?"

"I always have fish and chips. I've not yet got my palate round deep-fried haggis stick."

"Fish and chips will do for me then."

After paying, they made their way towards the bench on the edge of the park.

"Are you warm enough, or do you want to eat them in the car?" asked Tom, already tucking into his chips.

"The bench is fine," Justin replied, breaking the batter on his fish with a plastic fork. It was a bright afternoon for mid-November. The sun had been trying its best all day to push its way through. Justin seemed lost in his thoughts; Tom could see him staring out into the distance. Scanning the area, Tom wasn't able to see what he was looking at.

"Do you still believe in God?" asked Tom.

"Since taking Nina's life my heart has been closed to him. I've really struggled to reconnect. Ironically, since punching you I feel I can start seeking him again," said Justin.

"Oh cheers, so much for forgiveness," laughed Tom, holding his nose.

"I never said I was a pacifist," replied Justin.

"Obviously," said Tom.

After finishing the fish and chips they put their empty cartons in to the rubbish bin and ambled back to the car. Every few yards Justin would stop and scan the area. Not wanting to interrupt, Tom continued walking in silence.

"Just what I needed," said Justin as he opened the car door.

Tom started the engine and set off down the road towards home. Both were silent and in their own way were embracing the healing that forgiveness brought.

"When am I going to meet Viv?" asked Justin.

"Whenever you want," replied Tom. "She'll be back from her mother's later today. Would it be too soon to see her tonight?"

"You're obviously missing her," said Justin.

"I am, but I'm glad we've spent this time together."

"She must be special if you're prepared to put up with her husband," stated Justin.

"She is. He's a strange one, though. Since finding out about me and Viv, it's as if I'm to blame for everything bad in his life," said Tom.

"Rather you than me," said Justin. "I feel knackered. I fancy a lie-down when we get back. Afterwards we can sample some of that whisky we've bought."

"Great idea, I'm knackered myself," replied Tom.

————

Needing to change his clothes, take a shower, and lie down, Ken was making his way to his marital home. There were a few clothes in the wardrobe, as he'd left some in case of an emergency. Ken deemed this to be such an occasion. With more than a smattering of desperation Ken smashed the Kitchen window with a hammer from his tool box which he kept in the car. This allowed him to open the window wide and then climb over the sink and drop down into the kitchen. This was a painful experience given that he had to stretch and twist himself.

"Fuck," he screamed as blood spurted from his right index finger, having caught it on the jagged glass. "As if I haven't got enough pain to deal with."

Plunging his finger under the running tap, he watched the blood seep away down the plughole. The pain was not too bad. Reaching into one of the kitchen drawers, he found some plasters. After applying one to the offending finger he made his way to the living room where the booze cabinet stood and grabbed a bottle of brandy. Pouring a measure, he removed a packet of painkillers from his coat pocket and swallowed two of them. Putting his head back, he moved the liquid round in a circular motion in his mouth. Then he took the bottle and glass from the coffee table and sluggishly made his way up the stairs. Tiredness was overcoming him. He opened the bedroom door and collapsed on the bed. He wanted to sleep but was finding it difficult to relax. The tension in his body was so great that his legs were now twitching involuntary. He attempted to stand up, but his legs couldn't hold him, making him fall back onto the bed. His body was crying out for sleep. Ken needed rest.

Having arrived back in Forfar, Tom and Justin were sitting at the kitchen table having decided a small whisky would help them to sleep.

"I'm sorry to bring this up again," Tom said, "but I was really surprised when you said you'd not worked since coming out of prison. You of all people know the importance of structure. I couldn't have got by without working. By the way I can always help you financially if you ever need anything."

Yeah, thirty pieces of silver no doubt, thought Justin. Thankfully he acted quickly to squash his cynicism, accepting that this wasn't constructive.

"Thanks, Tom. I appreciate your offer. The problem is I've got a criminal record and have to declare it every time I apply for a job. I will look for work, but I realise there might not be that many sympathetic employers out there. Can you imagine a restaurant finding out about me? They'd worry whether I'd be adding rat poison to the customers' soup."

"Don't be so daft. Mind you, I can understand what you're saying," reasoned Tom. "You could always move further north. They're looking for workers at the factory. The money's crap, but the banter can be good. Well, it was before Ken started hounding me. He gives me a hard time at work."

"It must be difficult having to work at the same place. That's not good at all. As for me working there, I'm not sure whether I'd be very good in industry," said Justin. "You know what I'm like with DIY."

"Destroy it yourself," laughed Tom. "It wouldn't be like that; you'd be working the machines, filling jars with fruit."

"I'm not sure if I'd want to move again so soon after leaving London, but I'll think about it," said Justin. "What can you do with a redundant doctor anyway?"

Moving into the living room, Tom picked up the telephone receiver and dialled Viv's mobile number.

"Hold on a second. I'll pull over; I'm driving," she said.

"Okay," replied an excited Tom. It was good to hear her voice.

"Right then," she said. "Are you okay?"

"Never better, in fact. Do you fancy coming over later for a spot of dinner. Justin's eager to meet you."

"So it's gone well then I take it."

"Yeah, after a rocky start. We certainly seem to be communicating again. It's great to see him. So, are you up for coming round? I'll make us all something to eat."

"Yes, all right, but I need to go and check on the house first, put some washing in and collect the post."

"I'm looking forward to seeing you," said Tom with no embarrassment, sounding confident and upbeat.

"Yes, me too," responded Viv. "Oh, and by the way, my mother wants to meet you."

"Hell, I must be in your good books. Here I was getting all paranoid thinking you might not want to see me again," confessed Tom.

"You're still not worrying about me going back to Ken are you? Come on, Tom; give me some credit. I can't keep reassuring you," remarked Viv. "I'll see you later."

"Okay," said Tom. "See you later."

Having put down the receiver, Tom told Justin he was going for a lie down. He climbed the stairs, and lay down on the bed, his heart the happiest it had been for a very long time.

Pulling up outside her house, not having noticed Ken's car parked around the corner, Viv had no idea what was waiting for her. On entering the hallway she gathered up a large amount of post then sorted it into two distinctive piles, one for her and the other for Ken. The house did not feel like home anymore. She had made up her mind. It would be sold, whether to Ken or not she no longer cared. She might just abandon it. What she needed was to leave everything behind, including the memories that were stored within these four walls. Sitting down for a moment, she scanned the room. The photographs on the walls and the sideboard were evidence to seven years of shallowness. Her wedding picture was on the wall above the fire. This would now be discarded. There would be no room for it when she moved into a new house, and there was certainly no room for it in her heart. Manipulated over the years, her identity had been subjugated to a man she didn't like never mind loved. Her mother had sounded the first warnings about Ken. On first impressions people thought he was interested in them. With immaculate manners, he appealed to the majority of people he met. But ultimately, he was a player adept at luring people into his way of thinking. Becoming their confidante, he ceaselessly manipulated those he could gain from. Why Viv had ignored this side of him over the years she couldn't say. Chipping away at her confidence on a daily basis and slowly making her become more reliant on him had been Ken's master plan. Looking back to her kick-boxing days, she realised his opposition to her retiring had been about him wanting to control her. Having become tired of competition, she'd been finding it more difficult to compete with younger fighters that were quicker and possessed greater power. It had been Ken who had convinced her to continue another year. Retrospection was enabling her to see the truth. There had been no love in his heart for her; she had been his possession. This had now changed. The influence that Ken had held over her had been broken. She was free.

There was a chill in the air, and Viv thought it best to turn the heating on, seeing that frost had been forecast overnight. She unpacked her travel bag and placed the dirty washing into the machine. *I need to get some clean clothes from the wardrobe in case I stay with Tom,* she thought.

On leaving the kitchen it was only then that she noticed the broken window. *No wonder I'd felt cold.* Suddenly aware of how loud she had been, Viv switched the washing machine off and silently stepped into the hallway, taking a minute to scour the area. There was nobody there. Slowly moving into the living room, she saw that nothing had been disturbed. She cautiously climbed the stairs, conscious that she might have to act quickly if there was a burglar. Opening the door of her bedroom, she was greeted by Ken sitting up in bed.

"What are you doing here?" she screamed.

"I've been waiting for you," he said. "Care to join me?"

Enjoying the game, he also genuinely believed that Viv would want to join him. *Why wouldn't she?* He considered himself a good lover.

"Oh please!" castigated Viv. "I've only come to check the house. I'm not stopping."

"You are," threatened Ken, trying to get out of bed.

"What the hell happened to you?" she asked, seeing him flinch when he tried to move.

Providing an elaborate story of deceit, Ken made out he had rushed to the aid of an old man cornered by three thugs.

You're a liar, thought Viv. *You've been up to no good again.*

Although the tale sounded plausible, it did not convince her, not anymore.

"Do you want to kiss me better?" he baited.

Ignoring him, she began collecting some clean clothing, placing the items neatly in her bag.

"I hope you're going to fix the kitchen window. Anyway, why are you here? I thought you were staying with Gemma," said Viv.

"You don't listen, do you? You and me are getting back together. You know I love you. In time, you'll come round. We're made for each other," Ken said.

"Oh shut up. I'm sick of hearing you. It's finished. I don't want you. I don't love you."

"Do you really think I'm going to let Tom steal you from me? No, Viv, you're mine and nobody else's!" he screamed.

"Is it registering in that thick head of yours? I'm not coming back – not now, not ever." shouted Viv.

"He won't have you, Viv. He'll never have you," he repeated.

Knowing that conversation with Ken was pointless, she picked up her bag and made to leave the bedroom. Lunging forward, he caught hold of her left leg. She easily freed it from him, and he let out a scream. He'd had no choice but to weaken his grip as the pain in his ribs was excruciating. He dropped back onto the bed with his arms across his ribcage, trying to relieve the discomfort. Ken began swearing. Making no attempt to look back, she quickened her pace. Slamming the front door shut, Viv headed towards her car. She threw her bag inside, jumped in, and then sensibly locked it. Viv closed her eyes and took slow, deep breaths.

Was there no getting away from him? He seems more deranged by the day; I swore I saw the devil in his eyes. That's the creepiest I've ever seen him, thought Viv. Hoping Justin wouldn't mind, she decided to go straight to Tom's house.

Concentrate, Viv. Concentrate.

Over the years she had been in many tough bouts, but Ken's mind games were scarier than any kick-boxing opponent she had faced. She decided to stay still for a few seconds and continued to concentrate on her breathing, all the while with her eyes closed. When she opened these, her stomach almost left her body – there was Ken staring at her through the driver's side window and threateningly dragging his forefinger horizontally along his neck.

"You're bloody sick!" Viv screamed, setting off with wheels screeching. She managed to keep control and steady both herself and the car. Looking in the mirror, she could see Ken hobbling after her laughing manically.

What's happened to him? I knew he'd been a bully. But this?

After driving for ten minutes she pulled over, no longer able to see the road. Fumbling through her handbag, she found a small packet of tissues.

How has my life come to this? It's not as if I've done anything wrong. He cheated on me.

"Wake up, Justin. There's a cup of tea," said Tom, pointing at the bedside cabinet as he walked out of the room. "I'll leave you to come to."

"Thanks," Justin replied, rubbing his eyes and trying to come to. *Amazing, I haven't had a nightmare. Thank God.*

Tom made his way downstairs to prepare the evening meal. He was to make a winter lasagne with potatoes, onions, root vegetables, and red split lentils. If they wanted pudding, there was plenty of ice cream in the freezer. Expecting Viv to arrive within the hour, Tom was excited, evidenced by how often he checked his watch. He was also worried that Justin might start to bad-mouth him. Although a form of miracle had taken place at the distillery, Tom thought there might be further periods of instability between them. Yet against the odds, they had made moves towards reconciliation. Both had acknowledged the shifting of defences and a cracking of the wall guarding their broken hearts. They still needed to continue driving out the hurt and bitterness that stood in the way of their healing. Starting the cheese sauce on the hotplate, Tom thought about how and when he was going to tell Viv the truth. Feeling exposed, he wasn't sure whether tonight was the right time, but keeping a secret as monstrous as this would surely form a barrier between them. Once again Tom talked to a God he was not sure existed. Then he thought about Chrissie. He smiled, knowing that she would have given him grief about talking to a God she believed to be nothing more than an illusion.

Stumbling into the room, Justin cursed after tripping over a pair of shoes that Tom had discarded.

"Ha ha, watch your step, you blind bugger," laughed Tom.

"I think I need a whisky after that. It was a close one; a whisky will help steady my nerves," chortled Justin. "Do you fancy one?"

"Why not?" Tom smiled, thinking how less burdened Justin was from when he'd first arrived. It was beginning to feel like old times again. It felt good having Justin around.

"Can I help?" Justin asked.

"You can. Will you peel the spuds while I cut up the onion?"

"Sure," answered Justin, dragging out a chair from under the table.

"I haven't told you about my nightmares, have I?" shared Justin. "Well, ever since Nina died I've experienced four different ones."

"Did you have one about four o'clock this morning? I heard you having a shower," Tom interjected.

"I did," said Justin, nodding his head. "Actually, if you don't mind, I don't think I can be bothered describing them just now. I'll tell you tomorrow. Anyway, I think they might have left me."

Tom was hoping that he might forget to tell him altogether, as they sounded appalling.

"I'm going for a smoke," said Justin, making his way outside. Once in the street he immediately wished he had put his coat on. Gazing across the road, he saw no hint of Ken's presence. *It's all very strange that Ken should be spending all his energies in such an infantile manner. Does he not have anything better to do?*

Leaning against the front windowsill, he noticed a car parking directly opposite. Unless Ken had acquired a new motor, then it was unlikely to be him. Justin stamped out his cigarette and was picking it up when he saw a woman heading towards the house. This had to be Viv, and Tom hadn't been wrong about her being attractive.

"Hello," she said, holding out her right hand. "You must be Justin."

"And you are Viv," he replied, shaking it.

On first glance, Viv thought Tom and Justin had a look of each other and could almost be brothers. This was not a new observation. When they were younger, many people had got them mixed up at first glance. On further observation, Viv thought Justin looked the older of the two; he was also paler and thinner and seemed more dejected than Tom, as if he could do with some good food down him.

"Come on then, Justin. Let's go inside. It's a bit cold out here."

Following behind him, Viv noticed that Justin dropped his shoulders when standing and his head when walking. It seemed to her that he had a lot on his mind.

"Hi, Tom," called Viv as she walked into his warm house.

On hearing her voice, Tom turned and met Viv with a long hug. Holding on to each other, seeking reassurance, they instantly began feeling safer. Viv had decided not to tell Tom about Ken's latest tricks, thinking Tom had enough on his plate dealing with Justin. It could and would wait.

Justin observed the bond between them. How could he deny their happiness? Yet the animosity he was feeling towards Tom was still alive, slow burning and festering. Observing their embrace, Justin suddenly had a pang of resentment towards the two lovers and an overriding compulsion to defend his sister's memory. Chastising himself, he knew these thoughts to be absurd, remembering that over the years he had witnessed the depths of love Tom had shown his wife.

The resonance of Viv's soft, inviting voice brought him back to the present. Turning round, he saw Tom release her from his embrace.

"Viv, Justin; Justin, Viv," introduced Tom.

"We know," they said in unison.

Justin felt a little uncomfortable but tried not to show it. Noticing this, Viv immediately engaged him in conversation, beginning with the usual pleasantries around how the journey had been, what he thought of Scotland, and where he was from. Justin appreciated her efforts, and her warm eyes helped him to feel more at ease. Her Scottish accent was easily understood. Reaching out towards the kitchen table, she accidently dropped her keys on the floor. When she bent down to pick them up, Justin realised that he was in the presence of an athlete. Her muscles were strong, defined, yet still feminine. When it came to exercise, he was a disgrace, hardly a role model for a healthy lifestyle. He wasn't one for partaking in sport.

Assembling the lasagne, Tom was happy that Viv and Justin seemed to be getting on well. Curious as to which sport had produced such a body, Justin could see that she hadn't overdone the weights. *She's not a runner; her frame's too large for distances and not bulky enough to be a sprinter.*

"I'm intrigued as to which sport you do," said Justin.

"I'm a kick-boxer, though I no longer compete. I still go to the club and work out twice a week. I also go running a couple of times, usually in the morning," she replied. "And you?" she asked. "Are you sporty?"

Both Tom and Justin laughed.

"He's a lazy sod to say he's a doctor," said Tom.

Immediately a silence fell upon the room. Swallowing hard, Tom could feel his face turning red. Coughing nervously, he turned his body away from Justin and Viv, wishing he could turn back the clock to before opening his mouth. Given the atmosphere, Viv didn't feel it appropriate to make any comment or ask the obvious questions, such as where he practiced or whether he was a GP. Feeling ill at ease, she sensed that the agenda between them had not yet been fully realised. There were obviously outstanding issues to tackle. Suddenly Tom became busier around the kitchen, a sign that he was hiding something and didn't want to talk about it. Staring into space, Justin was saying nothing, which seemed incongruent given that a few seconds earlier the conversation had been flowing. What was going on? She knew all was not well between the two friends but was clueless as to what had suddenly contaminated the atmosphere. The disconnection between Tom and Justin had taken her by surprise. She wondered whether to ask Tom what was going on but thought better of it, accepting that she had no legitimacy to interfere in his life.

"Let's have a drink," said Viv, trying to lighten the atmosphere.

All three wanted a glass of the white wine she had brought. Sitting back in his chair, Justin was moving his legs quickly from side to side. Viv could feel his tension. Seeing Tom was upset, she put her hands on his shoulders and gave him a reassuring peck on his right cheek. He turned towards her with tears welling up in his eyes, and she gave him a smile that only lovers could understand. Studying them both, Viv was concerned that the barrier between them had resurfaced and would be locked down, forever cementing a rift that could never be healed. Standing up, Justin made to go outside. Removing a packet of cigarettes from his coat pocket, he walked out the front door. Seeing Tom and Viv together reinforced his own loneliness. He had no family, no partner, and no friends to help ease his sadness.

"Come here," beckoned Viv to Tom.

As he felt the warmth of her arms around him, his heart pounded.

"You're sweating," she said.

Holding his head against her chest, she stroked his hair in an attempt to soothe him. They remained silent without need for words. This was a new situation for her, never having held Ken in such a way; he would not have responded to her arms the way Tom did. It seemed so easy, so natural for both of them to share their hearts and feel each other's love. This love had eluded her and Ken. There was something deeply comforting in realising she had much love to give. This was real. She just hoped that the secret both Tom and

Justin shared would not catapult her awakening self into the realm of disappointment and shatter a growing optimism that Tom was her soulmate. Holding Tom in her arms transported her to a timeless place, although she knew she could not keep him there forever. She thought about Tom's situation with Justin. She would encourage him to continue working towards a resolution with Justin. Life was too short. On hearing Justin re-entering the house, Tom and Viv released themselves from their embrace. Witnessing them gently touching each other's faces as though communicating that they were strong together made Justin want to scream. Instead of joining them, he climbed the stairs and went into his bedroom. Throwing himself down on the bed, he was ready to pack his case and go home. Rather than acting on impulse, he decided it was best to take a few minutes to contemplate his dilemma. With his eyes closed, trying to clear his mind, he was hoping to hear the voice of God. He had to reconnect. Listening to his own breathing, Justin was conscious that he needed to slow this down. After a few minutes more he felt calmer. Past memories were randomly entering his thoughts. Lying there, Justin remembered Fr Hennessey advising a fellow noviciate that if he was finding it too difficult to love his enemies, he had to pretend. This had seemed rather ridiculous until Fr Hennessey had explained that God might perform miracles, but he also expected effort from people. And those who were unforgiving needed to put more in than most: pretending to love showed that the heart was open to change, and in time the pretence would become real. The heart would be open to God's love. Fr Hennessey had been keen to stress that the heart needed discipline, as without this, love became an illusion. To forgive a person of a wrong they had committed was an act of love. He took time to remind himself that love was a verb, a doing word; it required action. These thoughts helped relax Justin. His breathing was returning to normal, and his hands were no longer clammy.

Love is also painful, thought Justin, fighting a tendency to dismiss change. Yet he knew the action of love was his way to liberation.

Work was giving Gemma some much-needed respite from worrying about whether Ken would turn up. Not only this, she also had some good news to share.

"Are you losing weight?" Alistair asked, walking towards the bar.

"Probably," she replied. "Anyway, enough of that Alistair, look what I've got."

Alistair pointed to a brown envelope in her hand. "What's that then?"

"Our future," she said, rubbing her stomach. "The housing association has said I can have a house. It's got two bedrooms. I can't wait."

"That's fantastic news, Gemma. When can you move in?"

"Soon, whenever they've finished decorating it. I can't wait. It'll be a new start for me and the baby."

"It certainly will," remarked Alistair. "Good for you."

———

Gucci Boy slowly awoke from a sleep he had sorely needed.

What can I do now? I know exactly what I want to do, see Tom squirm in front of Viv. I think I'll sit outside his house again, check out the enemy.

Slowly turning to minimise the pain, Ken put his head down on the pillow and fell back to sleep.

———

On returning downstairs, Justin noticed Viv and Tom sitting at the kitchen table talking. Viv gave Justin a smile, and he returned the same. Looking for signs that he was coping with the situation, Tom nodded. This was reciprocated. Justin sat silently as Tom served the lasagne. Viv poured the wine, and raising her glass, she made a toast to everybody's health, not knowing what else to say. It seemed to be an appropriate gesture. Both Tom and Justin responded by raising their glasses.

"You've not lost your skill," said Justin after a mouthful of lasagne.

"Thanks," replied Tom.

"I can't believe my luck," said Viv. "Tom really is a good cook."

I bet you can't, thought Justin just able to stop from calling her a gold-digger. He was fighting yet another rising tide of anger. It was proving difficult to sublimate. *Nina should be sitting opposite me, not you*. Having a strong impulse to tell her this, Justin once again bit his tongue. Thankfully, the words of Fr Hennessey were now in his mind: "It's about seeking truth, Justin. You have to search for wisdom."

The truth was that there was no evidence to suggest that Viv was anything but genuine in her affection for Tom. Since her arrival both had shown genuine fondness for one another. After all, it wasn't Viv's fault for his and Tom's mess; she couldn't help falling in love with him. Feeling relieved he had held his tongue, Justin continued the conversation without any awkward apologies or feelings of guilt for his earlier disappearance. After assessing Viv's body language and sensing no hostility towards him, Justin decided to open up a little to her.

"I used to be a GP," he said, looking straight into Viv's eyes. "But I was struck off."

"Justin," interjected Tom.

"No, Tom, she has a right to know."

Sitting silently, Viv speculated why he had suddenly volunteered this information and what he was expecting her to do with such a revelation. After such a statement, she couldn't help but mull over what it was he had done to deserve such a drastic end to his career. No wonder silence had descended on their earlier conversation.

He must have done something terrible; doctors don't get struck off for no good reason. Had he been stealing drugs? Had he been negligent and misdiagnosed? Maybe it was for financial mismanagement or fraud.

"I killed Tom's wife, my sister," he said.

Staring at Tom for support, Viv suddenly went frail at the knees, overwhelmed by a feeling of horror. So much so that she remained speechless. With his head in his hands, Tom caught sight of the confusion in Viv's eyes and the look of fear on her face.

"Tom?" she said.

"It's not what you think," he replied, hoping this might help reassure her.

"I killed my own sister," said Justin.

Needing to find some space and a huge gulp of fresh air, Viv made her way to the front door. There would be time to hear their story, but first she had to calm herself. She didn't want to be accused of not having listened properly. Taking in the icy November air, she began questioning whether she knew Tom at all. The revelation that Justin was Tom's brother-in-law had surprised her.

What else has he been keeping from me?

"Viv," Tom said, having followed her outside.

"Not now, Tom. Let me have a few minutes to myself. I'll come back in, and then you can explain it all to me," Viv replied.

Saying nothing, he returned inside to Justin. Looking at each other, they assessed what was going to happen next.

"You're going to have to finish what you've started," Tom said. "You can't take back what you've said."

"I know," snapped Justin. "I know."

By the end of the evening Tom would know his fate. This might see him being thrown back into a world of memories and death sealed by a leaving kiss with Viv walking out of his life forever. He wouldn't try to stop her. Her decision would be made as to whether he warranted her love or not. Although fearing the worst, he would hold no bitterness towards Justin. In a strange way, he was thankful that Viv was gracious enough to give him the opportunity to explain the situation to her.

"You all right?" asked Tom.

"I think so," said Justin. "I didn't mean it to come out so dramatically."

"What's done is done. To be honest, it's probably for the best. At least Viv will know what a coward I've been."

Sensing a presence behind him, he turned around to see Viv looking straight at him. Taking a seat at the table, she suggested that they all have a strong drink.

"I'm listening," she said.

Justin said, "Nina, or Chrissie as she was known to everybody except to me, contracted a brain tumour and underwent unsuccessful surgery. Her condition was incurable. She was funny, loving, and at times a pain in the arse."

As Justin continued to provide a colourful account of his sister, Viv laughed at Chrissie's sense of fun and, at times, tunnel vision. Justin felt a need for Viv to know the amount of pain Nina's death had caused not only him but also Tom. A picture of Justin's faith was now forming in Viv's mind.

"As for the Hippocratic Oath, you probably think you've turned that one right on its head," stated Viv.

"Precisely, being a doctor doesn't make it easier. In fact for me, it makes what I did worse," replied Justin. "I know there's an increasing amount of medics that believe people should be helped to die. I still can't accept that. What is medicine about if it isn't to save lives?"

"What you did was right," interjected Tom.

"Oh, come on," said Justin. "Haven't you heard a word I've said since being here?"

"Don't be too hard on yourself, Justin. She was your sister who needed your help," said Viv.

"I don't think you can grasp the spiritual degradation I've felt ever since. I stuck a needle in my sister's arm and then watched her die. Every time I close my eyes I see that moment. It's horrible. I shouldn't have had to do it. Tom was supposed to be there, but he chickened out."

Viv said, "What you did was to give up your life for a loved one and sacrifice your career. That's martyrdom. It was an act of bravery. As far as I'm concerned, you liberated Chrissie. It seems to me that she had no life. Better to be dead than the living dead. Although, I can understand it's one hell of a position to be in."

"You're telling me," replied a tearful Justin.

"There's no getting away from it, Justin," Viv said. "You did go against what you believe, and that surely must hurt. You're a man of principle, but you have to move on and lift yourself out from your despair."

"I'll second that," Tom added.

"I'm glad I've come to Scotland. We've had a positive day today," said Justin, turning towards Tom for affirmation. "Maybe the healing has begun."

"I think it has," stated Tom, more in hope than certainty.

"People would think your actions brave, not cowardly," Viv said to Justin.

"Many have said that, but it holds no comfort for me. Be honest: you must have memories of having done something you're ashamed of, something that you can never forget about," replied Justin, looking straight at Viv, who nodded in agreement. "When that memory rushes into your head, does your stomach not drop through your body like lead hitting the ground and then bounce back even more ferociously? Admit it: does it leave you feeling sick and ashamed? Well, think of that moment, and multiply it by a thousand thousands. That feeling won't leave me. This must sound strange to you, but I can understand people's views on assisted suicide, but I still can't accept it as a treatment for death. Can't you both see how difficult it is for me to let go of what I did? I feel so hypocritical."

"You've got to learn to let go, Justin," pleaded Tom, giving a sideways glance towards Viv, hoping for some support.

"It's just too difficult to look at myself and feel that I have any credibility. How many times in the past have I called out others for not having a backbone? Come on, Tom; you know how important being true to my principles has always been for me, the amount of times I got into trouble for not towing the line. This is it, you see; I hate myself for my weakness."

"I know this is probably irrelevant, but a few years ago you'd have received a much heavier sentence," said Viv.

"I don't want to appear rude, but every day is like a prison sentence to me. Being locked up or walking the moors is the same experience. Prison for me is my heart and mind, the torture chamber of my memories. In some ways being in prison was easier to handle. Everybody knew why I was there. I didn't need to answer to anybody from going into jail to leaving."

"I know that only you can change the course of your life, Justin," Viv said. "Nobody can take your pain away. There is hope, though; look at you and Tom. For the first time in three years you're talking again. You both need to be honest with each other. You've already said that your God is a forgiving God. Surely he expects you to forgive yourself first before being able to forgive others. I don't know. I'm not someone with faith, but it makes sense to me."

All three were now involved in trying to find some way forward for their lives. The more Viv listened to Justin, the more she was able to empathise with him. In her mind, he had risked everything for his sister. *Where was Tom? What happened to him on that dreadful day?*

"Tom, can you remember after I was sentenced turning your back on me when I was being led out of the courtroom? That feeling of desolation walked with me into the prison van and remained until it turned to fury, which until yesterday had been as raw as the moment of its conception."

"It's hardly surprising you've found it difficult to forgive Tom," said Viv, glancing at Justin and feeling his pain.

"It felt like my life had ended. You were the one person I thought I could rely upon. But you deserted me. Left me for dead," explained Justin, looking at Tom for a reply.

"I thought you were his friend," said Viv. "What have you got to say for yourself?"

Waiting for his reply, she reached across the table and poured out a good measure of scotch in all three glasses. Taking a sip, she probed Tom's face for answers he might be hiding. She was conjecturing as to why he hadn't kept his word and hoping that he was still the man she had fallen in love with.

"I'm so sorry; I've no excuses, only that I couldn't lose Chrissie and was in a deep state of shock. I needed to blame someone. My behaviour throughout that time is indefensible. I failed to free the woman I loved. I was so bloody selfish, thinking only about my own hurt, believing I couldn't live without her. I wouldn't do that now. Seeing Justin in tatters has shown me that by hiding away that day I let down two of the three people I loved most in life. I'm not sure if I can ever forgive myself for that. And I understand if you can't forgive me, Justin," said Tom, bowing his head and avoiding eye contact.

"Even so, you left your best friend right in the shit," said Viv, doing her best to understand her lover's lack of action.

"I've held on to this letter that Chrissie left me," Tom said, holding it in the air. "I'd like you both to read it. Chrissie knew me more than I knew myself. Will you read it?"

"Not just now," replied Viv. "I think you need to continue explaining yourself to Justin first. Don't you?"

"Yes, you're right. But the letter will help with that. Anyway, that aside, I did want to visit you, Justin. I just couldn't bring myself to do so. I also thought about writing. For some reason I couldn't do it. Deep down I knew what I'd done was wrong, but I kept blaming you. I tried to justify to myself that it wasn't my fault. I couldn't face looking into your eyes. I kept telling myself it was your fault that you should have known not to go ahead when I refused to answer your calls."

Shifting her position on the chair, remaining silent, Viv was feeling unnerved. Nevertheless, she urged Tom to continue.

"I moved to Scotland because whenever we'd holidayed there Chrissie had always enjoyed the place. And the other reason was quite simple. It provided a distance between you and me, Justin. I thought by running away my life would change and I'd be able to forget about you, but I couldn't. I also thought moving away from London meant that by the time you were released from prison you'd have no idea where I lived. This was nothing but folly, as time passed by, it became even more difficult to live with my guilt. I did see you when you were led out from court. I can see you now, confused, rejected, and distraught. That look has haunted me for the past three years."

Reaching across the table, Tom took hold of Viv's hand. Thankfully, she didn't pull it away.

"Viv, when you entered my life, I began transforming myself. I felt resurrected and knew I could live a new life. I felt alive again. You touched my heart, reignited my love, and without you, I would still be lost. Please don't leave me."

"I'm not going anywhere," she replied, squeezing his hand.

Taking hold of Justin's hand as well, she asked them both to stand up. In between these two great friends stood Viv, strong and loving, a symbol of hope. She was the Madonna, a woman of succour and the conduit of change. Although she could not wash away their sins, she could provide them with emotional shelter. Stretching her arms around Tom's left and Justin's right shoulder, Viv became conscious that she was holding two unique individuals who once had held a great love for one another. Without warning, a feeling of power surged through her body and then transposed itself into both friends' hearts. They were transfixed, silent and still. Not understanding what had happened, Viv could only think that she had been chosen by a higher force. Standing in the middle of the kitchen interdependent for survival were two hurting people that had let Viv absorb their fears and channel them into the ether. Stepping backwards, she encouraged Tom and Justin to continue embracing each other until they finally reconnected. She stood by the window watching the stars form in the sky. The beauty of the moon was beginning to make her giddy. She could have sworn it was smiling at her. As Tom and Justin let go of each other with tears flowing down their faces, Tom asked his friend for forgiveness. Justin did not speak but replied by giving a confirmatory nod of the head. The act of forgiveness had been freely granted and at the same time willingly received.

"Let's start again," said Justin, smiling at Tom.

"I reckon we should," replied Tom.

"Today is a good day," pronounced Viv. "Let's finish our meal."

"Why not," agreed Tom and Justin.

In the few hours she had been in their company, Viv was already gaining an insight into their history, knowing that in future meetings she might at times feel an outsider but would never be excluded. Looking to the heavens, she thanked God for her new life. The energy in the room was changing. All three sensed a new force as sorrow gave way to joyfulness. Laughter filled the whole house as the best friends began reminiscing. Their laughter became even more raucous when Tom relayed an incident from work that had seen his foreman slip on his backside.

Tonight is a special night, thought Viv.

"Thanks," said Justin from behind her. "Tom was right about you. You are a life changer. In fact, you're a miracle weaver."

"Well, I'm not sure about that. I can't explain what's just happened, other than I sensed a greater power direct my love towards you both. It's never happened to me before. It's all a bit weird," said Viv.

"Well, I feel different. I feel forgiven. I have purpose back in my life," said Justin.

"That's brilliant," said Viv.

"He's a lucky man," said Justin.

"Thanks," she said. "I do know that it's meant to be."

"Maybe now Tom can get some peace. I know it seems we've despised each other, but it's actually the opposite. The fact we were so close over the years made our separation even harder to live with. He'll be kind to you. He was brilliant with Nina. She could be a real handful at times. He's a lot of love to give, that ugly bastard over there," cracked Justin, pointing to Tom who was staring into space enjoying his newfound peace.

"Aye, I'm looking forward to getting to know him more and you for that matter," said Viv. "I can see why you two get on so well."

"We've had some real arguments over the years, yet we still remained friends. Except for when Nina died. I know I've only known you a few hours, Viv, but I really believe he has found the right person in you."

"That's a lovely thing to say. I know I feel lucky having found him. You two must continue to reconnect with each other. Promise me you'll try."

"I promise," said Justin, crossing his heart.

They stood in silence observing Tom and loving him in their own inimitable way. All three were reborn and ready for the challenges that love surely would bring. In the moment, Justin and Viv were able to see into each other's souls. They knew that something very special had taken place. Both were willing to grab the mantle that change required. Rejoining Tom, they laughed about past times but more importantly the future. Talking until the dawn had been and gone, they were thankful that none of them had to go to work. Viv was smiling. She had taken the week off and was looking forward to spending it with Tom.

"Hey, Tom, where's the nearest shop? I've smoked all my ciggies," said Justin.

"There's a paper shop down the road. It's 6.50 so it'll be open," replied Tom.

Justin never liked to be without a packet of cigarettes. They were his comfort blanket, and without them he would become nervous and edgy. He also wanted to walk and feel the air caress his lungs and wanted to catch the majesty of the morning light. For him, this was to be a walk of freedom, the first venture into the world as Justin Ivens reborn. No way did he want to sleep; he would talk to God confident that their relationship was also restored. Today Justin felt forgiven. Today was a good day. Opening the door, he felt a slight drizzle and grabbed Tom's waterproof coat and hat. Before closing the door, he was about to shout to Tom and Viv that he would see them soon but noticed they were both curled up together on the settee asleep. Walking out into the morning was a new man who had learned forgiveness was the greatest act of love. For the first time since Nina passed away he felt worthy of his existence. Sensing a renewal of faith, he began speaking to Nina, believing she was with Christ. He told her about his reconnection with Tom. His heart was now bursting with happiness in the knowledge that she would be delighted. Her letter had stressed the need for them to remain friends. She had understood that their strength lay in their friendship. Filling his lungs with fresh Scottish air, Justin continued talking to Nina, telling her all about his meeting with Viv, insisting that she would have approved of her.

"You can rest, Nina. Viv has restored Tom to life," Justin said.

Stopping to take in the morning, Justin looked up towards the sky in recognition of his God. The rain was gently falling down his face, leaking into his mouth. These were spiritual waters washing him clean, holy waters returning grace upon his soul.

"What's heaven like then, sis?" laughed Justin. "Is it everything I imagined?"

The burden of guilt was now slowly being cast aside. Hope was returning, and light was re-entering his soul. Life was being restored to Justin Ivens. As he walked the streets of a town unknown, his footsteps were lighter than he had felt them for the past three years. "Guess what I'm doing, Nina. I'm thinking about living the rest of my life! You know me; I've never been too adventurous. Mundane, that's me. I'm going to get a job, maybe even move to Scotland to be near Tom. I want to do everyday things again. I'm sorry I abandoned, Mark. I'll make it up to him. I'm going to take him to the theatre and watch the Rovers again. He'd like that, wouldn't he?"

This fresh-found optimism expanded with every footstep of Justin's new life. For a mad moment he even considered tackling his well-established tobacco addiction. At this thought, he laughed out loud. For some reason, he was reminded of St Augustine, who had once pleaded with God to make him chaste, but not just at that moment. Engrossed in his thoughts, he didn't hear the car that had been tailing him swiftly pick up speed with a lethal power. Unaware of the vengeance growing within the dark soul that was Ken, Justin didn't feel a thing as the car hit him from behind. The impact immediately broke his spine in two and split his head open as he smashed down to the ground. The weight of the car on his now-shattered body forced Justin to breathe out his final breath, his heart restored with faith in a loving and forgiving God.

Lightning Source UK Ltd.
Milton Keynes UK
UKOW06f0255170415

249816UK00002B/130/P

9 781504 937252